kissing her crush

a Sugar City novel

OPHELIA LONDON

Entangled Publishing, LLC
2614 South Timberline Road
Suite 109
Fort Collins, CO 80525
Visit our website at www.entangledpublishing.com.

Bliss is an imprint of Entangled Publishing, LLC. For more information on our titles, visit http://www.entangledpublishing.com/category/bliss

Edited by Alycia Tornetta
Cover design by Heather Howland
Cover art from iStock

Manufactured in the United States of America

First Edition November 2015

Bliss
an Entangled imprint

To my sister Eileen, who first gave me Seaside, and then Hershey. xo

Chapter One

Natalie lowered her cell and stared bug-eyed in shock across the lab. Happy shock. "We…" She blinked a few times, then slid her safety glasses on top of her head. "We got it."

Ivy lowered the test tube in her hand. "What'd we get?"

"The foundation's endorsement. The lab space for our pilot trial. The *grant*."

"Stop—shut up." Test tubes clinked together when Ivy dropped the whole tray onto her workstation and held up one latex-gloved hand. "Since when?"

"Since ten seconds ago." Natalie displayed her phone, feeling the rush of endorphins the good news was bringing on. "I didn't want to say anything until it was officially happening. And now it's…"

"Happening?"

They gazed at each other for a silent second, then they both exploded in cheers that rattled the glass partitions of the lab.

"Buckle up, baby," Natalie said. "Starting Monday, for the next three weeks, you and I are heading the newest pro-tem research team at Penn State Medical Center." She smoothed down the front of her white lab coat, running her fingers over the Hershey logo.

"That's amazing!" Ivy's red ponytail bounced as she jumped up and down. "We need something to toast with, but not this stuff." She pushed aside a tray of caramel-colored blobs. "Not quite edible."

"Those'll do," Natalie said, gesturing to the row of brown squares on the counter. "Toss me one."

Ivy lobbed over one of their newest experiments: Peanut butter and honey-soaked wafers between shaves of coconut, covered in one layer of milk chocolate and one of Hershey's Special Dark. It would never make it past the test kitchen, but one of the best perks of being research and development food chemists in the "Sweets and Refreshments" lab was creating new products, no matter how unconventional.

"Cheers." Ivy lifted a square of chocolate.

"To us!" Natalie air-clinked their bars. "Mmm, man," she moaned, as velvety-smooth cocoa melted down her throat. "Whoever says chocolate doesn't stimulate positive brain function is high on cray-cray."

"Agreed. *And* that's the whole basis of your research project's theory," Ivy replied with a full mouth. "You gotta tell the rest of the team the news, and your family. Your mom will freak."

"I know—it's huge." Natalie couldn't stop beaming, due to the combination of succulent chocolate and the exhilarating, validating turn of events.

"This calls for a special celebration." Ivy twirled the end of her ponytail while finishing her candy. "I'm thinking never-ending tapas at the Lounge. Drinks on me!"

Natalie felt an even bigger smile about to break, but a second later, it dropped. "I can't. There's so much to do before Monday. I have to gather the data, store the files, order the base supplies—most have to be FedExed from Brazil—"

"Nat, chill. There'll be time for that. Right now, you need to stand still, breathe, think about chocolate, and be happy."

Natalie obeyed and took a deep breath. *Happy, yes. Chocolate, yesss.*

Not only was Ivy her best friend and R&D lab partner, she also had a knack for talking Natalie down when she was about to board the train bound for Stressville.

But she couldn't help it. She'd been submitting for pilot seed grants for two years, needing major coinage to fund the first phase of her research project on the rare Amazonian root that, when mixed with cocoa found in the same region, had been shown to safely elevate serotonin levels in adolescents.

Of course the theory that chocolate equals happiness wasn't anything new; women had been singing that song for decades. But this study was unique.

And for Natalie, very close to home.

Ivy opened her arms wide. "Congrats, superstar," she said, giving her a big hug.

"Thanks, seriously. I know it's going to take up a lot of time and you're only doing it to get your research hours in, but I really appreciate it."

"Nat." Ivy frowned. "I believe in your theory just as passionately as you do. You know that."

Natalie felt another surge of gratitude for her best friend.

Ivy stepped back and gave Natalie the old up-down. "No-no, you're not going out like this."

Natalie glanced at her outfit. Nothing unusual. Hershey-issued white lab coat covered in chocolate smears and spatters, jeans, and hot pink trainers.

"Since you're a big-shot medical researcher for the next three weeks," Ivy said, "we gotta make you presentable. These go." She removed Natalie's plastic goggles and tossed them on the table. "Pull your hair out of... Is this a *scrunchy*?"

"Who cares what I look like at work?" Natalie defended, just as she caught her reflection in the glass partition behind her microscope. Egads. Out of its updo, her blonde-streaked hair was wilder than usual. She combed her fingers through the ends, but taming it at this point was impossible. She might as well go for the purposeful lion's mane/1980 rock star's girlfriend look.

"Don't walk out in your uniform," Ivy added. "Even though it's super-fashionable."

Natalie laughed and slid out of her lab coat. "You coming now?"

"I'll meet you there in a few." She walked a tray of used measuring cups to the sink. "Um, I'm making a quick stop first."

Natalie cut between Ivy and the sink. "No. No, you're not."

"Not what?" Ivy asked, giving her the innocent eyes. But that hadn't worked in years.

"You are *not* going to see Jake." Natalie put her hands on her hips. "The guy's trouble. If I have to spend all night talking you out of it again, I will." Just a few days ago, she'd spent three hours saving Ivy from making a similarly huge relationship mistake. If Natalie wasn't around to police her, who knew what kind of trouble Ivy would get into?

"Fine," Ivy said after a dramatic exhale. "I'll stay strong, like you said."

"Good." Natalie stuffed her uniform down the laundry chute, grabbed her purse, and wound her long, cottony-soft scarf around her neck. "So you'll meet me at the Lounge later? *Alone*?"

Ivy rolled her eyes, making Natalie laugh.

She didn't mind if her best friend thought she was a pain in the derrière.

Solving Ivy's love life woes helped Natalie keep her mind off her own relationship issues.

"I promise," Ivy finally said, begrudgingly. Then her face brightened. "Now, call your parents and tell them the news!"

Natalie joined Ivy in one more celebratory squeal, then left the lab, the place she'd called her work home for five delicious years—fifty more years, if she had her way.

At every red light as she cruised up Chocolate Avenue, she called a different number. Not surprisingly, neither her mother nor her father picked up. She left voicemails everywhere, telling them she had big news and to meet at their regular table at the Lounge ASAP.

No shock they weren't there by the time she arrived. She scanned the room, picking out familiar faces of the locals she'd known her whole life among the tourists that hit spots like the Hershey Lounge on their way through "The Sweetest Place on Earth."

A tall guy stood alone at the bar. He faced the other

way, so Natalie allowed her dude-starved eyes a little stare, to pass the time, admire beauty in the world. He had waves of dark hair cut short; nice, broad shoulders; a *very* nice… um…posterior inside dark wash jeans that fit him like an Armani model.

When it was clear her quick glance had turned into a full-on ogle, she slid her gaze in the other direction. The decision she'd made to stay away from men was what made her resort to extended ogles.

She was about to call her mom's cell again when the guy turned and leaned an elbow on the bar. He looked at her briefly, looked away, then did a double-take. Natalie swallowed, not used to getting double-takes from men in Armani jeans. Maybe she should bend her own rule for once, saunter over, and…

Or maybe she'd been sampling too much product at work and was having a sugar hallucination, because she could've sworn she was staring into the blue eyes of—

"Luke?" Her diaphragm pushed the single syllable up her throat and out her mouth without too much of a choke.

"Nicole."

"*Natalie*," she corrected…then wanted to go play in busy traffic.

Luke Elliott. It had been six years since she'd seen him. What had been the occasion? Ah, yes. His engagement party. Awesome. She hadn't said one word to him that day, tried to not even look at him. Ever since one night when they were thirteen, Luke brought out every possible insecurity her teenaged self-esteem could handle, and some she couldn't. During the few times she'd seen him since graduating high school, those insecurities always came back.

Why she let someone who didn't even know her name have any kind of power over her was a mystery. A mystery she did not want to solve.

"Sorry—Natalie, of course. Hi." Luke slid his cell into his pocket and strolled over. "It's good to see you."

She felt the ridiculous impulse to greet him with a hug. But that was nothing more than a silly urge brought on by how damn good looking he was. All the Elliott offspring came from a moving assembly line of perfect hotness. Luke was the oldest, and in Natalie's life-long opinion, the most perfect.

"Good to see you, too." She was about to fold her arms but stopped halfway, unsure what do to with her hands.

Back in high school when they'd run in the same far-reaching social circle, she and Luke had never been even relatively close; for sure not close enough to hug each other now. Although the nicely fitting blue cashmere sweater he was rocking looked temptingly huggable.

No hugging, Nat.

For all she knew, he was still married.

The Hershey grapevine was notoriously unreliable. Just because she'd heard Luke got divorced two years ago didn't mean it was true. Still, she couldn't help but notice the way his sweater stretched across his chest, and how the color caught the deep-blueness of his eyes.

In case of another impulse, Natalie gripped her purse with both hands. After all, it had been a similar impulse that had made her humiliate herself in front of the guy when they were thirteen.

"It's been a while," Luke said.

"Six years," she replied, then mentally *thwapped* herself

on the forehead. Did she think she'd wow him with her memory? Or was she going for the whole stalker vibe?

He rubbed his square jaw that had a rugged five o'clock shadow going. "I think you're right."

"Six years," she repeated. What kind of small talk was called for when you practically grew up with someone who seldom gave you the time of day…until one stupid party and one "seven minutes in heaven" dare?

Polite small talk, Nat. That's what kind.

"So, what brings you to the Lounge?"

"Buddy of mine works the bar. Or used to." He ran a hand through his dark hair. "A lot's changed since the last time I actually spent more than a weekend in town."

Natalie had to laugh. "Nothing ever changes in Hershey!"

Luke smiled. The fact that it still made her stomach turn a cartwheel certainly hadn't changed. She was supposed to have gotten over her one-sided infatuation the day they'd graduated and he'd left for the big city.

"Yeah." He dipped his chin. "This town is pretty sleepy and slow. I haven't forgotten that." When he looked up again, his smile had vanished, and his sky-blue eyes looked a little cloudy.

She wondered about his subtle mood swing. She also wondered what he was doing in Hershey. The other four Elliott kids didn't live at home, either, but they came to visit all the time. Maybe it was someone's important birthday that finally brought Luke back.

"Anyway." He glanced behind her. "Are you meeting someone?"

"My parents and brother. They're not here yet. Are you alone?"

He took a beat before nodding. "For over two years now."

"I didn't mean…" She bit her lip. "I heard about the divorce."

"I'm sure everyone in Hershey's heard about it." He chuckled, but with no bitterness. "I'll wait with you until your family shows up."

She fidgeted, tugging at her sleeves, feeling like her awkward, tongue-tied teenage self.

"You don't have to. I'm sure you have better things to do."

Luke flashed a smile. "A lady should never wait alone."

Damn. He was charming, too. She'd sensed that about him when they were kids but hadn't been around him enough to know for sure. Totally unfair to be blessed with money, a perfect family, and perfect manners to go with that perfect face. Not that being hot and charming equaled a nice guy. In fact, in Natalie's most recent experiences, it meant anything *but*.

"That's very nice of you. Thanks," she said, holding up her end of the good-manners game.

"Family dinner on a Thursday. What's the occasion?"

"We're celebrating. I got a pretty big break at work. Not work-work at my day job but a new thing I'll be doing over at the med center for a few weeks."

Luke lifted his eyebrows. "Sounds impressive. Let me help you celebrate." He waved at the bar. "At least start it off."

"No, no, that's okay. They should be here any minute. Um, I think." She flipped her phone in her hands. "I haven't been able to get a hold of anyone."

"Then how do you know they're coming?"

She sighed. "I guess I don't."

"Well, then." He gestured toward the dining room. "After you."

Dang his good manners and smile. She was not about to get all weak-kneed over Luke Elliott again—the first time had been disastrous enough. And especially not now, when she was about to start on the most important project in her career. She didn't need the distraction, no matter how blue the eyes or huggable the sweater.

"We'll sit there," he said to the approaching hostess, pointing to a table next to the windows.

Looks, manners, and a dash of bossiness. Natalie thanked her lucky, chocolate-covered stars that the newly single Luke Elliott didn't live in Hershey anymore.

When they got to the table, he pulled out her chair. "Thanks," she said, unwinding her scarf and wishing she was more dressed up. No one else at the Lounge would care that she was in a plain white, long-sleeved T-shirt and hot pink Nikes, but they didn't go with Luke's cashmere polished manners.

Water and a basket of bread appeared at their table. "Thanks, Roy," she said.

"You must come here a lot," Luke observed.

"Small town."

"But you didn't grow up here. Or you didn't go to Hershey High, right?"

"Right." She opened her menu, although she'd had it memorized forever. "I'm from Inter—" As usual, she choked halfway through the word. "Intercourse."

Luke lowered his menu and eyed her across the table.

She tried not to feel the embarrassment she'd felt as a kid. She might have grown up in a tiny Pennsylvania non-town with the most mortifying name on the planet, but she'd had her own apartment in Hershey for years. The town was small, but at least it had its own post office.

"Ahh, that's right." Luke nodded. "Your father ran a farmers market in Lancaster County."

"One of them." She glanced across the dining room, hoping the subject would die.

What was it about being around Luke—or any of the Elliotts—that made Natalie feel like a barefoot hillbilly? Was it that big house on the hill where he'd grown up, while she'd been raised forty miles away in the sticks, surrounded by Amish dairy farms?

Or was it because she always seemed to be sporting exceptionally unruly, lion's-mane hair and jeans and Barbie-pink sneakers whenever she happened to see him?

Maybe it was all of the above, plus the fact that she'd had a crush on him since birth.

"Does he still have a farmers market?" he asked.

"It's smaller and only one weekend a month. But there're plenty of others in Lancaster."

"But yours had the apple cider."

Natalie couldn't help smiling. "You remember that?"

"Are you kidding?" He rested his forearms on the table. "We had that stuff year-round. *Holden Apple Farms.* I can picture the label."

So could Natalie—way too vividly. "I haven't had any in ages."

"Why?"

She gave him a long look. "I had to pick those apples

instead of going to parties."

His grinning eyes crinkled at the edges. "I hear ya."

While he went back to studying his menu, Natalie stopped to think how, in the last ten minutes, they'd exchanged more words than they ever had. Definitely more than during those dimly-lit moments inside the boathouse. The memory made the hair at the back of her neck stand up.

Luke chuckled.

"Does your entrée page have a comic section mine doesn't?" she asked.

"I forgot how huge bologna is around here. I know it's an Amish thing, but I never liked it, even as a kid."

Natalie crinkled her nose. "Me neither, but the tourists expect it. That and chocolate-covered everything."

"Of course." He smiled again, all broad and manly, and right at her. Jeepers. "So, you mentioned the med center. You didn't go into the family business? No farming?"

"No farming. But I didn't stray far." She draped a napkin over her lap. "I work at the Hershey factory."

"And at the med center? How do you swing that?"

"*That* is a long story." She lifted her water glass and took a drink, not wanting to get into the nitty-gritty of her upcoming research trial. Not that she didn't want to shout her excitement from the rooftops, but for someone who didn't know her family history, the root of this project was personal.

Having come from a perfect family, Luke wouldn't understand, anyway.

"What about you?" she asked. "You didn't follow in your father's footsteps, either."

"No, I did not." He took a sip of his own drink.

The Elliotts were easily the wealthiest non-chocolate-connected family in Hershey. Mr. Elliott ran one of the most successful software companies outside Silicon Valley, with three offices in Manhattan and a tiny one in Hershey. She admired that Luke had gone his own way, instead of the big corporate route like the other Elliotts.

"Last I heard, it was music," Natalie said.

Luke's eyebrows arched and he lowered his glass. "Where did you hear that?"

"You know Hershey. The grapevine isn't particularly accurate, but there's always plenty of information."

"That I *do* remember." He ran a finger along the rim of his glass. "I could never give up music. It's my first love. Tough to get over your first love."

Sure is, Natalie thought, looking away from him. *At least not without a whole lot of work, years apart, and mucho Kit Kat bars.*

During their senior year, Luke was never more than an arm's length from his guitar. He was an acoustic guy, stripping down rock songs; Ed Sheeran before Ed Sheeran existed. To Natalie, Luke's cool style stood out.

"It's tough to make a living at music," he added. "My father saw to it I had something to fall back on."

Unfortunately, Natalie suspected this about Luke Elliott, too. How nice it must be to have a cushy inheritance so you could cross the country with a guitar on your back. She tried not to feel envious.

Roy appeared to take their orders. "What do you recommend?" Luke asked Natalie.

"Anything but bologna," they said together, then looked at each other, laughed, then fell silent.

Luke held eye contact for a good three seconds longer

than was socially acceptable for two old "non-friends," causing Natalie's cheeks to flush and the back of her neck to tingle. She knew she'd be in full-blown blushing mode if she didn't break the silence quickly.

She scooted up in her seat, reached over, and pointed to the center of Luke's menu. "You look like a beef man," she said, crossing her legs. "You'll find nothing better than the filet."

"A beef man? I can't wait to hear why you think that," Luke said, right as Natalie felt his foot slide against hers under the table.

L uke's eyes couldn't move from the woman sitting across from him. He wasn't sure if he was pathetically out of practice, or if he'd just accidentally hit on Natalie Holden.

Why did he feel the need to stretch out just as she moved?

When he'd spotted the curvy blonde with the big eyes waiting by the hostess station, he hadn't recognized her. But when she'd called him by name, something flickered inside his brain, the shred of a memory from a million years ago.

Natalie Holden.

Until he'd pictured the label on the apple cider, he hadn't remembered her last name— Hell, he'd even gotten her first name wrong. In the past decade, the woman hadn't so much as crossed his mind. She'd seldom crossed his mind in high school, either.

Why was that? Five feet away from him now, with that cute little button nose and bright smile, she was zigzagging all over his mind.

As he continued to pretend to read the menu, he felt her large, long-lashed eyes on him, but he chose not to look up. It had been two years since the divorce. There'd been lonely nights and accommodating women, but Luke was miles away from something more than a friendly dinner with anyone who had even the slightest…potential.

No flirting, not even an accidental game of footsie.

He cleared his throat. "Filet sounds good, but ladies first."

She seemed to be deciding for an awfully long time for someone who came to this place so frequently she knew the staff by name. "I think I better have a Cobb."

"Cobb salad for the lady," he said to the server. "And the filet for me, rare."

After the server left, Luke finally glanced at Natalie. She hadn't minded him ordering for her. That was another difference he'd noticed about some city and country women. It used to annoy his ex-wife, Celeste, when he showed the tiniest amount of polite authority. Yes, he was perfectly aware she could order for herself and open her own doors. That wasn't the point. His father taught him and his brothers better than that, and his mother and sister never expected less.

"So?" he said. "Better?"

"Better what?" She tore off a piece of bread.

"You said you *better* have a salad." He pushed the butter dish toward her. "Why?"

"Today at work, we finished the cycle of a test product."

"Meaning?"

She took a bite and tilted her head. "I've been eating chocolate all day."

Her straightforward answer made him laugh. "Not a lot of green vegetables in that."

"Not enough if I want to keep up the sampling and still fit in my clothes."

Funny, she didn't give off the impression of being the kind of woman who stressed about what she looked like. Not that she wasn't attractive— She was. More than that, she seemed comfortable in her skin.

With that thought, Luke couldn't keep his gaze from dipping to the healthy triangle of skin exposed by her low-cut V-neck, then a little bit lower. "A balanced diet, yes," he said after a throat clear and a quick glance up at her face. "All the studies say how important that is. We gotta keep a balance; I'm all about balance."

And now he was babbling. In front of Natalie Holden. Farmer's daughter from Intercourse. That quiet sixteen-year-old who used to catch his eye then disappear around a corner before he could say more than hello.

Now she sat across the table, intriguing him.

It was a good thing she was the exact opposite—right down to her blonde hair—of anyone he'd ever been with, starting with his first middle school girlfriend, Misty, and ending with Celeste, his ex. He'd always gravitated toward assertive, polished women, lethally classy, with big, fast-paced lives. Never a dull moment. Those women were the right fit for his own fast-paced lifestyle.

Natalie was good looking, but not his type.

"Balance, right," she said, while buttering another piece of bread. "Of course, I'm in favor of the scales tipping a little more on the chocolate side."

"Job security."

"Exactly." She slid half the piece of bread into her mouth and pulled back a sunny smile. Smiles like that could only come from the goodness of the country. Back in Philadelphia where he'd lived the past decade, they were few and far between. Or maybe it was that he hadn't had much to smile about lately.

"How do *you* deal with the whole job security thing?" Natalie asked when the server returned with their food.

"What do you mean?"

"You're a starving artist."

When she reached for the salt, and that deep V-neck started sliding off one shoulder, Luke caught a peek-a-boo glimpse of flesh-colored lace.

"Um, what?" He blinked up at her face.

"I'm just saying, it's a pretty insecure field."

Luke had no idea what she was talking about. "I've got inner security."

She laughed and pointed her fork at him. "Bragger."

He'd never thought of himself as a bragger, but when Natalie said it, it sounded like a compliment. He smiled and shrugged. "I try."

And so they ate, while watching and giving commentary about a family with five kids who'd taken over the middle of the dining room.

"How often do you play?" Natalie asked.

"Play?" The way she slowly slid her fork out of her mouth and looked at him made Luke's imagination shoot to one kind of *play*. Or maybe that was his pent-up mind drifting.

"Your guitar." She laughed lightly, femininely. "You're so funny."

He wasn't sure what he'd said that caused her to laugh, but he hoped he'd say something funny again. He liked the sound of her laugh, and he liked her smile. She had a dimple on her cheek he'd never noticed. And a lacy bra strap he couldn't help but notice.

Damn. Natalie Holden is sexy as hell.

Her brown eyes blinked at him. "You were telling me where you play guitar?"

"Ah." He wiped his mouth on a napkin. "There's a coffee shop in Philly that's forced to allow anyone open-mike access Thursday nights. They have no choice, even if I drive customers away."

She batted the air between them, as if his last sentence had been absurd. "I'm sure you pack the place."

"Not even."

"You have a beautiful voice." Their gazes locked, then she blinked hard, wiped her mouth like she was wiping away her smile, and looked down at her plate, spearing the salad. "I mean, you did in high school."

"You heard me play back then? I had no idea you were a fan. Do you want my autograph?" He couldn't help grinning. "I'll sign it wherever you want."

He was flirting, and it wasn't accidental. He liked watching how her cheeks turned pink, and sometimes when she smiled, she twirled her hair around a finger.

"I wasn't a *fan*," she said.

He chucked into his fist. "Don't break it to me gently."

"I mean, I wasn't one of those girls." She rolled her eyes. "The ones who followed you around and went to all your concerts."

"I didn't have concerts."

She forked a cherry tomato on her place. "We didn't go to the same high school, but I know you played your guitar at assemblies."

"Hershey has a superior music program. Two choirs and three bands."

"Ah, I see." She toyed with the stem of her glass. "Which were you in? Band or choir?"

"Uh, neither," he admitted, narrowing his eyes at her playfully, which caused her to lift a tiny smile. No dimple appearance yet.

"And yet they asked you to perform anyway."

He grinned. "Okay. I guess I was kind of a spotlight hog back then."

"You mean, inner security."

His felt his smile broaden at the same time hers did. "That makes me sound less like a cocky jerk, thank you."

Natalie took another bite of salad. "I heard you play at Philip Arthur a few times."

"The ice cream shop?" He had a flashback. The school assemblies had been one thing—his buddies were there and whoever his girlfriend was at the time. Plenty of friendly support. But Phillip Arthur was public. Not even his mother could clap loudly enough when that party room fell silent.

"You were great."

Luke's seventeen-year-old self felt the warmth of gratitude. "Really?"

"You sound surprised."

"No one listened to me back then."

"I was listening." Her eyes lingered on his for a moment, then she glanced away, suddenly fascinated by a huge orange clock on the wall.

"Maybe I could play for you again. How about tomorrow night?"

Damn. He'd done it.

But how could he not? She was incredibly cute—no denying that, and she made him laugh. She was open and enchanting, yet with something mysterious and held back. It made the academic in him curious, and the rule-follower forgetful.

But Natalie didn't reply, didn't even look at him as a few long moments ticked by. His "inner security" was about to take a hit.

"I'm free tomorrow," she finally said, sliding her gaze to his. "Or maybe…"

"Maybe?"

She tugged a strand of her long blonde hair. "Do you have your guitar with you now?"

Warmth—that had nothing to do with teenage grati-tude—gathered in Luke's chest like tropical storm clouds. "It's in my car," he said. "Should we…" He made a check motion in the air with one finger.

When she smiled, not only did her dimple show, but her whole face lit up.

It had been a while, but Luke felt lit-up, too. She might not be his type, but Natalie sure as hell could distract him from stressing about work for a while.

His mind skipped from strumming his guitar for her to strumming his fingers across her cheek then into her hair, down her…

Suddenly, he had to keep his mind as well as his hands occupied. "Enough about me. We're here for you. A toast." He held up his half-empty glass. "Though it's belated, sorry."

"I appreciate the thought." She tilted her glass toward his.

"Here's to…wait, you haven't told me what we're celebrating."

"A research project I put together finally got funding for a pre-clinical trial," she said. Luke caught the appealing twinkle of pride in her eyes. "We start next week."

"Congratulations. What kind of research?"

"I guess you'd call it a supplement. In layman's terms, the idea is to insert my serum into chocolate and gauge its stimulants on the brain."

Huh. That sounds vaguely fam—

The glass in his hand slipped an inch. "What control group?"

"Teenagers suffering from depression. I was contacted a few weeks ago that we were awarded a seed grant. It won't be enough for phase two, but it's a start. I didn't find out until today that the foundation giving us the grant booked the lab for next week. It's either now or they'll give the money to someone else."

Luke felt himself nod stiffly.

"Anyway, we're a pretty unorthodox team. Just me, another chemist from Hershey, two medical interns from the university, and…" She paused to roll her eyes. "Apparently the NIH is sending a microbiologist to proctor the whole thing. Like the feds want to cover their asses before approving a grant—which I get, but it's a pain. The proctor's probably some new-age health flunky they dug up."

Before unhinging his jaw, he took a breath, then calmly rested his palms on the table. "Flunky?" he repeated. "Why do you say that?"

"For one thing, I don't think it's common for the National Institutes of Health to bother proctoring tiny projects like ours. It puts the spotlight directly on us, and I'm already under enough pressure. But it's as though the guy lobbied to be added to the team, like he has a grudge against the project." She shrugged. "I don't know. Maybe he's not a flunky, but a vegan who's never had a bite of chocolate his whole life."

"Or maybe he's someone who champions healthy living."

"Yeah." She snorted. "Like I said, new-age."

If that snort hadn't been so adorable, Luke might've been insulted. "First of all, my specialty in holistic medicine for mood disorders makes me more than qualified," he said. "Second, the NIH promotes the absolute importance of proper diet, especially in those whose brains are still developing and susceptible to foreign stimuli."

Natalie was staring at him, her glass still outstretched in mid-toast.

"And third, I'm not a vegan."

Chapter Two

The meaning of his words didn't register in Natalie's brain at first. Then the truth released like a mental dam had burst. She lowered her glass, not about to toast her success with the enemy.

"*You're* the flunky?"

"No, I'm a specialist." Luke's expression didn't change. "But you're right about the NIH. They won't give you a dime if they don't see the importance of your study."

Just then, Roy came whizzing by with their check. When Natalie reached for it, Luke slid it away. "It's on me."

"Thanks," she muttered, suddenly too annoyed—or disappointed or *something*—to be grateful. "What are you, some kind of sugar Nazi?"

"That's one way of putting it."

"So I'm assuming dessert is out."

Luke was stuffing bills into the leather folder, but Natalie could swear he was smirking. "If you want to fill your body with pollutants, go for it."

Natalie huffed. "Says the NIH."

"Wait." He closed the check booklet and looked at her. "You're angry about this?"

Before replying, she managed to reign in her temper. "Frustrated, not angry. This trial is really important to me, and it's already being messed with before day one."

"Not by me."

She exhaled slowly and gripped the sides of the table. "Look, I'm not angry with you. We should drop it. Thanks for dinner. It was nice to catch up." She scooted back her chair and stood, regret mixing with relief as she glanced down at his dreamy, chiseled face.

At least she wouldn't have to worry about more of those old feelings resurfacing—the awkwardness and crippling inadequacy. She'd always sensed Luke Elliott thought she wasn't good enough for him. Now, it wouldn't matter. She was romantically distraction-free once again, just the way she liked it.

Luke was still seated when she left him and walked to the exit. But by the time she'd made it to the parking lot, he was right behind her, calling for her to wait. She tried to ignore how hearing him say her name, her correct name, made her stomach flip.

"Wait for what?" she said, turning around. Dammit. His eyes were even bluer under natural light.

"I thought..." Luke began, "you wanted to see my guitar." He nodded toward a black ragtop Jeep a few spaces away.

Of course he drives something panty-droppingly sexy like that.

"I don't believe this," she muttered.

"It's fine if you changed your mind. I can handle rejection."

Of course, he could. So then why was Natalie the one feeling rejected—just like when they were kids? "You haven't been exactly truthful, have you?"

"How so?"

"You *just happened* to run into me after ten years, and *just happened* to be assigned to my research team." She couldn't stand the idea of being misled about something to do with work. Not for a second time. She planted her hands on her hips. "And since when is a starving musician also a microbiologist?"

"Since it's what I studied in grad school."

Why hadn't she heard about that? Stupid unreliable grapevine.

"And I never said I was a starving musician."

"What was all that open-mike talk?" she asked, trying to ignore the way his blue eyes fixed on her.

"I still do that, or used to."

"And wanting to play for me."

"The offer stands."

Seriously? "Don't you think that's a bad idea? It's an ethical conflict."

Luke opened his mouth but then shut it. "Yes, it's a conflict," he finally agreed. "I'm here to represent the NIH, but that doesn't mean we're automatically on opposing sides."

"I don't see it that way."

"Look, I didn't…" He ran a hand though his hair, giving him that sexy disheveled look. Like she really needed him to be any sexier while she was trying to stay focused. "I didn't know you were heading this trial. Hell, I haven't seen you since high school, Natalie."

"*Nicole*, you mean."

Luke looked at her, then down at the ground while blowing out a breath. It made her smile to know she'd needled him.

"That was a mistake, and I apologized," he said, back to Joe Cool.

"I just don't understand," she said. "The Baldwin Foundation already approved their grant. Why does the NIH care at this point?"

"They hired me to gatekeep any future grants they might award you," he said, being furiously logical. "I'm not a fed, but helping kids get healthy and happy *naturally* is important to me."

"Me, too!"

He crossed his arms. "I guess we have different views about how that's done."

"You can say that again." She'd had enough and turned to leave. But when she swung around, one strap of her purse fell off her shoulder, causing half the contents to spill onto the parking lot. "Great," she muttered.

Luke kneeled to pick up miscellaneous pens and lip-glosses before she could stop him.

"I got this," she said, crouching down, probably most inelegantly. But what did she care how she looked to Luke now? She couldn't count the ways this guy was off-limits.

"Here." He passed over her compact mirror and a few crumpled Mr. Goodbar wrappers. "And this." He held the travel-sized bottle of her Pink Macaroon perfume. "Nice." He waved it under his nose. "Sexy." When she growled and grabbed for it, Luke actually laughed. "If it makes you feel better, I'm only on your team to observe and give my opinion when necessary."

Natalie reached for more of her fallen stuff and crammed it in her purse. "I don't need a babysitter. I need carte blanche. With lab space for only three weeks, I won't be able to have that with the NIH's spy breathing down my neck."

A little breeze picked up, scattering stray wrappers around their feet. Luke moved to gather them. "I'm not a spy," he said, as he bumped into her back. "But if the NIH wants me to breathe down your neck, Natalie, you'll learn to like it."

He was behind her, close enough that she felt the warmth of his body, causing her traitorous temperature to rise.

"I'm practically breathing down your neck right now," he added in a low voice. "You don't seem to have a problem with it."

Natalie couldn't stop more heat from spreading across her cheeks, under her hair. She had to nip this thing in the bud, so she rotated around, her lips peeling apart to say something back. To shut him up. But his face was so close to hers. She could see the notch between his eyes, the light scar that ran along his left temple, the sexy way his mouth curved.

Her pulse galloped, sending out a warning that she was about to make a very unwise decision…

"Nat? What are you doing?"

Natalie sucked in a gasp and knocked her head against Luke's when she saw her mother staring at them. "Mom. Hi." She straightened, hoping her face wasn't as flushed as it felt.

"Did you just get here, too?" her dad asked, then glanced at Luke. "Hello there."

"He was just leaving," Natalie cut in, shooting Luke a blatant go-away glare.

He didn't react at first, but then nodded. "See you Monday."

She watched his butt—for just a second—as he walked toward the Jeep, solely to make sure he was really leaving.

"Who was that?" Mom asked. "Cute and tall."

"*That*"—Natalie paused to sigh—"is living proof karma is a bitch."

"Don't say that word, dear. And who's Carmen?"

"Never mind, Mom." She laughed under her breath. "You guys were late so I already ate. Let's go back to the house. Will you drive and I'll leave my car here?" She peered behind them. "Where's Muff?"

Her parents glanced at each other.

"Your brother didn't want to come," Dad said. "He wasn't up to leaving his room."

Natalie's heart sank like a stone thrown in a pond. She loved her little brother more than anything, and his illness rendered her helpless. "Did something happen?"

Mom shrugged as they walked to their car. "Not that we know of. With Brandon, sometimes there's no rhyme or reason. That's what his doctor says."

Natalie nodded, feeling even more helpless.

Dad didn't hold Mom's door open. The kind little gestures Natalie used to notice between them had disappeared. And they might never return. Her parents had been through hell—were still in hell. Natalie knew darn well that a high percentage of couples in their situation split up for good. At least her parents were still together, still trying.

"What's your big news?" Mom asked as she buckled her seatbelt.

Only this particular subject change could make Natalie's mood lift like she'd been injected with her own serum. "Mom, Dad, we got the grant."

They stared at her blankly for a moment, then her mom's eyes grew wide. "You're joking."

Natalie beamed with pride. "Start Monday."

As they drove to her parents' neighborhood, she filled them in on the details, though skipping over everything about Luke's involvement. She hadn't had enough chocolate to stomach that.

L uke took the long way through town. Not that he dreaded going home. He just wanted a few extra minutes to think. As he idled at the light on the intersection of Cocoa and Chocolate Avenues, he felt himself smiling. Then he actually laughed out loud.

That Natalie Holden. She was something else. The way her cheeks turned pink then bright red when he unleashed that crack about breathing down her neck. It made him laugh again.

But this laugh was short-lived. Dude, he'd really dodged a bullet there. If he hadn't asked what she was celebrating, or treated her the same as the other getting-him-over-his-divorce women, Luke would've woken up in the morning having made the biggest mistake of his career.

It wasn't only that hooking up with the head researcher of the trial would be unethical, but at his company—thanks to a major HR shake down—every employee's personal behavior was under the microscope.

Not to mention the tiny fact that Luke was currently being headhunted by the NIH.

Yes, definitely dodged a bullet.

As he headed up the hill, he saw in the distance that every light in the house was on. He wondered if his parents were hosting a party they didn't tell him about. Things with his siblings were almost completely smoothed over now, but it had taken longer with his parents. Not that he blamed them for reacting the way they had to the decisions he'd made. At the time, he thought he'd been doing the right thing, going along with Celeste. He'd sided with his wife to make their marriage work. But the repercussions of that decision still weighed heavily on him.

He roared into the driveway and set the parking brake. Probably not a party after all, since there were only two extra cars. One, he knew was as his brother Dexter's. The other, he didn't recognize, but when he eyed the license plate, he had a hunch.

"Hey, loser."

Hunch confirmed.

"Hey, snoozer," Luke fired back. "What are you doing here?" He walked to the front door where Roxanne stood under the porch light. The top she wore showed too much skin. Luke didn't like that one bit and still couldn't wrap his brain around how his baby sister was about to graduate from college.

"Where've you been?" Roxy asked.

Luke took the porch steps two at a time. "Again, why are you here?"

"Because I heard *you* were, and I couldn't stay away." She waved a dramatic hand in the air, then stepped into Luke's open arms.

Was she thinner than usual? Her hair was definitely shorter. Wasn't it? Luke cussed himself out for not keeping in better touch. She probably posted a million pictures on Facebook. He could've at least kept tabs on her that way, but after what had happened with Celeste, he'd sworn off social media.

He gave his sister one more squeeze, then stepped back. "You drove all the way from Jersey to see me?" He narrowed his eyes. "Why do I not believe that?"

"Dex is here, too," Roxy said, walking backward into the house.

"I saw his car. And you got a new Audi? Nice."

"Dad said it's an investment, and I didn't argue."

"Well played, Sis. Where is everyone?"

"You'll see." She leveled her chin and linked an arm through his, leading him into the formal living room, which was strange. That was where the Wedgewood and china was; they never used that room unless…

Luke stopped in place the second they stepped into the room. There they sat, as still as statues, peering at him: his parents and his brother Dexter, looking way too…something. Calm? Creepy? Creepy-calm was a good description.

"Vince and Danny are on Skype," Roxy said, squishing herself between her parents, looking up at him just as creepily.

Luke waved to the laptop on the coffee table, at his twin brothers' digital images. They waved back. Their solemn expressions gave nothing away, either.

Cloak-and-dagger behavior wasn't anything new with his family. Even now, with them all grown and out of the house, he and his brothers usually had some kind of prank war going. Not to mention the bets. Last time he'd lost a bet, he'd found himself on a sailboat bound for Nantucket with only a hotel towel as clothing.

He slid his hands in his pockets, attempting the image of "it's all good" in case they were trying to rattle him. Despite the creepiness of the scene, it made Luke feel like one of the gang again, as if things were almost back to normal between him and his family.

"Hey, Dex," he said, bumping his brother's outstretched fist. "Mom." He bent down and kissed his mother on the cheek. "Let me guess, this is an intervention." He was joking, but no one laughed.

"Sit down, son," his father said, motioning to the armchair.

Luke felt like he'd stepped into a trap instead of a reunion, but since he couldn't think of any way he'd soiled the family name recently, he sat.

"Eileen," his dad said to his mother. "Why don't you start?"

Mom glanced at him nervously and touched the side of her hairdo. "Luke, we love you. You know that, right?"

"Okay…"

"But this simply won't do."

Dad folded his arms. "Your mother's right."

Luke was completely lost. "Guys, I'm obviously not in on the joke. I have no idea—"

"We heard what you're doing," Mom cut in. "And we don't approve— We can't."

"What exactly am I doing?"

"Luke, bro." Dexter shook his head, pitifully. "Seriously, it's all over town."

Mom stood up. "Sweetie, don't get me wrong, we love that you're back in Hershey with us, but... You told us it's for a temporary assignment at the med center."

Luke wasn't any closer to understanding what they were going on about. "Is that an issue? Me proctoring a research trial?"

Dexter shifted his weight. "Bro, it's pretty lame what you're doing. In a town like this? You're vilifying its main commodity."

"How?"

The next thing he knew, the room was chaotic from everyone talking over each other. He couldn't hear Vince or Danny on Skype, but their mouths were moving.

"*Chocolate*, Luke." Roxy's voice broke through the noise. "After all this time, you ride up on your white health horse and expect everyone to be overjoyed?"

This was getting out of control. His family was reacting the same way Natalie had. "I'm not the enemy here. This assignment is a stepping stone in my career—an *important* one. It's nothing personal against Hershey."

Dad chuckled darkly and touched the knot of his tie. "Tell that to the fellas at the club. They have stock in Hershey. So do I."

Luke rubbed the back of his neck, trying to think. "I don't know how word got around so fast since *I've* only known for twenty-four hours. I ran into her at the Lounge, and she made a big deal about it, too. But I'm in no way vili-fying her." He felt on the brink of a smile, picturing Natalie's blushing face. When she'd bent over to pick up the things from her purse, he'd gotten a longer glance at more than her face.

"Her who?" Dexter said.

Luke blinked to shake the image from his brain. "The, um, head of the research team."

Dex tapped his chin. "Interesting."

"Well, we've said our piece, Son," Dad said, standing. Speech over. Luke wanted to laugh. Their "fly-by-parenting" hadn't changed over the years. "We trust you'll do the right thing," Dad added. You know we won't interfere in your decisions." He rested a hand on Luke's shoulder. Instead of laughing, he felt a lump swell in his throat.

Despite the way he'd treated them, practically cut them out of his life for a time, they still forgave and didn't interfere. They fervently expressed their opinions—yes. But never interfered.

"Thank you, Dad," Luke said, scratching his head. "I think."

"Good night, boys. Come home soon." Mom blew kisses to the computer, then his brothers disappeared and the screen went black. "Fix yourself a sandwich if you're hungry," she said, ruffling Luke's hair.

"Thanks, Mom, but I just ate."

"Bologna's in the fridge."

Luke almost gagged, then he chuckled as his parents left the room. "They were never any good at tough love," he said to his remaining brother and sister.

Dexter propped his feet on the coffee table. "So, who's the girl?"

Luke frowned. "Girl?"

"The one running the research team. You said *she*."

"Oh." Luke sat on the couch and slid a coffee table book onto his lap. "No one. A local."

"Which makes this even worse," Roxy said. "Hershey already thinks our family's a bunch of elitists."

"Since when?"

She rolled her eyes. "You haven't been here enough lately to get it. *I* was the last one left and had to deal with all that crap." She folded her arms. "You have no clue."

He didn't. He had no idea the town felt this way about his family. Had they always? Or was it a recent development? "The Hershey Company is a world-wide corporation," he defended. "This is an insignificant pre-clinical trial that won't go anywhere."

"Whatever," Roxy said. "Try seeing it from the other side. Being obtuse won't win you any friends."

"Thanks for the tip," Luke said with an indulgent smile as she left the room, then went back to the book on his lap.

"Okay," Dexter said. "Tell me about her."

Of course Luke knew which her Dex was referring to and tried hard not to smile.

"Yeah?" Dex added.

"It's nothing. She's funny, that's all."

"Is that code for hot?"

"No, that's code for saying charming things and having a sense of humor." He paused then pushed out a long breath. "But in this case, yes, it's also code for hot."

"Nice." Dex grinned. "Good to see you out there again, man."

"No one's out anywhere," Luke said, cutting off his brother's excitement. "We accidentally had dinner together, accidentally played footsie under the table, then she yelled at me and accused me of being a liar and a federal spy." He shrugged. "It was a nice moment."

"You said she's a local. What's her name?"

"Natalie Holden."

Dexter's brows furrowed. "Doesn't ring a bell."

That was a relief. Luke didn't want to discover she'd been one of Dex's conquests. Though, judging from the way Natalie's smile could knock the breath out of him, *she'd* be the conqueror in that scenario.

"If she's hot and"—Dexter waggled his eyebrows— "funny, you should ask her out."

Luke wasn't about to admit he already had and had basically been shot down. Even if Natalie wasn't in the picture, Luke was by no means "back out there." An emotion-free and uncomplicated night with a woman was one thing. But a relationship? Love? No.

He'd never let anyone manipulate him the way his ex had. Love had made him weak. Love had almost cost him his family.

And since any kind of uncomplicated night with Natalie was a non-starter, there was no reason to think about her.

"It'll never happen. There's an ethical conflict," he said, grabbing for the logical instead of personal. "Enough about me." He kicked his brother's feet off the coffee table. "How's life in New York?"

"I work hard so I can play even harder." He grinned like a wolf. "But my life isn't nearly as interesting as yours. New research project. Potential new job. New prospective lady…"

"No lady and no prospect," Luke said with an eye roll, while inside, he wondered if he'd catch Natalie blushing on Monday.

Chapter Three

Natalie followed her parents into the house. She'd been away at college when they'd decided to buy a home in Hershey and not live full time at the farm. Though it wasn't the house where she grew up, she liked it, and she knew it was easier on her parents to be closer to Brandon's doctors.

"You should go say hi to your brother," her mom said, glancing at the closed door at the end of the hall.

"Yeah." Natalie took a few steps then stopped. "Anything I should know? I mean, anything new?"

Mom shook her head, her face showing lines of sadness.

Natalie gave her brother's door a few taps in rhythm. "Muff? Can I come in?"

No response for a moment, then a quiet, "yeah," came through the door.

Brandon's bedroom had changed a lot in the last few years. If an outsider inspected it, they'd think he'd joined the "emo" crowd that was so prevalent with teenagers: lots of dark colors, angsty music, and obsession with the macabre.

But Muff wasn't emo.

Depression in teens wasn't uncommon—there was so much pressure to fit in and be popular, not to mention the hormones. Not everyone was allowed at the "cool" table. She'd been living proof of that. But Natalie had had a lot of interests in school. She was active and had friends who helped her through those awkward stages.

Until three years ago, her now sixteen-year-old brother had seemed like your average well-balanced kid. He *had* sat at the popular table, and there'd always been groups of friends coming over to the house. His attitude and upbeat personality hadn't change overnight; there'd been signs early on.

Luckily, their parents had been on the lookout because Dad's mother had suffered from depression for over a decade, passing that trait onto one of Natalie's aunts. Things like that could run in the blood.

Dysthymia with a touch of double depression was his official diagnosis, which meant it was chronic and longer-lasting than regular teen depression. His doctors said eventually—through meds and psychotherapy—Brandon should outgrow it. But after three years, the dark clouds hadn't lifted.

"Hey, bran muffin," Natalie said. One bedside lamp and the TV screen were the only lights on. Muff sat on the floor, leaning against the foot of his bed, knees pulled up to his chest.

He didn't look at her but continued to stare at the TV screen. It was one of those shoot-'em-up games. He didn't have the volume up loud—bugging everyone in the house to hear the constant gunfire and techno music like he used to. Now, Natalie could barely hear the soundtrack.

"What's the score?" she asked. The wording of the question used to get a rise out of him. But he didn't reply. Natalie glanced at the TV and noticed her brother's avatar wasn't doing much on the screen, like he was waiting for the enemy to put him out of his misery.

She sat on the bed next to his head. "Have you eaten? Mom and Dad were late meeting me so they're talking pancakes and bacon." She bounced on the bed. "You love breakfast for dinner."

Brandon sighed. "Whatever."

It wasn't the normal teenage attitude they were dealing with. When Muff said, "whatever," he genuinely meant he didn't care…that he didn't have the energy or ability to give a rat's ass about the subject. There'd been a time when Natalie would've yelled at him to snap out of it, or burst into tears, hoping to pull some kind of emotional reaction out of her brother. But that was a long time ago, and neither had done any good. Depression wasn't something you could yell out of a person.

For a while after that, they'd been careful to walk on eggshells around him, to make sure no one did anything that might make him worse. They'd even stopped using the family nickname he'd had since birth, wondering if the affectionate "Muff" bothered him. But he'd actually snapped at Natalie when she'd called him Brandon.

"I got this new job at work," Natalie said to him conversationally. "It's not a promotion or anything— In fact, it's basically an assignment 'cause we have to publish research papers and whatever. But it's pretty exciting." She glanced at Muff, and when he didn't respond, she stood up, knowing it was best not to coddle him. Treat the scene like it was normal was the best thing to do. "It's a research project at the med center," she continued as she turned on the overhead light, brightening the room. "Ivy's on the project, too. She's totally jazzed. Get this. Before I went out to celebrate, she gave me a mini makeover, like the head of a research team can't possibly walk the streets of Hershey with my hair in a scrunchy."

Muff exhaled a quiet breath, something that might've been a laugh, then he lifted his chin to look at her. "Those are tacky."

She laughed, thrilled his reply wasn't a single syllable. "Oh, please. There's nothing wrong with wearing a scrunchy while I'm at work."

"Then you're tacky, too."

"Hey, don't be mean." She stood between him and the TV. "I don't need another lecture about my appalling lack of fashion." She kicked his foot. "You're the one wearing mismatched socks."

"Like it matters. No one gives a crap about my socks."

Natalie's heart sank even deeper. Normally, she'd kneel beside him and tell Muff how much *she* cared, how much everyone cared and that if he tried harder, he'd see that. But words didn't work.

"Well, I care about the socks I'm wearing today because they're what I was wearing when I got the good news. They're my lucky socks." She hitched up a pant leg to display the item in question. "Huh, they're lame and white. Okay, so I'll call this my lucky bra—"

Brandon's head snapped up. "That's gross. I'm not

looking at my sister's bra."

"I wasn't about to show it to you. That *is* gross." She kicked his other foot. "Want dinner?"

"Don't feel like it."

"Will you do it for me? I've already eaten, and I know if there's leftover bacon, I'll scarf it." She extended her hand to help him up. He ignored it, but a moment later, he shifted his weight and stood on his own.

Well, progress is progress. Not that getting him to eat is monumental, but at least he's leaving his room.

His shaggy blond hair hung over his eyes, which used to be stylish when he wore the front flipped to one side like other boys his age, but now it looked like he was hiding.

As they were about to leave his bedroom, Natalie put a hand on his shoulder. "Hey, you okay? I mean, you know, how are you?"

"I'm okay." His usual reply. It was the tone she'd been listening for. This "I'm okay," didn't sound okay.

"I heard you're on some new meds. What do you think so far?"

He shrugged.

"No change? I mean, do you feel worse or…"

"I dunno. I guess I'm sleeping better."

"That's awesome."

"Yeah. Let's have a damn party to celebrate." His sarcastic tone was biting, and he walked off.

Tears burned behind Natalie's eyes as she watched him leave. It killed her to see him in pain. Even if he didn't feel physical pain, an emotional illness could be excruciating. On the other hand, Muff didn't usually make an effort to be sarcastic. Even though the remark was aimed at her, she was glad there was some animation in his personality.

Even if outside research wasn't part of her job, she still would've devoted all her spare time to this project. A lot of people—including the head of Hershey's R&D—thought she'd bitten off more than she could chew by gunning for an actual clinical trial. She'd read about Brandon's new medication. It had decent results, but everyone was different.

More than ever, she was pumped about finally starting the trial. There was an element all those doctors were missing, and maybe, just maybe, she'd found it.

On the way to the kitchen, she grabbed her purse, wanting to start a to-do list for tomorrow. She already had an appointment in the morning with the facilities administrator at the med center to see the lab and give him a list of materials they required. After that, she was meeting with Ivy and the team. Since they only had the lab for three weeks, timing was everything.

Excitement fluttered in her stomach as she thought about what might be accomplished. She dug for a pen, causing her tiny bottle of perfume to fall out. Instantly, she remembered the semi-smoldering way Luke had looked at her after smelling the perfume. "Sexy," he'd said, though he'd been the one looking sexy and smelling sexy and…

Another flutter erupted in her stomach, but not the good kind— Well, it *was* the good kind, but not the *productive* kind. She took a deep breath then pushed it out.

If she was going to focus on the trial, there was no room for thoughts of how a certain proctor made her flutter.

Luke sat in the parking lot. It had been a draining week-end since the "intervention," with his family giving him subtle though never-ending grief about his assignment. He was on the side of nutrition, so why did they deem his job as villainous?

Like Natalie. This was why he hadn't moved from his car yet.

He'd tried not to think about her over the weekend, because every time he did, he smiled.

She obviously wasn't interested. If she had been, she'd changed her tune the second she'd learned he'd been sent by the NIH. What had she called him? A new-age flunky? He chuckled into his fist but cut it short.

Head out of the clouds, man, and focus. You owe that to the team back in Philly. He also owed it to the NIH, who'd contracted him for this job, but mostly he owed it to himself and the future he was trying to build.

He'd been with *Perelman School of Medicine* in Phila-delphia for five years. It was a steady job, and he'd done some good in his field, but he felt stifled and knew there must be more. Because of his specialty, he'd been borrowed by foundations and research centers to lend his expertise. But this was the first time the NIH had asked for him.

That call from the big league boys had been a surprise, but Luke was more than ready for a new challenge.

He knew the NIH only borrowed people they wanted to hire—it was their last little "test." A job in Washington DC would be a huge leap in his career, and living in another face-paced city was exactly what we wanted. He could taste it, and this trivial proctor gig was going to seal the deal.

Before he mentally packed his bags, though, Luke had

to be the best damn proctor ever. At last word, he got the impression that his boss at Penn Med did not want this particular research project to be awarded additional funding. Luke had no problem with that. If the theory wasn't so potentially dangerous, it'd be laughable—the worst kind of quackery he'd seen. Feeding chocolate to depressed teens? If his boss or the NIH was testing him, Luke sure as hell wouldn't fail.

It was finally time to go inside. The more steps he took, his strides became longer and more confident, but as he rounded the corner toward the lab, he ran headfirst into something—someone.

"Pardon me." Reflexively, he grabbed ahold of the staggering form and found himself face to face with a familiar pair of brown eyes.

"Thought you'd bailed," Natalie said.

Besides that moment in the parking lot the other night, this was the closest he'd been to her. And for a second, he couldn't move.

"I think you can let go," she said. "I'm not about to swoon over you."

Luke realized he still had a firm grip on her. She felt soft under her lab coat. "Are you disappointed?" he asked as he removed his hands from her narrow waist and stepped back.

"That's some line. Hold on, now I might swoon." Her sarcasm was evident, but he could also see she was blushing. Hmm. Despite their professional differences, he got to her. He made a mental note of that.

"I meant, are you disappointed I showed up?"

"No, impatient."

"For me?"

"*No*—about getting started. I'm impatient for that."

She pressed a hand to her forehead and nodded toward the room she'd just come from. "Everyone else is here."

She seemed so flustered that Luke had no choice but to hold eye contact with her and smile.

Natalie blinked, groaned, and then disappeared into the lab. The same perfume he'd smelled on her the other night, the one in that little bottle that had fallen from her purse, hung in the air like a scented cloud. He breathed in the sexy fragrance for half a second, then held his breath and followed her inside.

The room was clean and bright, though smaller than the labs he was used to. It gave him an idea about how much weight this research project carried: Not much. He made a mental note of that, too.

There were three other people, a woman and two men. "Everyone, this is the addition to our team sent from the lovely suits at the NIH."

"I'm not with—"

"*You're* the fed?" the woman asked, sounding accusatory. She was short with long red hair and reminded him of Roxy.

"Technically, he's not," Natalie said in a begrudging tone. "He was borrowed by them to proctor."

"Nice to meet you. I'm Luke."

"Ivy," the redhead said. "This is Mark and Ken."

"You all work together at Hershey?"

"Just Nat and me," Ivy said. "Mark and Ken are on loan from the med center. They're usually on other projects, but we've all been working on this whenever we can."

"I see." Luke nodded, getting a clearer picture.

"So." Natalie clapped her hands. "Now that the introductions are over, let's get to it." She moved to a laptop and ran her fingertip across the touch pad. A blown-up image appeared on the white wall. She tapped a clicker and advanced to the next slide. "Now, as you can see…"

Luke had reviewed this PowerPoint when he'd been sent her research packet a few days ago. Some of it was well intended, but he couldn't get over the basic premise. When he'd read the proposal, he'd assumed the author was a full-on crackpot. The only information he'd been able to find on this rare Amazonian root was a study in a French journal from twenty years ago. The fact that this current research project was being headed by a food chemist *from Hershey* was beyond irresponsible.

Who had taken this study seriously in the first place?

He wasn't there to argue his personal opinion but to observe and report—report thoroughly, if that was what it took to sufficiently impress the NIH. If he saw anything truly dangerous, of course he'd crush it…no matter how cute Natalie looked in her lab coat.

"The flavanols in this particular cocoa bean are literally laced with anti-oxidants and magnesium, which make it an ideal carrier for the serum. Plus, the proven release of endorphins and other chemicals boost feelings of wellness in nearly ninety percent of subjects—"

"What about the sugar and fat?" Luke had to cut her off here.

Natalie sighed and didn't look at him, but kind of through him. "In small doses, there's little impact."

"What teenager do you know who's satisfied with one bite of chocolate? The city we live in is proof of that."

"You don't live here," she muttered.

He crossed his arms. "Does it bother you when I point

out the flaws in your theory, or do you plan to gloss over them?"

Another sigh, but with an impatient edge to it—like *he* was the slow one in the room. "We're talking controlled doses," she said. "Less than a quarter of a square of a standard Hershey bar, not the whole damn bar five times a day. Even so, we've seen no indications that even hint at a danger of overdose, aside from a normal stomachache that comes from eating five bars a day. And I'd appreciate if you'd hold your comments until the end."

He lifted his eyebrows. "I thought we were a team."

"I thought you were here to *observe*."

He inhaled a slow, deep breath. "Look, like I tried to explain to you the other night—"

"Other night?" Ivy interrupted. "What other night?"

Natalie pressed her lips together in a hard line and shot him a glare. "It was nothing, Ivy. I told you."

"No, you didn't."

"Well...I'll tell you later."

Something unspoken passed between the two women. They weren't just co-workers. They were friends, probably close friends. Yet Natalie hadn't told her about their dinner. Another mental note.

"Can we get back to the subject?" Natalie said, her gaze scanning over their faces, though barely touching Luke's. She was annoyed, and he thought about being a smartass but knew pushing her buttons wasn't professional. So he leaned against the counter and listened.

For a while...

"You're wrong," he said, finally, straight up, after ten minutes of trying to have a tactful dialogue with her.

"I'm not," Natalie shot back, getting red in the face. "You're obviously not listening, and we're all familiar with your *opinion*. You're a sugar Nazi."

"That's insultingly simplistic," Luke replied, regretting—for only a second—that he'd piped in. "Especially for someone who claims to be a scientist. You're way off."

"I'm right on target."

Now *he* was getting annoyed. Though it was hard to stay annoyed when she tugged at the ends of her hair.

"What would you say if I said we should agree to disagree?"

Luke grinned at her. "I'd say I won."

Natalie exhaled a growl. "The ego on you."

"Inner security," he tweaked. Then winked.

"Don't," she snapped under her breath.

"Don't what?"

"You know what."

"*Hey*. You two need to stop. Step back and regroup."

They both turned to Ivy. For a moment, Luke had forgotten there was anyone in the lab besides Natalie. She'd taken over the room, as well as his mind, and made him lose focus.

Ivy's hands were splayed on her hips, looking tiny but menacing. "I'm serious. Leave."

Natalie clicked to the next slide. "Right, like we have time for that."

"What we don't have time for is stopping every two seconds for you guys to argue the simplest points. Nat, I'm number two on the project, right? Right?" She waited for Natalie to nod. "As number two, I'm saying you're seriously slowing down progress. When you're both gone, I'll pick up where you left off."

"Sorry," Natalie said. "There's no need. Let's get back to—"

Ivy grabbed the clicker out of her hand. "You think I'm kidding? Does it *sound* like I'm kidding?"

She sounds a little scary, Luke thought.

Maybe their bickering had gotten out of hand. Something about arguing with Natalie brought out the teaser in him. But Ivy was right. It was the furthest thing from professional.

"Cool off," Ivy said in a low voice to Natalie. "Refocus and regroup. Whatever it takes, okay?"

Natalie stared at the redhead, but Luke could tell it was no longer a battle. He'd never been kicked out of a lab before. What was going on in his brain?

"Fine," Natalie said. "But I'm not leaving unless *he* is."

"Oh, he's leaving."

Luke lifted both hands. "I don't have a say?"

Ivy elongated her tiny stance. "I think we've heard enough from you for one morning."

Yep, he was getting the boot.

"Fine. But I'd like a copy of any notes taken today. You have my email."

"Sure, sure," Ivy said. When he didn't move to leave, she crossed her arms and glared.

He glanced at Natalie who was sliding out of her lab coat. She hung it on a hanger with the others and picked up her purse and a jacket.

"Well, that was a first," she muttered once they were in the hall.

"Yeah." When he realized his eyes were a bit too appreciative of Natalie's body free from her uniform, he looked away. "For me, too. She's tough."

"She needs to be. That was really unprofessional. I'm never unprofessional.."

"It was my fault."

"I'm not denying that." She glanced at him and exhaled a tiny laugh. Over the weekend, he'd tried to remember what her laugh sounded like, why he'd liked it so much. And there it was. "We didn't last one morning. We obviously need to figure out a way to work together."

"Agreed. Compromise and communication, then?"

"We've probably communicated enough."

Intriguing. "Okay. So, what do you suggest?"

She tugged at her bottom lip, thoughtfully. He liked her lips, too. "What I need right now is a major release. *Major* release. Know the kind I mean?" She looked him right in the eyes. "A tried and true one. Are you thinking the same?"

Luke's mind spun wild at the thought of "releasing" with Natalie. "Maybe," he said.

He was about to follow up with the classic "my place or yours" when she said, "Now. Let's go."

"Where?" he asked, following as she started marching toward the parking lot. Though he was so curious, he didn't care where she was leading him.

"I came with Ivy this morning, so you're driving. This is you, right?" She stopped at his Jeep.

He rushed to her side to open her door. She climbed in without a word, and Luke slid behind the wheel. "Where to?"

"Hersheypark."

That thoroughly awakened him, and he frowned in confusion. "The amusement park?"

She smiled at him, the same smile from the other night. "Race you to the SooperDooperLooper."

Hersheypark was just what Natalie needed when she felt stressed and wanted to bust out. It reminded her of being young and carefree. Of course Luke wouldn't come with her. He was an Elliott, after all. Dignified and polished, living in a city with actual traffic. He'd clearly shaken off the small town charm of Hershey a million years ago.

So she was surprised when he'd thrown the car in reverse and sped across town.

"What's your favorite ride?" she asked as they walked across the parking lot.

"It's been a while, probably twenty years," Luke answered.

She flashed her badge at the entrance gate. "You never came in high school?"

"Guess I grew out of it."

"Oh." No, she was not immature, even though she'd gone at least once a month for as long as she could remember.

"Where should we start? Ladies' choice."

"Hmm." Natalie couldn't help grinning like a kid as she glanced at the familiar shops, booths, and rides. "How are you with heights and freefalls?"

"They're my specialty."

"Let's hit Sidewinder." She pointed toward the roller-coaster across the park. "It might not look tall from here, but we're far away."

"I'll consider myself warned."

Luke was first to get in the waiting two-seater car.

Obviously, she'd noticed his body the other night, his chest and nice-fitting jeans. Those details weren't lost on her today when his long legs stepped into the car. She also took note of his thick neck and broad shoulders as he pulled the paddled metal harness over his head, securing it at his chest. Nice arms, too. Nearly perfect bicep muscles. Scientifically speaking.

"Ma'am?" the worker kid said, waiting to usher her in next.

"Sorry, yeah." She blinked awake and slid into the seat beside Luke, getting a closer look at those biceps. Damn, they were perfect, all right. Had he always been so muscular? He was this chiseled-faced, hulking mass taking up most of the space they were supposed to share.

She pulled the harness over her head, locked it in place, then stared straight ahead, trying to not feel the hard muscles of Luke's arm and thigh against her.

"You smell nice."

She continued to stare at the space in front of her. "That's the cotton candy stand behind us."

"No, it's you."

Right as she looked at him, their rollercoaster ride began...

L uke gripped the metal safety bar. He'd never been afraid of thrill rides. Then again, he hadn't been on a rollercoaster in years. As it started to creep up the hill, he glanced at Natalie. Her hair was blowing back from her face, a look of innocent excitement in her eyes, a twinkling smile of anticipation.

Caught up in watching her, he hadn't realized they were at the top of the track until they pitched over the hump. Wind rushed against his face as they flew down the track, first one loop then another then a corkscrew through a tunnel. Natalie laughed and squealed, their bodies bumping against each other. He couldn't help letting out a few whoops of his own.

After more loops, turns, and one sidesplitting jolt that probably gave them whiplash, the car slowed and crawled back to the start. His heart raced, and he was laughing so hard, tears blurred his vision. He hadn't felt this exhilarated in ages.

Beside him, Natalie was hiccupping a string of laughs. Her long hair was wild and tangled, cheeks flushing like starbursts. She had a glow of satisfaction.

From the way Luke's heart beat hard and fast, coupled with the rush of adrenaline, he couldn't help comparing how he felt right now to how he sometimes felt after having mind-blowing—

Whoa. Where'd that come from?

"You okay?" Natalie asked, breathless and winded. Again, reminding him of other activities.

"Sure," he said, wiping his palms. "That was a rush."

"Right?" She shook out her hair. "It never gets old."

Luke was ready to suggest they take the ride again, right then. He wanted to hear her excited squealing, see that nirvana-like joy in her eyes.

"What next?" she asked, already climbing out of the car. "Your choice now."

He sighed but quickly lifted a smile, a little preoccupied

by watching as she made her way to the gate. Had Natalie had such a tight body when they were in high school?

She must not have, otherwise, why the holy hell hadn't he noticed? He couldn't help noticing now how her jeans hugged her in all the right places, and her pale blue shirt brightened her already bright eyes.

Luke could've been content right here, watching her sway and toss her tangled hair. Right as his gaze reached the back of her jeans, she slid a hand in her back pocket. Uncomfortable heat filled his chest, and he was momentarily grateful he was strapped in.

"Coming?" she said, glancing over her shoulder.

Hell to the yes...

No, wait. There was to be no hell to the yes-ing with Natalie. As it was, Luke was going to have a hard enough time explaining to Penn Med *and* the NIH why he hadn't been in the lab for most of the first day.

Damn, man. Eye on the prize.

She's blond and unpredictable. She wears pink Nikes and is almost as tall as I am, he thought, reminding himself that she was the polar opposite of any woman he'd been interested in. There must've been a strong and logical, psychological reason why he'd always stuck to his type. He wasn't about to question that reason now.

Chapter Four

It had been months since Natalie had been on the Sidewinder, and it was the exact release she needed. She'd even caught Luke having fun. The top of his hair was tousled from the wind, and that child-like grin made his eyes all sparkly.

She might not be able to wipe that image from her brain for a while.

"You had fun." She pointed at him as they wove through the ride's exit queue. "Admit it."

"Gladly." He nodded, conceding. "It's a complete, natural rush."

She laughed and tried to tame her hair. "Natural, except for the gasoline and engines."

"I'm just saying, there wasn't any sugar involved and yet you're smiling."

"That's not part of the argument. The adrenaline rush from a rollercoaster is short-lived."

"Unlike sugar's?"

She tried to shoot him a glare, but the effort was half-hearted. She needed to behave like an adult, like the head of a research team. "I don't want to fight about this."

Luke opened his mouth like he was going to shoot back something triumphant, but instead he nodded and held the bar of the turnstile down for her to walk through. "No work talk?"

"If we're going to get along, we need to...you know... start over."

"You make us sound like a couple getting back together."

Her body's first reaction was her heart skipping a beat. But then "couple" echoed in her ears, and there was no more skipping.

When Jack the rat had pulled the plug on their relationship four years ago, he'd pretty much cured her of all desire to be part of a couple ever again. Especially with someone she worked with. Jeez, what a mistake that had been! One that not only left her with a severely broken heart, but a black mark on her professional reputation.

Note to self, Natalie thought, as she made herself look away from Luke who was still wearing that adorable boyish smile. *Never let the man you're living with, in love with, dating, or even almost kind of dating anywhere* near *the recipe you dreamed up that could revolutionize taffy. Or else said guy might one day get a huge promotion because he stole your intellectual property and passed it off as his own.*

Her heart was no longer broken over Jack the rat, but she'd never again get involved with a co-worker, never assume a guy would choose her over his job...love over everything.

"You're right, though."

Natalie blinked and looked at Luke. "About?" she asked, feeling strangely melancholy.

"Starting over is a very good idea." He ran a hand up the back of his head, the corners of his eyes crinkling as he gazed toward the sun.

"So, um." She cleared her throat. "Which ride is next?"

She watched as Luke's blue eyes moved from the sky and settled on the Comet, another fast-paced coaster.

"That."

While on the ride, it was hard for Natalie to not look at him every two seconds. It seemed like a new experience for him. If he hadn't been to Hersheypark since he was a kid, it was kind of like he was here for the first time — a rollercoaster virgin. She grinned at the thought of that towering beefcake of a specimen being an anything-virgin.

His dark hair was even more mussed as they disembarked the Comet, and Natalie's wandering mind wondered what it'd be like to run her fingers through that hair, to either mess it up more or smooth it into place. She wasn't sure which would look hotter.

"What were you like in high school?" he asked, as they stood in line to buy bottles of water.

The question was an immediate return to reality. He really hadn't known her back then.

"Angsty."

Luke laughed, pulling out his wallet. "Weren't we all? What was sixteen-year-old Natalie into?"

You, she could've said. *As if you don't remember.* "Why do you want to know?"

"We're not supposed to talk about work. Prompt: You

mentioned you picked apples for the cider."

"Indeed. I have the calluses to prove it."

He laughed again. Natalie was getting used to the sound. "Did you help out a lot on your father's farm?"

"My parents tried to instill a healthy work ethic in us." She rolled her eyes. "But I would've much rather been hanging out in town with my friends."

"Us?" Luke paid for the two waters, unscrewed his lid and took a drink.

"What?"

"You said us… You have siblings?"

Natalie froze mid-sip. "Uh, yeah. A brother."

"Older?"

"Younger."

"Would I know him?"

She shook her head, then took a long drink.

She felt Luke watching her, and she hoped he wouldn't press the issue. She didn't want to explain about Muff. Although, maybe if Luke knew about her brother's situation, he wouldn't be a hard-ass at the lab.

Not that she was intimidated by him or his questions. She could defend every detail of her research all day long. She'd never been more knowledgeable or confident about anything. But she also wasn't about to get into it in the middle of the boardwalk. Her family's business had nothing to do with him.

"Okay," he said after a moment. "Tell me something else about you."

"I love chocolate."

"You're exasperating."

"That too."

He scowled at her playfully, then nodded at a shop selling pretzels. "We're not supposed to be talking about work, remember?"

"Fair enough." As they got in line, she tried once more to comb her fingers through her hair but finally gave up. "Did you know the recipe for these pretzels comes from an Amish family in Lancaster?"

"Huh." Luke glanced at the sign. "Aren't these the same stores in malls?"

"Yep, they're a national chain now." She placed her order for a soft pretzel with no salt. Luke got the same. Natalie was tempted to jab him with something about trans-fat, but she'd already broken their no-shop-talk rule once.

So she cleared her mind of all jabs and boyish smiles and took a bite of pretzel. She closed her eyes, relishing its warm, doughy goodness.

"Honey?"

"Yes, Luke?" she replied, then froze. "I mean, what?"

He was holding out a small plastic cup. "I asked if you'd like honey to dip it in, but it seems you're content with what you have. At least, judging by those noises you were making."

She wiped her mouth with a napkin. "I enjoy food."

"Ya think?" He pulled back a half-grin, putting Natalie in danger of that inconvenient weak-in-the-knees feeling. "Eating's good for you. And that's all I'll say on the subject." He dunked one end of his pretzel in honey and took a big bite.

As he turned to gaze across the park, she noticed a tiny spot of honey on the corner of his mouth, which he began working at with his tongue. Her mouth watered, her breath stopped all together, and her knees were definitely about to give.

"How about another ride?" he said after running a napkin over his mouth, saving her from collapsing on a bench and putting her head between her knees.

She coughed. "S-something slower, maybe?"

"Are you feeling okay? You look a little…"

"What?" She lowered her pretzel.

He turned to face her full on. Was his gaze moving over her analytically? Or was he checking her out? Hot blood crept up her neck and bloomed across her cheeks. She couldn't stop it—she did have female hormones, after all. Preempting anything hormonal she might say, she shoved the last of her snack into her mouth.

"I guess you are feeling okay," Luke said with a grin, taking her wrapper, and walking all their trash to a recycling bin. "How about that one next?" He pointed to the ride on the other side of the food stand.

Natalie's breath stalled in her windpipe, and she couldn't swallow the rest of her pretzel. "You want to take me on the *Kiss* Tunnel?"

"Nothing slower than boats on a lazy river."

She still couldn't swallow. "But…"

He chuckled under his breath, a deep, manly sound. Then he rested a hand on the small of her back. It sent tingly goose bumps over her arms. "I don't think kissing is an actual requirement." He tilted his head. "Or is it?"

"Of course it's not," she blurted, making Luke chuckle again. Since she couldn't tell if he was flirting or not, she made herself smile breezily while trying not to breathe in his cologne. "I mean, sure. The tunnel sounds nice—um, restful. Darkness is easy on the eyes."

Why are you still talking?

Thanks to the short line, before Natalie could even process that she was about to enter a tunnel of love with Luke Elliott, they were escorted to an empty boat. The couple exiting looked like they'd taken full advantage of the five minutes in the tunnels. Her hair was halfway out of its bun, and he had lipstick marks all over his face.

Luke had already stepped into the boat and was reaching a hand out to help Natalie. She swallowed hard and took it. It was warm and as strong as steel, but he dropped her hand the second she hopped in.

Okay, fine. He probably regretted his joke about kissing being a requirement on the ride. Whatever. She didn't need his hand. Or his eyes. Or mouth.

It *was* a joke. Obviously. Just because the two-person seat was only the size of a single seat—their bodies were practically wedged together—didn't mean it was meant as a romantic ride.

Luke didn't seem to notice the forced close proximity. He settled in his seat with his legs outstretched. "You all strapped in?"

"Uh-huh." She made sure her lap bar was in place. Though the thing was nothing more than a safety precaution, it didn't get even close to her lap and had a good two-feet of give.

The boat lurched forward, water gently sloshing around them.

"This slow enough for you?" he asked after they'd moved no more than ten feet in thirty seconds.

"I like thrill rides, too. But taking it down a notch is its own kind of fun."

Their boat entered the tunnel, and it was suddenly pitch black. Without sight, her other senses perked up. She heard Luke's breathing, smelled more of that aftershave, felt the side of his body against her.

"Slower rides also give a guy opportunities."

"Opportunities for…?" Answering her question, Luke shifted, his arm settling around her shoulders. "Um, that's not a good idea," she said, forcing her voice to sound scolding.

"It's just an arm."

True. She nodded in the dark.

Around the next turn, soft red lights illuminated the tunnel, casting dark rosy shadows over the walls, over Luke's face, his profile, the strong cut of his jaw.

"Are you scared?" he asked. "You're gripping the bar."

Although she couldn't see them clearly, she felt her hands white-knuckling the thing.

"Relax." His voice was calm and lazy as he reached out to pry her grip loose using those steely-strong hands. "This is supposed to be chill, no adrenaline rush, change of pace."

She nodded about five times. "Exactly."

Being with Luke in the dark zapped her back to another time and place where they'd been together with the lights off. A time when she'd been so completely hardcore infatuated with him that her thirteen-year-old heart knew it was love.

Of course it *wasn't* love, but it was one heck of a crush. Just tapping into that memory made her palms feel tingly, and her stomach turn a backflip.

"Why did you call this the Kiss Tunnel?" Luke asked. "The sign says Lost River."

Ohmigad, Natalie's teenaged-self squealed. *You're totally in the Kiss Tunnel with Luke!*

"It's what everyone calls it," she said, trying to shush that voice, swat away those antiquated crushy feelings.

"Because it's where you come to make out?"

She shrugged. "In middle school, maybe."

"Ah. So kissing's required after all?"

"Not *required*." Her protest echoed off the tunnel walls, so she lowered her voice. "It's the only ride with privacy. Teenagers don't need much more romantic atmosphere than a room with the lights off."

Just when she'd almost wiped the image from her mind, she was back to remembering that night all those years ago. The two times they'd been alone this week, Luke hadn't brought it up. Either he'd blocked it out, or it had been so anti-climactic for him that he'd forgotten about it.

Which was worse?

"I see your point. This is the perfect place to make out," Luke said as his arm tightened around her shoulders. Or maybe he was only adjusting his position. "The sound of the water," he continued, his voice hushed like hers. "The rocking of the boat, up and down, up and down." His eyes shifted her way. "You next to me, bathed in this hypnotic, unearthly light." His free hand brushed across her cheek, tucked a strand of hair behind her ear.

Natalie tried to speak, but everything in her stopped. Everything except the recall of how familiar and amazing it felt to be crushing on Luke.

"Kissing is definitely a requirement," he added, leaning in.

Her eyes stayed open. Because her brain was mush. Because she was sixteen again. Because she was too dang shocked to breathe.

Luke Elliott was kissing her.

His arm around her rotated her shoulders so she angled toward him. Warmth rushed to her lips, pulsating blood at the spot where their bodies touched. They'd barely gotten started when Luke drew back, their noses still close enough to touch. He looked at her through the shadowy red light, his gaze holding, a glimpse of hesitation in his eyes. Before what that meant could register, she saw something else in his eyes, something he could probably see in hers.

Natalie grabbed his face and pulled him in. The tiniest voice in the back of her head was saying something about danger or rules or ethics, but the second Luke's lips parted hers, everything faded, except the taste of honey.

What were those rational, psychological reasons for why Luke shouldn't be attracted to Natalie? He'd just been reviewing them, but he couldn't even remember the basic food pyramid when he'd seen her under the glowing red lights. Instead, he'd babbled on and on about all the reasons why this was the perfect place to kiss…almost like he'd been talking himself into it.

Natalie's soft hands held his face, and she kissed him so hard that his legs went numb. Once he managed to suck in some oxygen, he tried to pull her to him, but something was stopping him, a physical barrier stronger than his need to hold her close.

So he made the most of it by sliding his hands into her hair, combing through the long, untamed strands. When his mouth touched her neck, she made a gasping sound that went straight to his head.

But then she pulled back.

Was she stopping them? Was there an annoying nagging at the back of her mind, too?

No, she hadn't done it to stop, but to slither under the safety bar. With blood rushing behind his ears, Luke slid to the middle of the bench seat, pushed the bar away as far as he could, then pulled her onto his lap, her legs straddling him.

His lips found her neck again, and he heard a soft laugh, that same little gasp. The sound made him hungry. She held his head and tilted his face, cupping his cheeks like before, kissing him squarely on the mouth until his mind emptied of all nagging voices.

Needing more of her to touch, he ran his hands up her thighs, feeling the rough denim between him and her skin. They trailed to the small of her back, up and down her spine, settling on the slice of bare skin between her jeans and shirt. But not settled for long. His needy hands were inside her shirt, holding her sides just under her ribs, feeling and hearing her breath hitch and turn ragged.

Blood pumped from his chest to hungrier parts of his body, reacting to her mouth finding his neck. Then the other side of his neck. The only thing Luke could do was lean back and hold on with his fingers digging into her sides.

With his face buried in her hair, he smelled sweet shampoo. Could it be chocolate-scented? His breathing was becoming more labored, and pretty soon his hands would not be satisfied with their current location.

"Sir? Sir, you'll have to pay for that."

The faceless, floating voice sounded like it was coming

from underwater, from inside a tunnel.

Tunnel? Water? Chocolate?

Oh, damn.

The first twinge of reality was sensing her soft weight on his lap. Luke opened his eyes to find Natalie staring down at him. He tried to blink away the bright light. Hadn't it just been dark?

She sat up straight, freeing her fingers from where they'd been knotting the back of his hair. They both looked toward the voice. It was the same worker who'd put them in the ride at the beginning.

"We have it on camera," the kid said. "We have proof."

"Proof," Luke repeated. "Don't tell me kissing on this ride is a crime."

"No, but breaking the safety equipment is." The guy pointed at the lap bar that was not only not across their laps, but pulled off one hinge and hanging at an awkward angle.

Hell. Talk about brute strength from an adrenaline rush.

He glanced at Natalie who was biting her bottom lip while trying to wiggle off his lap.

"Luke," she said in a pointed tone, "I can't get off of you if you're holding me…there."

"Oh." He removed his hands that were still way up the back of her shirt, and she slid off onto her feet, stumbling like a baby goat. "Careful."

"I'm fine," she said, not looking at him.

But he couldn't keep his eyes off her as she climbed out. Those limber arms, long legs, and that mouth. Damn, that mouth. He almost couldn't move, but then he noticed the glares of the worker and of the people in the waiting line, some with children. He quickly leaped from the boat.

"Whatever it costs," he told the worker, drawing him aside. "I'll pay for the repairs, all of it. It was completely my fault."

Natalie had a hand up, blocking her face like she didn't want to be seen. Like that would make a difference now.

"Take this form." The guy handed him a piece of paper. "Go straight to the administration office. They're waiting for you. It's over by the—"

"I know where it is," Natalie cut in. "Come on." She was already walking at a fast clip. Luke had to jog to catch up. "I can't believe that just happened."

"Which part?"

She glared over her shoulder at him. "Not funny."

"Kind of funny."

"Hi, Natalie," a man said, strolling by.

"Hey, Milton!— *Walk faster*," she hissed at Luke.

The administrative building wasn't far, and they walked in silence the rest of the way. Luke was surprised at how many people greeted Natalie by name. Though he got a few looks, no one acknowledged him.

"That's it." She pointed at the first door.

"After you," he said, holding it open.

"Jeez. I *so* don't want to go in there," she said, gnawing at her bottom lip. Luke didn't ask why, because after a deep breath, she did go in.

"Well, well, Natalie Holden," said a woman with gray hair and peach lipstick. "You and your friend put on quite a show."

Natalie pulled at the neck of her shirt, looking flustered, but cute. "Sorry about that."

"You're lucky. If my grandson was working the office

today, it'd already be on YouTube."

"YouTube?" Luke cut in, thoughts of cuteness gone.

"She's kidding," Natalie said.

After that pseudo-lecture the other night, his family would murder him if he was caught on tape making out at Hersheypark. He was trying to repair their relationship, not rip the stitches.

Worse, though…no one at work could find out. This was exactly what HR was looking for: an example of ethical misconduct. Not that he had to maintain a squeaky-clean reputation to be hired by the NIH, but this wouldn't exactly help his cause.

How had he let it happen? Well, he *hadn't*…it just *happened*, like he was out of control. Which was complete BS because he believed in the exact opposite. Mind over matter could overcome just about anything, like craving sugar and fat, as well as irresistible women.

Something about it made him smile, though. Luke couldn't think of the last time he'd made out with a woman that didn't result in clothes hitting the floor. They'd just kissed, like they really were a couple of kids taking advantage of the tunnel's privacy.

"Ah, yes. It's you."

Luke snapped awake to see the gray-haired woman looking at him while adjusting her glasses. She smiled like he was something to eat. "There aren't many good shots of you when Natalie was on your lap. She's either leaning over you, or you're at her neck like Bela Lugosi. Though there's one really good part at the end—"

"Anyway," Natalie cut in. "He'll pay the fine and we'll go."

"All right, dear." She adjusted her glasses again. "But I must compliment both of you on your style."

Luke cleared his throat, passed the women a credit card, didn't bother looking at the charges, and signed his name blankly.

"Come back any time," the woman said. "*Any* time." He couldn't help laughing, but when he turned to share the moment with Natalie, she'd gone.

By the time he'd made it outside, she was a good ways away, and he had to take her by the elbow so she'd stop. "Are you mad?"

"I must be, right? Freakin' loco in the cabeza."

"I mean, are you angry about…what happened?"

"Oh." She bit her lip. Luke remembered how it had felt between his teeth, soft and full. "Why did you do that, anyway?"

"Kiss you?"

She stared up at the sky. "Um, *yeah.*"

He slid his hands in his pockets and shrugged. "It was an impulse. You were saying that stuff about it not being a requirement and then the lights went out and, I don't know. It was entrapment. I had no choice."

"You always have a choice."

Luke sighed. Of course, she was right. It might've been an impulse, but he could've squelched it. Truth was, he'd been dying to kiss her; he just hadn't known it until that moment.

"Okay then." He looked her dead in the eyes. "Why did you kiss me back?"

She rubbed her nose and glanced away. "Yeah, um, I claim entrapment, too."

They looked at each other, a moment of heavy silence,

then Luke said, "We broke the ride."

Finally, a big smile curved those lips. "And we looked worse than those kids who were in the boat before us. I was straddling you like it was prom night, and your hands were about to unhook my—"

"No they weren't," Luke jumped in, grinning. "But if that's what you want, I can certainly—"

"No!" She huffed and crossed her arms. Natalie Holden was just as tempting post-kiss as she was pre-kiss. "We can both call it entrapment or caught up in the moment or whatever, but it will never happen again."

"Was it that bad for you? I might be rusty at the whole first kiss thing, but you seemed into it."

Two starbursts of red spread across her cheeks. "That wasn't our…I mean, it's not that," she said, dropping her voice as well as her chin. "I'm not about to screw up this trial because you're an awesome kisser."

He cocked an eyebrow. "I am, huh?"

"We have to drop the subject. Let's just silently agree to never speak of this, either."

"Either? Do we share other secrets?"

Her face went pale and then she blushed again. Her expressions were like a living Monet. "The importance of my job is only one item on the laundry list of reasons why it was a mistake."

Luke was about to ask what her other reasons were, but didn't, since he had his own laundry list.

"Fine." He was capable of controlling himself around her. And since kissing hadn't legitimately crossed his mind until the moment it happened, it wouldn't be a problem to not do it again.

Then Natalie bit her bottom lip. And Luke could taste it.

"If you're serious about not wanting me to kiss you, you better stop."

"Huh?"

"When you bite your lip like that, it's damn near… I'm only human."

"I won't bite my lip if you won't…" She paused and her eyes did a quick sweep up the front of his body, causing a fist of heat to punch through his chest. "Um, just like, wear a bag over your head or something."

"Like a grocery bag?"

"Yeah, that'd be great." She smiled and rolled her eyes. "As hilarious as it might be, we're done with this subject. The more we talk about it, the more I want to…"

He didn't interrupt. She might not be biting her lip, but the thought of never finishing that kiss made his brain ache.

She slid on a pair of sunglasses and turned into the breeze. "The subject is officially dropped forever. Okay?"

Though Luke wasn't quite ready to not think about what they'd done in the tunnel, he did agree with her. Nothing was more important than landing this job at the NIH.

"Okay by me," he said, facing the other direction. "Anyway, it was only a kiss."

Chapter Five

After refusing a ride home from Luke, Natalie didn't have the guts to wait for Ivy to finish at the med center. Her best friend would have questions about why she'd dragged Luke to the park, what they'd done there, and why she was now standing at the entrance gate alone. Fuming.

So instead, she called Muff.

"What were you doing here?" her brother asked while Natalie fastened her seatbelt.

"Working," she said, as he maneuvered though the parking lot.

"Since when do you work at Hersheypark?"

"I don't." So much for no nagging questions. She rolled down her window for fresh air and immediately spotted a black Jeep tailing them. "Son of a— He's *following* me."

Muff hit the brakes. "Who?"

"Don't stop!" Natalie slid down in the seat, though it was too late to hide. Luke obviously hadn't left the park but had waited until someone came to get her. She wasn't sure if she should be flattered or ticked.

It was only a kiss. Luke had actually said that to her. *Only a kiss.* Nothing could've ticked her off more or made her feel like she had when they were kids and Luke never gave her the time of day. Even after the boathouse.

He hadn't noticed her back then, so why would he notice her now?

Before her heart could fill with the familiar disappointment that should've been buried deep, she decided to think of it as *only* a kiss, too. She was a grown woman and could kiss anyone she wanted without it meaning anything.

"Who's following you?" Brandon repeated.

Natalie bit the inside of her cheeks. "No one. A work colleague."

"You said he."

"Yeah." She scrunched lower in the seat, practically eating her knees.

"Since when do you work with guys?"

"Since always. I don't tell you everything."

"Liar."

Natalie turned to him. "Why are you being a pain in the ass?"

He adjusted the rearview mirror. "You caught me on a good day."

"I like it. I miss your pain in my ass."

"Gross. My good day is over."

Normally, she'd be thrilled to get more than two words out of her brother. And she was tempted to circle back to the subject he seemed interested in.

Only a kiss. She inwardly scoffed. *Bite me.*

After they passed through an intersection, she casually glanced behind them. The Jeep was gone.

Good. No reason for him to follow me like he's my brother.

This made her turn to Brandon. His shaggy hair wasn't blocking his eyes. Probably because he was driving. Muff wasn't a danger to himself or others, and ever since he'd gotten his license, he was very careful behind the wheel. Driving was one of the only times he seemed almost like a normal kid.

"Do you mind if I ask why you're in a better mood?"

He shrugged. "I don't know. Right before you called my cell, I finished my homework and was about to turn on the TV when I heard Mom on the phone. I usually don't care what she's saying, even when it's about me—and it's always about me. She was saying something about you and…what you're doing at work. For me."

Natalie hadn't told Brandon the subject matter of her research, or what she hoped to accomplish if she proved her thesis. "Is that okay?" she asked. Even if it wasn't, she was going through with the trial anyway.

"I guess." A corner of his otherwise flat mouth twitched. It could've been a frown, could've been a smile. Either way, emotion was a good sign. "But, um, I mean, thanks for at least trying to help."

"Of course," she said, feeling so much love for her little brother it actually hurt her heart. As they drove home, more than ever, Natalie knew she had to get through this first phase and secure another grant. Nothing and nobody would stand in her way.

Even after she'd refused a ride home for the tenth time, Luke hadn't been about to leave her standing at the entrance gate alone. He wasn't a complete ass. So he'd sat in his car and waited, keeping an eye on her from the side mirror.

Huh. She had a temper, too. He'd never been into annoyingly stubborn women—not that he was into Natalie. He'd meant what he'd said. It was only a kiss. And just a kiss—even an extraordinarily hot one—would not make him forget his reason for being in Hershey. He'd finish this job, go back to Philly, then hopefully begin planning his move to DC.

Now that he was far removed from that kiss and could think, he also had to admit his brain was in no way ready to be *into* someone. The lies, the manipulating, the total betrayal of trust. Even the memory of what led to his divorce was enough to stop his irrational attraction to Natalie Holden dead in its tracks.

He didn't have to wait in the Jeep for long. A silver car pulled up and she got inside. Luke was too far away to get a good look at the driver, but it was definitely a dude. Tall, from the looks of it. But not nearly as tall as Luke. He could take him.

Take him? Where the hell had that come from?

On the heels of that, a chilling thought landed in his mind. Luke hadn't once considered that Natalie wasn't available. Had she mentioned a boyfriend? If she did have one, what was all that in the tunnel? Sure, he'd started it, and he still blamed most of it on the atmosphere of that stupid ride—"entrapment," they'd both called it. But she'd been into it, because Luke wasn't in the habit of breaking innocent amusement park rides without just cause. And there had definitely been cause.

He ran a tight fist over his jaw. Not that "cause" mattered. The thought of her having a boyfriend was the basic equivalent of jumping in the freezing cold ocean. He'd never pursue someone who wasn't 100 percent available. Celeste's betrayal was too fresh on his mind to put another guy through that. Ever.

He only followed the silver car for two blocks, because he was sure he'd been made when Natalie poked her head out the window. After that, he hung a right at the light and headed to Derry Woods Road, up the windy hill toward his parents' house.

Roxy had driven back to Jersey the day before, but Dexter's car was there when he pulled into the driveway.

"Rough day at the salt mine, bro?" Dex called from the porch.

Aw, shit. Had someone told his family about what happened in the Kiss Tunnel? He kept his sunglasses on to hide his expression. "What's that supposed to mean?"

Dexter pointed at his Apple Watch. Did Dad know Dex was wearing their competition? He was also in a suit and tie. Even away from his Manhattan corner office, his brother dressed the part.

"It means it's not even three-thirty and you're done for the day. How do I land a cush job like that?"

"Oh." Luke reminded himself to breathe. "No, um, yeah, we finished early." *Three hours ago, actually.* "First day. Still feeling each other out."

Dexter's eyebrows shot up. "Feeling each other out? Are you referring to the girl from the other night?"

Damn. Luke was so not in the mood to talk about Natalie or give any details about what went on today—in or out of the med center. "Don't read into anything. We're completely professional." *Lie.* "Speaking of work, why are you here and not back in the city? Enjoying another four-day weekend?"

He and Dex walked into the house. "Not even. Pop and I have been on conference calls all day. Sometimes I think you made the right move by not working the family business."

"You make us sound like the Hershey Township mafia."

Dex moaned and looked at the ceiling. "Actually feels like that on days like today. Good thing I'm a workaholic."

"As I recall, you lost your shirt in a certain bet we made about me finishing grad school."

"Don't remind me," his brother said with a laugh. "So really, how was the first day?"

"Fine. Nothing unusual." *Big fat lie.* They entered the kitchen, and since it was too early for a beer, Luke tossed Dex a water.

Despite his mind over matter philosophy, Luke knew if he didn't stay distracted, he might spend the rest of the afternoon trying not to think about Natalie's bottom lip.

"Feel like going to the club and hitting balls?" he asked.

"Dude, you've been away from home too long. We don't go to the club. We have our own driving range."

"Since when?"

"Since I turned the balcony of the guest house into one."

"What about all the balls?"

"Ya know the Voyles family down the hill with all the

kids? I told them they can keep whatever they find. Clean shots over three hundred yards go straight into the pond."

Luke crossed his arms. "Isn't that bad for the fish or ducks or whatever Mom stocks it with?" Not that Luke was a bleeding heart, but he didn't like the idea of purposely polluting the environment.

"I had a filtering system installed."

"In the pond?"

Dex nodded. "And I tip the pool guy to run a net over it once a week. He said he's never fished out a single ball."

Luke put a hand on is brother's shoulder. "That's because golf balls don't float. That's physics."

"Huh." Dex scratched his head. "Hadn't thought of that. Anyway, it's a perfect day to work on your terrible backswing."

"My backswing kills yours."

"Care to make it interesting?"

For the next two hours, Luke and Dexter smacked Titleists, accompanied by plenty of sibling trash talk. By the time their parents came home, Luke had practically forgotten about Natalie. And her bottom lip.

Natalie hadn't slept well the night before. Not only did Luke keep popping into her dreams at the most random times, but after their short drive from Hersheypark, Brandon went straight to his room and didn't come out the rest of the day. Not even for dinner.

One step forward sometimes means three steps back, she had to tell herself.

After dinner with her parents, she drove to her apartment. Ivy had called twice, wanting to recap the rest of the day. But Natalie didn't feel like talking.

Her first session at the med center had been a colossal failure. The next morning, as she threw on work clothes and minimal makeup, she could barely look at herself in the mirror.

How could she have blown an entire day just because she couldn't stop arguing with Luke? And then, after the humiliation of being kicked out of her own lab, when she'd tried to play nice, they'd played *too nice* and it had turned into a full-on teenager make-out session, hot enough for Instagram.

What the hell had come over her?

The simple truth was, she hadn't been with a guy in three years, not even a kiss, and she was overly ripe—and Luke's gorgeous, willing face just happened to be there, along with feelings she *used* to have.

Frickin' inconvenient time for those feelings to make a brief comeback in that tunnel.

She made it a point to arrive at the lab early to catch some alone time and read Ivy's notes. Instead, she found Luke leaning against the locked door, his hands in his jeans pockets, his long legs crossed at the ankles. The epitome of relaxed and confident dude made her lips start to tingle.

"Hey," he said.

Damn, he looked good. His brown hair had some sexy bed-head going, and he was rocking the unshaved look. She couldn't help noticing his muscles flex when he saw her. From the way his blue button down shirt strained over his chest and biceps, she had a heck of a time replying to his greeting.

"Hey," she managed to utter. "Why are you early?"

He pushed off the door. "No email from Ivy, so I need to get caught up from yesterday." He nodded at her. "I take it you had the same idea?"

"Yeah," she said, trying not to notice how blue his eyes were the closer she got to him. Really, very bluey-blue. Had they always been such a bright color? Or was it only when they were aimed directly at her?

No! She slammed her eyes shut and turned the other way. *That's a childish thought, juvenile, the foolish daydream of a silly teenager who knows nothing—and I'm done with that. I just won't look at him all day. No problem.*

She unlocked the door, pushed inside, dropped her purse on the workbench, and went straight for her lab coat.

"Speaking of yesterday…" Luke said while putting on his coat beside her. "Should we talk about it?"

"Um, no." She exhaled a laugh/scoff combo as she fingered her hair into a ponytail. "That's the last thing I need."

"Why?"

"Because we need to be professional. This is work—really, really important work—and I can't allow myself to be distracted."

"Is my being here distracting you?"

She still wouldn't look at him. "Yes."

"But I haven't done anything. I'm just standing here."

Right! she wanted to say. *And that's enough!*

While thinking about distractions, she got sucked into a memory of the way he'd turned to her right before the kiss. Then his mouth had covered hers, his lips everywhere. Natalie knew darn well if they hadn't been confined on that ride—never mind the broken lap bar—she wouldn't have stopped with *only* a kiss.

Knowing she was capable of that, that Luke's mouth and hands and aftershave were capable of making her completely lose herself in a split-second made him dangerous…to her career, the clinical trial for Muff, and to her heart. She'd never really gotten over being rejected by Luke—when she'd been too young to know how to build a brick wall to keep out the boy who was sure to break her heart.

Well, that brick wall was in place now.

"Thought we had a deal," Luke said, stirring her awake. "You're already breaking your side of the bargain."

Finally, she looked at him. "How?"

He pointed at her. "No biting your lip."

She hadn't been aware she was doing it. Or had she done it subconsciously because he'd admitted it made him want to kiss her?

No. She'd never been into head games. In her experience, guys were the big teases, making promises they didn't keep, painting pictures of a future they'd never have, disappointing her, not putting her first. Not remembering her name…

She was done with that crap. Over the past few years, she'd convinced herself to be fine with what she had now. No messy feelings or heartbreaks or games.

"Sorry," she said, unlatching her teeth from her lip. "I didn't mean to."

Despite his messy hair and stubbly chin, he smelled amazing. He was wearing something classic like Old Spice. Somehow the scent drifted through her mental brick wall and made her mouth water. "Aren't you supposed to be wearing a bag over your head?"

"Maybe I didn't want to."

"Luke," she said firmly, "I might be small town, but I'm perfectly aware when a guy is trying to flirt with me—don't."

He exhaled like he'd known this was coming. "Just kidding around. I swear; we'll never talk about what happened in the tunnel."

"What tunnel?"

Natalie flinched and nearly gave herself whiplash as she jerked around to see Ivy in the doorway.

"What tunnel, Nat?" she repeated.

"The one at, um, Hersheypark."

Ivy's eyebrows smashed together. "That's where you went after I booted you?" She put both hands on her hips. "What happened in the tunnel that you don't want to talk about?"

Both Natalie's heart and brain froze. "We um…I, uh, it—"

"Broke," Luke finished. "One of the safety bars came off its hinges while we were, um…"

"*Riding*?" Ivy cut in.

Luke shot Natalie a not-so-subtle glance, and she felt her cheeks flame red. "R-riding, yeah." She forced a laugh. "It was the damnedest thing. It just broke."

"Right in my hand," Luke added. "Like I was fueled by super-power strength." The way he looked at her made Natalie's blush deepen. *Crap, no blushing in front of Ivy.*

"You should sue," Ivy said as she pulled her lab coat off a hanger. "Get some of those Hershey billions."

"Yeah, I should!" Natalie's next laugh was a little too loud and horsey. "Anyway, what'd I miss yesterday?"

As Ivy gave them her report, Natalie tried very hard to concentrate and not look at Luke, not smell Old Spice in the air, taste honey on her tongue, or bite her lip.

"Sounds like you were productive without us," Luke said, capping his pen. He looked at Natalie, who'd barely glanced at him during Ivy's summary. "Maybe we should get kicked out again."

"*Stop it*," she hissed, barely moving her lips. Enough time had passed that she wasn't blushing anymore, but damn, that comment about breaking the safety bar while she'd been *riding...* Luke couldn't think about it without wanting to smile.

Smiling was one thing. Doing something about it was another. And Luke was not about to do anything. Besides his current job, his future job, and bitterness from his ex, there was another glaring reason to keep his mind off Natalie: He'd never be the "other guy."

"Anyway," he said, pushing up his sleeves. "Sounds like we've got a lot of work today."

"We?" Natalie said, opening her laptop. "You're here to observe."

He leaned against the counter between a row of microscopes. "That's what I meant." He tried not to *observe* Natalie's curves beneath her lab coat, the upstairs curves as well as the curves downstairs.

He had to stop his dirty thoughts right there, and the ridiculous semi-flirting. Otherwise, he might be tempted to semi-kiss her. After that, there'd be no semi-anything.

Just then, the interns arrived with a box of donuts that everyone descended upon but him. Seeing Natalie with dots of empty-caloried powdered sugar on her nose and the corners of her mouth should have revolted him and should *not* have been attractive in the least.

The rest of that day and the next went smoothly. Though their subtle wisecracking never completely disappeared, Luke behaved. The following morning, Natalie started off by giving instructions on how they'd prepare the initial test. This phase didn't sound like a first attempt. She'd gone through this before, if only theoretically. They were prepared.

It shouldn't have surprised Luke that her team had been priming for this. To them, it wasn't some preposterous theory. Perhaps the NIH dropping him on the scene was more of an inconvenience than he'd thought. That didn't mean he didn't belong there, of course. Every first product development stage needed checks and balances. He'd always been a stickler for that. Maybe that was the reason the NIH was interested in him.

As Natalie instructed the team, every time she mentioned sugar, she'd send him a steely glance. He wasn't about to argue now that he'd reverted to his proctor position at a desk in the corner.

While silently typing notes, he did some observing of a more personal nature. When he left her alone to do her thing, the head of this research team was on the brilliant side, an expert in her field, and eloquent in her explanation. He'd always been drawn to highly intelligent women, ending with Celeste.

Ruminating about his ex was helpful when Natalie stooped to pick up a pencil she'd dropped. Did the woman have any clue how dangerous it was for her to bend in half right in front of him?

"Any thoughts?"

Where should I begin? "About?"

Natalie crossed her arms. "I asked if you have anything to add. You've been so quiet."

"Trying to be respectful," he replied, grabbing for something to say instead of how he'd been mesmerized by the act of her picking a pencil off the floor.

"Just don't want you reporting back that I didn't give you a chance to retort."

"I'll retort when there's need."

She rolled her eyes, but behind them was a hint of that playful gleam.

While the others ran the first series of tests, Luke hung back with Mark the intern. After mixing five ingredients in the high-pressure blender, Natalie took a sample and spun it in a machine. Everyone waited in silence for the results to spit out.

She looked nervous, pulling at her ponytail, shifting weight from foot to foot, though thankfully not biting her lip.

When a green light flickered on, she and Ivy looked at each other but didn't move. Luke stepped closer, noting the exact moment when the tension in Natalie's shoulders relaxed.

"It's a match," she said. Ivy whooped like a cheerleader while the interns gave high fives. "Step one is complete," she said, recording the data on a spreadsheet. "Ready for two and three?"

Another whoop, then they immediately split up to take care of their individual prep jobs for the next test.

Because of his need to argue, Luke hadn't bothered noticing before that Natalie was also a born leader. Maybe she was only that way in her lab. Though he'd kind of loved it when she'd stolen his lead in the tunnel.

But he shouldn't think about that. What he should be doing, what he was being *paid* to do was make sure every *I* was dotted and every *T* was crossed. So far, he had no complaints.

Well, he had plenty of complaints about the project in general. In his soul, he knew pouring chocolate down teenagers' throats—even if it was some rare, tropical, seemingly-*healthful* variation—was no way to treat depression. If there was a plus side to her theory, it was a quick fix. On the negative side, it might promote childhood obesity and diabetes or give hope when there was none.

But his personal ethics weren't why he was there, and he knew even if her trial passed all the mandatory criteria, even made it through a clinical trial, there was no way an actual product would see the light of day.

It was too absurd, which was a puzzlement when he considered how bright Natalie was. Why would she waste her time with something that would never make it onto a pharmacist's shelf? Was she a glutton for punishment?

He had a few questions while they ran the next two tests. Again, while waiting for the results, Natalie and Ivy were dead quiet. But their celebratory cheers grew louder each time.

Luke enjoyed watching her laugh and cheer. He wasn't selfish but happy she was getting the results she wanted. Results in the lab, though, and a real-life blessing from the FDA were two different things.

For a moment, his happiness for her warped into protection. All her hard work would be for nothing in the long run. He knew how this world worked. She'd lose in the end.

The bigger question was why that bothered him?

Chapter Six

"That's five out of thirty in the bag," Natalie reported a few hours later. It was late, she was brain tired, and her fingers were raw. Her spirits, though, were sky high. She couldn't have been more jazzed about their progress.

She was also starving and ready to be off her feet for a solid eight hours. She glanced at Luke who had been quiet most of the afternoon. Not that she minded. He was nothing but a proctor.

Still, his silence made her suspicious.

"Um, Nat?" Ivy was halfway out of her lab coat while reading her phone. "You better check your email."

Hearing Ivy's tone, Natalie's pumped-up, accomplished feeling froze. Something was wrong. With a nervous knot in her stomach, she fished her cell from the bottom of her purse and tapped the envelope icon. After reading the first line, she stepped into the hall to read the rest.

When she came back into the lab minutes later, her

agitation must have shown, because Luke marched straight up to her. In any other situation, the concerned expression on his face would've made her swoony, but there wasn't even a thought of that now.

"You're *freaking* kidding me," she muttered through a clenched jaw.

"Right?" Ivy said, just as outraged.

"What is it?" Luke asked, still in his worried face. Honestly, they'd kissed one time — well, one and a half times, even if he didn't remember the half. No reason for the guy to go all boyfriend-protective.

"We're losing the lab," she said after pushing out a long exhale.

"Today?" Luke asked.

"End of next week."

"Oh, that's good."

Natalie shot him a glare. "Good for who? You? You're that keen to leave Hershey and jet back to Philly?" She held up a hand, preempting whatever reply he was planning. "We're supposed to have this lab for three full weeks because that's how long it takes to run the entire segment. Don't you understand? We're screwed."

"Royally," Ivy agreed.

"Can't you speed things up?" Luke suggested.

"So typical that a guy wants to rush to the next step."

"That's not..." Luke actually broke into a smile. How dare he look cute? "That's not at all what I meant." He gave her a long, knowing look that she easily inferred. But it was her fault for throwing out the innuendo in the first place.

"No, we can't speed anything along," she said. "The chemical combinations have time specifications on how and when they can be intermixed. Thought you read the proposal."

Luke rubbed his jaw with a knuckle. "I did."

"So then you know."

He didn't speak for a moment. "Why are you losing the lab a week early?"

Ivy displayed the face of her phone before Natalie could explain. "Temporary staffing cutbacks is what they *say*. But I call bullshit. They probably double booked the lab, and we're getting booted because they think our trial isn't as important."

"That doesn't seem fair," Luke said.

"Fair?" Natalie laughed bitterly. If she didn't laugh, she was afraid she might cry.

What Ivy didn't know, what none of them knew was that the second she'd read the email, she'd called her boss at Hershey, the head of research and development. Scott had been an important sounding board while she'd been vying for grants. So naturally, she'd called him to complain.

Their conversation had been short. But informative.

"I warned you this was too big," Scott had said.

"I know you did," she'd replied.

"And now Ivy…"

"I know."

All midlevel R&D chemists were expected to participate in an original research study in order to extend their contracts. Natalie knew that, and she'd already completed her first during her third year at Hershey. Those who didn't would be suspended from contract negotiations and lose credentials. And if the economy was just right…maybe even their jobs.

Last year, Ivy had been part of two research teams that had folded. Her contract end date was in four months. If Natalie wasn't able to complete this project—that had suddenly been cut short a week—neither would Ivy.

Because Natalie insisted on going for the time-consuming, complicated, and unpredictable route of a clinical trial, her best friend's job was a stake.

Even without looking at Ivy across the room, Natalie knew her partner was fully aware of the consequences if this thing went under. More tears threatened her eyes. Instead of letting defeat win, she lashed out.

"Fair?" she repeated, directed at Luke. "Do you have any idea how long I've been trying to get the grant to pay for this trial? *Any* idea?" Annoyance boiled under her skin at Luke's blank expression. Of course someone like him would have no idea what it was like to struggle for years and years over something he couldn't control. He had all the money he wanted and lived a charmed life.

"No," he replied. "I assumed you'd recently applied because the assignment was short notice on my end."

She couldn't help huffing a dark laugh. "That's because it was the only time frame they gave us. We've been busting our asses for this. Yes, it's amazing that we got the grant, but they gave us seventy-two hours between the phone call and the day we got the lab. We had no other choice than to start immediately or we'd lose the funding. Luckily, we're prepared."

"Damn straight," Ivy said.

A rock sat in the pit of Natalie's stomach. Lashing out wasn't helping. Pointing fingers wasn't either. She shut her eyes and put a hand over her mouth, trying not to lose it. "I can't believe this. I seriously can't." Just as she was about to release a long, defeated moan, she pictured Bran Muff.

Her little brother needed this. Especially now that Muff knew what she was doing, she couldn't give up.

"I see on the schedule we should be done for the day," Luke said. When Natalie opened her eyes, he was flipping through the proposal on his tablet. "But is there something we can do tonight? Get the next step rolling? Anything?"

Natalie blinked at him. For someone who was dead set against her theory, Luke was more gung ho than she was. "Um, let me think a second," she said, running the schedule of the next few days through her head. She could not cut even one corner, couldn't give the NIH any reason to shut her down. But maybe…

"Step five?" Ivy asked, reading her mind.

Natalie nodded, her heart picked up speed. "That's exactly what I'm thinking. We can skip ahead to five and start preparing the sample prototypes to absorb the injection."

"The what?" Luke asked.

"She means, make the chocolate," Ivy replied, sending Natalie a quick, though grateful, smile.

With a renewed plan and a fire in her soul, Natalie rushed to her laptop and pulled up a spreadsheet. "That could save us one day at least. The samples must be less than forty-eight hours old, but if we work fast with steps three and four, that'll give some cushion."

"Okay," Luke said. "So chocolate making is moved ahead to tomorrow—"

"Tonight—*now*," she corrected. When she looked up, four sets of eyes were on her.

"That'll take hours," Ivy said. Then she spoke low. "I

know what you're trying to do, Nat. But this project is way too important. Don't jeopardize it because you're rushing it through for me."

"This will work."

Ivy pressed her lips together. "Are you sure?"

"Totally. I can do this part in my sleep. Oh, sorry, everyone. I didn't mean we all have to stay here overnight. Nothing's being made in bulk; the sample numbers are tiny. It's a one-man job." She put her hands in the pockets of her lab coat, feeling for any hidden chocolate. She'd have to draw energy from somewhere to pull an all-nighter.

"The rest of you can go, but be here first thing in the morning to start early."

Ivy looked a little guilty. "Nat, you know I'd stay, too—I'll sleep in the lab for the next two weeks, we're a team, but...Sharona just flew in from Sydney. She brought her fiancé, that shark guy."

"Ivy, I swear, it's fine," she said, sincerely. "You know as well as I do that two people here for this is a waste."

Ivy chewed a thumbnail. "Yeah, I know."

"Go. It's not a problem."

Ivy nodded then went to get her purse. "First thing in the morning."

"Bright and early!" Natalie replied with a chipper chirp. "Have fun with Sharona and her shark man, then get a good night's sleep."

The interns said good-bye and Ivy followed them out. Good, now she could get to it. Just as she opened a new document, she noticed Luke leaning against the doorframe, still wearing his lab coat. How could that boxy piece of unisex clothing fit him so well?

"You can go, too," she said, needing him and his distracting body to be gone.

But Luke shook his head, slowly. "I don't think so."

Natalie's eyebrows arched into a sharp V as she looked from him to her computer. "Didn't you hear what I told everyone? I can do this myself. One-man job. Go home, Luke."

For working nearly twelve hours already, she still seemed energized. How did she do that? Luke hadn't noticed her consuming massive amounts of caffeine or shoveling endless Hershey bars into her mouth.

"I heard you," he said, admiring her spunk. "But I'm not about to leave you alone."

She rolled her eyes. "I appreciate the macho protection act, but the med center has round the clock security. I'll be perfectly safe."

"It's no act. I am macho," he pointed out, for fun. "But that's not what this is about, and you know it." As he walked toward her, the closer he got, the bigger her eyes grew. If he didn't know better, she looked like she expected to be kissed.

Or actually, *feared* that she'd be kissed.

Kissing that sassy mouth had drifted in and out of his mind all day, but that wasn't what this was about, either.

"My job is to observe everything that goes on in this lab."

Natalie's shoulders lost some of their tension "And?"

"And...if you're here, I'm here."

"That's not necessary. I won't be doing anything with the serum. I'll be mixing and molding chocolate bars."

"Wouldn't be ethical if I report back that research was being done in the middle of the night without my presence."

This made Natalie huff, but there wasn't genuine annoyance behind it. "You honestly have to oversee everything?"

"Observe," he tweaked. Sometimes it seemed like she really didn't want him there, but other times...

Never mind those other times.

"So." He clapped his hands, taking her silence as concession. "What's first?"

Weary suspicion shown in Natalie's eyes initially, but then it seemed as if she didn't want to waste energy on it, and she turned to her computer. "We mix the chocolate, put it in the molds, then it's all about time."

"You said we." He leaned on the counter and tried not to smile. "Thought you said this was a one-woman job."

"Oh, um, right." She rubbed her nose. "Well, since you're here..."

He did smile now, pleased as hell when she smiled back. Felt like an eternity since he'd seen that smile.

"Okay, so yeah, we set the molds then wait three hours because we don't refrigerate. After we make sure the molds are set, we'll practice on a few, make sure the consistency of both products are what we want."

He liked how often she said we. It might have been his job that required him to stay, but an instinct that had nothing to do with work wouldn't let him leave.

"Sounds like a plan."

It really was a one-person job, but Luke appreciated how Natalie allowed him to help. They used a small mixer, bigger than the kind sold at any kitchen store, but not as massive as the industrial sized ones he'd seen around. Those were used for mass production. A tiny headache stabbed at his temple, knowing those machines would never be used for Natalie's product.

But that wasn't his problem.

Only a few times did he catch himself watching her in a way that wasn't even close to being appropriate for co-worker conditions, let alone since she had a boyfriend.

"About the other day in the tunnel," he broached, oh so smoothly, while adding five cups of sugar to the bowl, "I hope that didn't make life difficult for you."

She lifted her chin, her safety glasses balancing on the tip of her nose. "Didn't we agree to never bring it up?"

"I know. But that whole YouTube thing—"

"The video wasn't posted, Luke. You don't have to worry about your precious reputation."

He had worried about that—a lot. But he wasn't now. "I'm worried about yours."

She crossed her arms. "Ah, you're saying a woman has to be concerned about protecting her reputation when a man doesn't, for the exact same thing?"

He covered his laugh with a fist. "That came out wrong. And no, that's not my opinion at all." He paused, searching for an indirect way to bring up the subject. When he couldn't think of one, he considered just dropping the whole thing. But the rock in his gut wouldn't let him.

"I goaded you into it. I'm not saying you didn't goad me back, but I started it." He took a beat, thinking carefully about how to articulate the next part. "After I left you at the park gate, I waited."

"I know you did."

"I know you know. And I saw."

"Saw what?"

He groaned. Why was nothing easy with this woman? Except wanting to kiss her.

"Believe me," he said, "I wouldn't have started anything or asked you out that first night at Hershey Lounge if I'd known. I have experience with the short end of that stick, the bad end, and things like that can begin so easily—an innocent email, a friendly dinner, at least that's what my ex said, and I guess I believe her."

He stopped speaking after he realized he was rambling. He'd never been a rambler until Natalie.

"I'm still not sure what you mean."

He turned and faced her straight on. "I'm deeply sorry I kissed you."

Her expression went slack. "Deeply…?"

"Not that it wasn't good—it was. It was a great kiss, the way you…" He forced himself to stop talking and take a breath. "I read the whole situation wrong from the beginning."

"Am I that unkissable?"

"No! You were amazing." He slapped a hand over his heart. "I just…I'm usually better at reading people. I didn't realize you had a boyfriend until I saw you get in his car." He let his hand drop. Saying the words made him feel sick.

"You mean the silver Honda with the Hershey High bumper sticker?"

Luke rubbed the back of his neck. "Yeah."

"The one that belongs to my *brother*?"

His hand froze. "Brother? So you're…"

"I am, or I'm not—whichever."

"Oh." Suddenly, he was at a loss. The sickness over potentially—though unknowingly—helping Natalie cheat on her significant other was gone, leaving behind one singular desire. To kiss her.

She must've read that in his expression because she held up both hands. "Stop."

"Stop what?"

"Stop whatever you're about to do. I see it in your eyes. I feel"—she pressed a hand at the base of her throat—"I feel it in the air. But it can't happen."

"You're single."

"I might be single, but we talked about this. A lot. *Way* too much."

Before his sails had fully hoisted, the wind died.

Of course she was right. How many times would he have to be reminded? What was it about this woman that made him a stupid pile of teenage hormones?

"Fine, I'll stop." But he couldn't help staring at her mouth, thinking about her mouth. She couldn't stop his thoughts, could she? He took a full step back and watched while she finished blending the liquid mixture with the Amazonian cocoa. The way she adjusted her gloves and pushed up her goggles should not have been so alluring.

"Those are the molds there," she said, snapping him awake. "Could you put them on this counter?"

Luke obeyed, happy she was letting him help, even in this small way.

"Grab two of those measuring spoons over there. The tablespoon size. Fill the molds on your pan with a full scoop. Make sure it's level."

"Yes, ma'am."

She rolled her eyes.

"What? It's *candy* making."

"It's *chemistry*. And it's extremely precise."

"Okay, okay." He handed her a measuring spoon. "I'll watch you do one first so I won't screw up."

Natalie mumbled something under her breath, and Luke could've sworn he heard the word smartass preceded by a highly impressive curse. He was dying to kiss that dirty mouth now.

By the time he'd finished with his pan, Natalie had filled the other five. Man, she was fast. And while he'd made a huge mess, her chocolate had made it into the molds and not a single drop anywhere else. Well, he was a newbie while she'd been doing this for years.

They lined up the pans.

"So, if I understand correctly," Luke said, "we wait three hours for them to set." He peeled off his gloves. "You know what they say about how a watched pot never boils. We should grab dinner while we can."

"It's after ten, the only thing open this late is McDonalds, and I know you're against that."

He laughed. "True."

She rubbed a hand over her stomach, unknowingly drawing Luke's attention to more of those sexy curves. "I am hungry, but I don't have much at home."

"We'll go to my place," he offered. "I'll whip up something both nutritious and full of healthful calories to keep us energized."

"That'd be great. I didn't consider going without food all night when I adjusted the schedule."

She began unbuttoning her lab coat. It wasn't exactly a striptease, but to Luke's eyes, that coat had been as impeding as lead to Superman's x-ray vision. Underneath, she wore a long-sleeved T-shirt, the front tucked into a pair of jeans that were created solely to mold to her body.

"You can't think of everything all the time, right?" he sputtered. "Let's go. It's kind of a drive up the hill."

Natalie stopped in her tracks. "When you said your place, you meant…"

"Sorry, yes, my parents' house."

She remained frozen in front of the laundry chute. Did she look…nervous?

"I've never been to that house. It's a mansion, though, right? I mean, technically because of the size."

"Um." He rubbed the back of his neck. This was why he used to resent being a part of the Elliott legacy. His name and that stupid house were intimidating by reputation alone. He thought after moving away he'd never have to deal with that again. But here was Natalie, clearly daunted.

"I suppose it's one of the bigger houses in Derry Township, but I don't think of it that way. It's where I grew up. Nothing special."

This was a major stretch, but the thought of Natalie not coming home with him made him severely unhappy.

"I'm sure everyone is asleep by now," he added. "We'll hang in the kitchen. I make a mean omelet."

"Well." She shifted her stance. "I guess that's okay."

The second she agreed, a weight lifted off Luke's shoulders that he hadn't known he'd been carrying.

Chapter Seven

This was a bad idea. It was hard enough for Natalie to be alone with him in the lab, what with his gorgeous face not being hidden in a paper bag like he'd promised. She'd never sparred so much with a guy before. She was at her sassiest with Luke, and she could tell he liked that about her.

Which was getting in the way of work—as she had to tell herself whenever he'd scratch his jaw or run a hand through that dark, wavy hair, looking all hot and whatever.

For most of the drive across town, they chatted about meaningless subjects. Not until they turned to head up Derry Woods Hill did Natalie feel a pang of distress. She'd been on this road a few times, but never on the path at the very top of the hill where the Elliott estate loomed.

Oh, she'd seen the house from afar but never had a reason to get close, aside from her curiosity to see the home where her crush lived. It was dark, and besides the dots of light shining from various front porches way back from the road, only Luke's headlights lit up the night.

When he shifted into second gear to make a turn, Natalie clutched her seatbelt. Luke shot her a glance. "You okay?"

"Sure," she said in a squeaky voice. *Calm down, it's just the house of a work colleague. You don't have a crush on him now, so take a breath. Dinner. That's all this is.*

"Don't tell me you're afraid of old, secluded homes built deep in the woods."

"N-no."

"Good." He slowed down, went into first gear, then headed up a steep driveway lit on either side by gas lamps. The place was illuminated like a castle on a hill—which, it kind of was. It was three stories, no, four. Or five? Did those watch towers count?

"Damn," Luke muttered. "So much for them being asleep. Every light in the house is on."

Natalie's stomach tightened. Since when was she so chicken? Yeah, sure, besides Hershey, the Elliotts were the most influential family in town, but did she have to grip the sides of her seat like she was about to make the free-fall without a harness?

"We can go somewhere else if you want," she said. Like a coward.

"No, it's fine." He parked behind three shiny cars. One had a New York license plate. Was one of Luke's other brothers home? Or Roxanne? Last she'd heard, the only Elliott daughter was finishing college in New Jersey.

Luke was already climbing out, so Natalie took a stabilizing breath and joined him on the path up seven stone steps to the porch. After another breath, she felt only slightly terrified, which was ridiculous. She was a grown woman, head of a research project at Hershey Medical Center, and yet she felt fourteen and as out of place in her jeans, T-shirt, and pink trainers as a clown at Windsor Castle.

Luke waited on the top step. "You look pale."

"I believe in sunscreen."

He chuckled. "I was joking earlier about the house being secluded." He pointed past her shoulder. "We're surrounded by neighbors. Though once I have you inside, the walls are thick. You'll have to scream really loud for anyone to hear."

"Funny." She rolled her eyes, his joke relaxing her as they walked inside.

Crap, man, the place was massive. The entryway had a vaulted ceiling that shot four stories up. The landing of each level looked down to where they stood, like a ski lodge in Aspen. Also similar to a ski lodge, the front of the house had huge windows of varying shapes. She could only imagine what the view must be like from the top landing.

"Kitchen's this way," Luke said, his hand touching her shoulder then skimming to the small of her back. "But I'm afraid that has to wait." He steered her in the opposite direction, and into a dimly lit living room surprisingly sparse of furniture. Just a large off-white sectional, that would probably fill her entire apartment, a coffee table, and two over-stuffed armchairs. Three bodies sprawled across different sections of the couch, all facing a TV screen showing…*The Walking Dead*?

"Dad," Luke said. No one moved. "Mom." Not even a blink. Luke stood right in front of the TV. "Hello? Anyone awake?"

"Move," ordered a voice from behind a stack of pillows. "The governor's about to get it."

"Hush!" a female voice said. "What did I tell you about spoilers, Dex?"

"Sorry, Mom."

"It's like *Breaking Bad* all over again." Mrs. Elliott was stretched out on the chaise lounge part of the sectional, a bowl of popcorn by her bare feet.

"Dexter," Luke said. "The remote is right there, would you pause it for two seconds?"

After a sigh, Dexter lazily lifted the remote and paused the show. "This better be good."

"Um, yeah," Luke said. "We're pulling an all-nighter but stopped in to grab a bite."

"An all-nighter?" Dexter laughed. "Sounds like you…" The second he caught sight of Natalie, he shot into a sitting position. "Whoa, shit."

"Language," Mrs. Elliott said.

"But shit, Mom, look."

"You heard your mother," chimed in an authoritative voice seated in one of the recliners.

The room illuminated as Dexter turned on a tableside lamp. "See?" When her eyes adjusted, Natalie saw Dexter pointing straight at her.

Mrs. Elliott gracefully tilted her chin to look over the back of the couch. When she met Natalie's eyes, she too sat up, then slid off the chaise. Natalie hadn't seen her in a few years. She wore dark blue stretchy jeans and a man's button down shirt that— judging by the oversize fit—was most likely her husband's. Even though both articles of clothing were probably designer, she also had charming bed head, and housed a few stray kernels of popcorn in her dark hair. "Luke didn't tell us he was bringing someone home," she said.

"I didn't *bring*…" Luke sighed. "Forget it."

"How do you do," Mr. Elliott said, walking over to them. "I'm Braxton." Natalie knew who he was. Everyone in Hershey knew who he was.

"Natalie Holden," she replied, shaking his hand.

"This is my wife, Eileen."

"Delighted," Mrs. Elliott said. "And this is Dexter."

"Hey-o." He wore a grin as he sidled up to Natalie. A younger version of Luke, Dexter's eyes shot from her to Luke then back to her. "You said you're pulling an all-night-er, huh?"

Luke crossed his arms and glared at his brother. "For *work*," he uttered between his teeth.

Dexter's gaze returned to Natalie. "This is her? Your hottie boss who yelled at you?"

"She's not my boss."

"When did I yell at you?"

Luke knocked her shoulder playfully. "When *don't* you?"

Natalie laughed, though she hadn't missed that Luke had described her to his brother as a hottie. The sixteen-year-old in her might've just suffered a fainting spell. But… what else had Luke told him? Did Dexter know about the broken park ride? Did his parents know? She felt a raging blush coming on and wondered if they'd think she was crazy if she made a lunge to turn off the lamp so no one would see it.

"You two work together?" Mr. Elliott asked. "You're heading the research trial at the med center?"

"You brought him home," Mrs. Elliott added, staring

starry-eyed at her.

Natalie didn't know which to address first, so she said, "I, um, yes. Though I didn't ask for Luke specifically." She was about to continue that she hadn't asked for an NIH proctor at all when Mrs. Elliott cut her off.

"Luke hasn't been home for more than a weekend in years."

"Mom," Luke said. "It's a job, it could've been anywhere."

"Oh, hush." She batted the air in front of his face. "And it's so wonderful that he brought you here to meet us."

"I didn't—" One withering glance from his mother made Luke shut his mouth and roll his eyes good-naturedly. Maybe his family wasn't scary after all.

"Are you connected to Holden Farms in Intercourse?" his dad asked.

"That's my father. It's where I grew up."

"Well." Mr. Elliott slid his hands in his pockets and leaned back in the same way Luke did. "I'd love to meet him. I'm a big fan."

Natalie felt her eyebrows lift. "Really?"

"I'm just…" Mrs. Elliott put a hand over her mouth. "I'm just so happy about all of this."

"All of…" Natalie began, but before she finished, Dexter took her elbow and was ushering her and Luke away.

"These guys don't have time to chat; they're in a time crunch," Dexter said over his shoulder. "Didn't you say it's a quick break from work?"

"Yeah—yes," Luke said, sounding overly apologetic. "Necessary sustenance then straight back to the lab."

Dexter had nearly pushed them all the way out of the room.

"Oh, well, it was lovely meeting you, Natalie, dear," Mrs. Elliott called, waving her fingers.

"Nice to meet you, too—both of you."

Taking over for Dexter, Luke grabbed her hand, tugging her down a hall and into the kitchen.

"Dude," Dexter said, staring at his brother while braced against the kitchen island. "Don't *do* that."

Luke dropped his chin and his shoulders relaxed as he exhaled. "I know."

"Mom was two seconds from—"

"I *know*."

"You're lucky I was here."

Luke rounded his lips and blew out another long breath. "Dude, thanks for that."

"You owe me." Dexter's eyes slid to Natalie. "I've heard a lot about you."

Maybe because she hadn't understood a thing about what just happened, she felt her cheeks prickle again and willed the blush to stay away. "Have you?"

"Yep."

"Don't be a dickweed," Luke said. "He's just giving you crap. He knows nothing, I swear."

Dexter laughed and tapped his chin. "Well now, I *was* talking crap, but that was before I knew there was something to know."

"Drop it," Luke muttered, a warning in his voice.

Dexter lifted both hands in surrender. "Fine, whatever, it's dropped. So, what are you guys doing here so late?"

"I told you, we're working all night but want food."

"Food, uh-huh."

"You're an idiot."

"It's my fault," Natalie cut in before the brothers threw down. "Our days in the lab got slashed, so I'm being a slave driver."

"My brother's a very hard worker. Ask anyone. I'll give you a list."

"Just…shut up," Luke said, punching Dexter's arm.

"Fine, I'll leave you to your all-nighter." He rubbed his arm and turned to Natalie. "It was a great pleasure to formally meet you." Just like his father, he held out his hand for her to shake. It was warm and strong, friendly. In fact, everything about the Elliotts had been extremely friendly. Why had she always been so in awe?

When she noticed half of one wall of the kitchen was floor-to-ceiling windows looking out over the lights of Hershey, she remembered why.

"Well, that was fun," Luke said when they were alone.

"Barrel of monkeys," Natalie replied.

"Sass," he said under his breath, as he opened the refrigerator. "Omelet still sound good?"

"Sure. Can I help?"

"No, you can sit." He pointed to a bar stool at the island. "You've been in charge of food all night. It's my turn."

She smiled and sat, more than happy to be taken care of for a change—if only for one meal. "What was with all that 'dude, don't *do* that,' half sentence brother lingo with Dexter?"

Luke cracked six eggs into a mixing bowl and started to whisk. "When it comes to the marital status of their offspring, our parents are very…eager."

"They seem down to earth," Natalie said, unable to sit there and not help. While Luke whisked the eggs, she added milk and threw in some grated cheese. "I'd never picture them as fans of *The Walking Dead*."

"Why not?"

"It seems too…normal."

Luke stopped whisking and looked up. "We're as normal as anyone. I know they've got this big house up here like some freaking monument, but that doesn't mean we're untouchable."

Natalie knew for a fact just how touchable Luke was. She couldn't stop her gaze from sliding over the muscles of his arms, up his chest and neck, to his face.

The way he was looking back at her gave her the overwhelming desire to bite her bottom lip and let the chips fall where they may.

But that was asking for trouble.

"So, back to what Dexter was saying?"

"Dex, right." Luke took a step away from the counter and sucked in a breath, running a hand up the back of his head. "My parents come from a long line of Massachusetts families dating back to the Plymouth Rock. A whole lot of *wasps* in the bloodline, couples that stayed together when they had no functioning marriage to speak of. Even in the twenty-first century, my divorce threw my parents for a loop. It killed them, actually."

Natalie nodded, while her heart twisted into a little knot.

"The divorce was finalized two years ago, but it's longer than that since my ex and I separated. Our marriage was over, but some of that *wasp* fortitude was in me because I kept hoping we could work it out." He paused and looked across the room, his expression showing weariness, leftover defeat. "But when trust is broken and there's no love to speak of on either side, what's the point?"

Even with the Hershey grapevine, Natalie couldn't remember hearing why Luke had gotten divorced. Maybe she had heard the why, but ever since graduation, she'd made herself stop thinking about him. Her feelings had been self-strangled—dead.

Until six days ago.

"I'm sorry."

A corner of his mouth formed into a non-happy half smile. "Thanks."

"When you thought I had a boyfriend, you mentioned something about how easy it happens. Were you talking about…" She let the sentence fade.

Luke flipped their omelet with more force than necessary. "Yeah, that's what I meant."

So, she'd cheated on him. Luke's ex-wife had broken their marriage vows and hooked up with someone else, destroying their life together. The thought made her sick.

"And then we…in the tunnel… And you thought I had a boyfriend afterward." She felt even sicker. When he still wouldn't look at her, she pried his hand off the handle, shut off the burner, and pushed the pan off the heat. "Luke." She turned him so he faced her. "I'm sorry."

"For what?"

"For…" She bit her lip on accident. "For making you feel guilty about what happened at Hershey Lounge and in the tunnel. Thinking we were doing something wrong. I'm sorry I put you through that."

Finally, he lifted his eyes to hers. "It's not your fault. I just never want to put a guy through what I went through; it was hell. I don't know, you—*it* happened so suddenly. And when I stopped to think, it seemed out of the blue that you'd kiss me like that."

Looming embarrassment rose in her chest, but the confession had to happen now. Luke deserved to know. "For me, it wasn't out of the blue at all."

"No?"

She glanced down at the pan of eggs, ruined. "I, uh, kind of had a crush on you."

His eyes blinked in surprise. "When?"

"High school, middle school, probably from the womb."

"That was years ago."

"Yeah, well, it was pretty intense—which sounds creepy, I know—and my feelings didn't just evaporate the day we graduated. But it's not like I'm some crazy stalker chick. I moved on, so you don't have to worry that I've been carrying a torch all this time. And *you* pretty much started it, *again*. I'm only telling you so you'll know I don't go around straddling random guys at Hersheypark without some feeling behind it." She paused to take in a breath, prepared for Luke to immediately drive her back to the lab and dump her off in the parking lot. "So yeah, there's that."

But he didn't freak out. "Interesting story," he said, tilting his head.

"No need to smile all cocky like that. I said I was over you."

"Uh-huh, that's what you said. What do you mean though, that I started it *again*?"

Her stupid, stupid babbling mouth. How had she let that slip? "I don't want to say." She crossed her arms. "It's embarrassing."

Luke looked at the ceiling and chuckled, causing Natalie

to notice how the muscles of his thick neck flexed. "Now you have to tell me."

"It happened a million years ago. You don't even remember it."

His smiled dropped. "This is about me? And you?"

She nodded.

"Well"—Luke shifted his weight—"You said it's embarrassing. For which one of us?"

Natalie couldn't stop a dark laugh from escaping her throat. "Definitely not you."

"But you said I don't remember."

"You've never said anything," she said. "Not now and not back then."

"Sorry. I'm at a loss here. Looks like you'll have to remind me."

She didn't want to. She didn't want to be having this conversation at all. It wouldn't be embarrassing for Luke, which made it even more mortifying for Natalie. What other choice did she have, though?

"Do you remember the summer before seventh grade?" she asked. "Justin Bay had a birthday party in Bird-in-Hand. It was my first boy/girl party at night."

"Mine, too."

"Justin's mom put on a DVD, but all the cool kids snuck out—*you* snuck out. Do you remember?"

He thought for a moment, then nodded.

"My cousin and I snuck out a little bit later, not to follow your group, but we found you anyway. You guys were using that old boathouse to play seven minutes in heaven."

Luke laughed under his breath. "I haven't thought about that in fifteen years."

"When we got there, you and Melissa Mallory were about to go to the boathouse around the corner from the group. You went in first and shut the door, and Melissa was supposed to go in after you." She paused and looked away, tugging at the neck of her shirt. "But she just stood outside the door, then walked off."

Luke blinked. "That's not what happened. Trust me. I remember that experience vividly."

"Then why did you never say anything to me about it? Not then, not the day after or the millions of times we crossed paths?" She swallowed. "Imagine for one second how painfully embarrassing that was for me, Luke. We saw each other all the time and you never gave me one word, not a look meant just for me. But don't worry, I figured it out on my own. You thought I wasn't good enough. You made that perfectly clear when you pretended it never happened."

She'd worked herself up so much that she was about to storm from the room. Until she remembered she didn't have a car.

"You lost me again," Luke said. "Why would I tell you about what happened in the boathouse between me and my girlfriend?"

Since there would be no storming out, and since Luke still didn't get it, Natalie took in another deep breath. "She left you in there alone. I saw the whole thing."

"That's impossible." He stared into the middle distance, his forehead crinkling as he strained to recover the memory.

"Luke, how can you not…?" Finally, Natalie understood the miscommunication going on, and her mouth fell open as she blinked, connecting the dots. "Wait. So, you didn't know?"

"I *still* don't know." He lifted both hands. "Would you please finish? You're saying Melissa wasn't in the boathouse?"

"Yeah." She squinted and ran a hand over her throat. "I felt bad that she ditched you like that. Then my cousin dared me to go in, like it was a peer pressure thing. But the truth is, you were in there. Luke Elliott. And I wanted to do it. So I…"

"That was you?"

She closed her eyes and confirmed the ancient memory with a nod.

"In the boathouse with me." His voice was incredulous. "That was you."

Natalie was still a bit incredulous, herself. Suddenly, so much made sense. Luke hadn't blown her off or ignored her. He simply *hadn't known*. "You and Melissa were like the hot seventh grade couple, so I assumed you'd know I wasn't her right away, even in the dark."

"We hadn't started going out yet. That party was when we got together." He looked down at his hands and rubbed them together. "I remember she came in—*you* came in while my back was to the door. I was trying to remember the last thing I ate and wondered if she would be able to taste it."

"Strawberry cake," they said together.

He dropped his chin and a laugh rumbled from his chest. "You came in and touched the back of my shoulder."

"I felt you turn around," she said, tag-teaming the story.

"Then I just went for it. I had no idea what I was doing."

"Ha! *Such* a lie. I was the inexperienced one; you knew exactly what you were doing, where to put your hands, my hands, you even stopped to hug me right in the middle of it." She felt her heart pound for that silly thirteen-year-old kissing bandit.

"So wait. All this time, you thought I knew it was you with me?"

"Yeah. While we were together, I forgot you were with Melissa, or I didn't care. I mean, you were this *amazing* kissing sex god, and she got to make out with you all the time, and I knew there was no way she liked you more than I did, so it seemed fair."

"Melissa and I hadn't kissed before then. I hadn't kissed anyone before then."

"What?"

"It's the truth. And you're telling me my first kiss…" He pointed at her.

"Was my first kiss, too."

"Whoa."

"Huh." She twisted her lips. "Sorry."

"Don't be. That's one hell of a story." He smiled and looked at her with those blue eyes she'd fallen for before she could even drive. "Now that I think about it, I should've known." He leaned forward. "You bit your lip back then, too."

The air between them came alive, sparked, crackled. Natalie couldn't move. If she could, would she be responsible for her actions?

"We…came here to eat, Luke," she said after wetting her dry throat. "I think our omelet is dead."

"What should we do?"

"You don't happen to have an all you can eat Chinese buffet stashed in one of those rooms upstairs?"

A muscle in Luke's mouth twitched. "Nothing up there but bedrooms."

The word hung in the sparking air between them, making Natalie's mind reel, her palms sweat, mouth flood with the memory of the taste of honey, the taste of him.

Breaking the spell, Luke took a full step back and crossed his arms tight across his chest. "We probably shouldn't go upstairs any time soon."

"Ya think?"

He smiled that hunky, dreamy smile she remembered from high school. "Since my parents have the TV so loud I can actually hear zombies eating each other, I don't feel like hanging out in here, either."

"We should go back to the lab. We still have two hours until the molds are set, but we can always—"

"I have a better idea. Give me five minutes." He yanked open the fridge. "You like cold fried chicken?"

"Yes, but—"

"And you have no lactose intolerance?"

"I can tolerate anyone," she said. "You, of all people, should know that."

He glanced at her over his shoulder. "Hilarious. I'll grab food, and the wine rack is over—no, wait, we're working. There's a beverage fridge in the back of the third pantry." He pointed across the kitchen. "Why don't you grab us some water or whatever you want."

"Beverage fridge?" She repeated deadpan. "*Third* pantry?"

"Seven people used to live in this house. Five were male, one of those being Dexter who has literally, *literally* eaten a horse."

"Eck." Natalie cringed. "For real?"

Luke tossed her a cloth reusable bag for the drinks. "He

lost a bet to me and I made him pay."

"Boys." She shook her head. By the time she'd stocked the bag, Luke had already made two trips outside. The third time, he took the bag of drinks and ushered her down the front steps. "We're not eating now? Luke, we have a long night ahead of us, who knows when we'll—"

"I'm feeding you, Ms. Holden. Just not here." He placed her bag in the backseat of the Jeep, which she noticed had three other bags, a pile of blankets, and two camping lanterns.

Chapter Eight

The necessity of a Plan B hadn't occurred to Luke until he'd found himself staring into Natalie's chocolate eyes with the word bedroom echoing in his ears. Then he pictured spreading her across the kitchen table beside his mother's flower arrangement.

Dude. That thought had been enough to metaphorically dump cold water down his back.

By the light of the dashboard, he caught Natalie's eager, animated smile as he drove down the hill. Near the bottom, he hung a left. The place was mostly dark, illuminated by the moon and a single street lamp in the parking lot. He was glad he'd thought to bring the kerosene lanterns at the last minute.

"We're stopping here?"

"Yes, indeed." He reached back and grabbed three bags, the blankets, and one lantern. Gauging by the dim light but mostly by memory, Luke led them across the grass, over the bridge, and a few yards down the paved trail that forked at the foot of the greenbelt.

Natalie was holding onto the back of his shirt the whole time, not knowing the terrain like he did. He grinned and glanced over his shoulder at her. Her trust pushed his "inner security" up to the stud level.

"I've never been on a picnic in the middle of the night."

"Classy, huh?"

"Creative. But it's cold and pitch black."

"It won't be." He set down his haul, passed her the warmest blanket, crouched before the lantern, then lifted the glass chimney from the burner. "There's a book of matches in your pocket."

"No, there's— Um, how did these get in the back pocket of my jeans, Luke?"

"Magic." He smiled in the dark as Natalie lobbed them at his head. He caught them before they made contact, struck a match, then lit the wick, adjusting the level as it began to smoke. A minute later, both lanterns were shining bright.

"I love this smell." Her voice drifted to him. "Reminds me of camping."

"Me, too."

With one blanket around her shoulders, she unrolled another and spread it across the grass. "You used to camp?"

"Still do."

"Huh. I never pictured the Elliotts roughing it."

"I'm an expert at rough."

His attempt at an innocent flirt was rewarded with one of her soft, feminine laughs.

"I camp mostly with my brothers." He smiled at a memory as he helped Natalie unload the food. "There's this one time when Dex, Vince, and I drove to the mountains at the foot of the Ozarks—middle of the night, spur of the moment, no map and zero cell reception. When we were sufficiently lost, we got out and walked for a while then crashed out on the ground. We woke up surrounded by a flock of hungry and very pissed off Canadian geese."

"Geese?" She grinned and handed him a pile of napkins. "How terrifying for you."

"Those things are damn mean. Bite your frickin' hand off if they think it's food."

"You're a regular Daniel Boone." Her musical laugh filled his ears. "Where are the plates?"

"Must've forgot."

"You forgot plates for a picnic? Talk about roughing it."

"Don't make me bite you like a goose, woman."

"I'd like to see you try…"

Though he was tempted, he didn't take the bait but walked to the Jeep for the last of the supplies.

No, he would not take her bait, no matter what she did. It was his fault they had to leave the house in the first place and rough it in the chilly autumn air. If he hadn't made that crack about the bedrooms, then he wouldn't have pictured Natalie on the kitchen table and then in one of those beds. That was about the time he'd needed to get the hell out of there before fantasy became reality.

Natalie was smart, funny, sexy as hell…and she was available. Hell, man, she'd been his first kiss.

The instant she'd told him the guy in the car was her brother, he'd felt like that kid in the boathouse again, waiting to kiss a girl for the first time. Happy and nervous and alive. So alive.

That sexy woman wrapped in his blanket in the dark was single, but still off limits. And that was really starting to mess with his head. It was a good thing he was only in Hershey temporarily. The noise and energy of Philly and DC would take his mind off of her in no time.

"Are you coming back or what?" Natalie called. It made him smile. *Damn, this girl.* By the time he returned, she'd divided the food, a slightly larger plate-less pile for him, though he knew full well she could eat.

"Oh, phew." She looked up at him. "Thought you might've been attacked by geese."

Don't kiss her. Do not kiss her.

"Why am I not surprised to see you drinking that?" he said, desperate for small talk, pointing at the two cans of orange soda by her pile of food.

"I'm not a sugar Nazi." She took a long swig.

"You better brush your teeth after that."

"Thanks, Mr. Surgeon General," she said, teasingly. "On sample days, I probably brush ten times, so we're good." She gave him a sparkly grin, pulled off a large purple grape from its bunch with her teeth, then chomped it like a sexy pig. "Why aren't you eating? Sit."

Luke took a second to wonder what it would be like to be that grape, then steeled himself and sat.

"What's that?" she asked, pointing behind him.

"My guitar." She stopped chewing, like what he'd said made her nervous. He grabbed an apple and took a bite. "The other night at Hershey Lounge, you mentioned you'd seen me play at Phillip Arthur."

"And you casually mentioned you play at open mike nights." She threw a balled up napkin at his head. "You totally had me going. I thought you were a sexy starving artist."

"Aren't I?"

"I think we better stop this line of conversation." She tore off a hunk of bread and tossed it to him. "Eat."

They ate in silence for a while. The distant creek, the odd car, crickets, and other nocturnal elements the only sounds.

"It's still too dark to see exactly where we are."

"Bullfrog Valley," Luke replied. "It's one of the suburban parks out here in the sticks that share a trail."

"Oh, okay." She glanced around. "I love running these trails."

"I didn't know you run."

"With my job, I'd be bigger than your parents' house if I didn't stay active."

He scoffed. "You'd look good no matter what size you are. Women get too hung up on scales and dress sizes and calorie counting."

"So says the holistic microbiologist."

"All I'm saying is, men don't care about that. Yes, I think it's important to have a healthy lifestyle—it's my job to want that—but not to the point of obsessive exercise or starving yourself."

Natalie tipped her chin to finish the last of her orange soda, then threw both arms open and pointed at her stomach. "Does it look like I starve myself?" she asked, then hiccupped.

"You look damn perfect."

She lowered her arms and gazed across the darkness at him.

"I, um, meant *you* as a generalization, not actually you.

I know you're healthy." He couldn't stop his gaze from sliding over her upper body, focusing on a singular area that had nothing to do with a healthy lifestyle, only about being a woman. When his temperature shot to fever pitch, he cleared his throat. "We need to get back to the lab now. Right? How long have we been out here?"

"Thirty minutes."

"Oh." Only a half hour? They had way too much time left out here alone in the dark. "Cool, that's cool. The night is still young, or *we're* still young, or..." He needed to shut up before he said or *did* something he couldn't take back. But he couldn't just sit here, either, looking at Natalie by lantern light. It was like the tunnel all over again.

So he pushed his food to the side and grabbed his guitar.

Natalie lowered the pear she'd been nibbling and didn't care that her eyes were ready to bug out of her head. Luke was going to play.

"It's been awhile," he said, sitting cross-legged then adjusting the strap around his back. "Can't think of the last time I played at all." He held a pick between his lips and strummed. "This thing's really out of tune."

Natalie waited like an anxious groupie while he adjusted the nobs on the neck of the guitar. Soon, strums became a melody, one she recognized as a song by the Eagles, that one about having peaceful, easy feelings.

"Sing," she asked.

"It's been a *really* long time since I sang for anyone." He glanced up and met her eyes. "Okay, but not this one." His tune morphed from the Eagles to the Beatles. First it was a few bars from "Twist and Shout," which made Natalie giggle, then it slowed into the opening of "I Will."

Luke Elliott was singing.

The melodic words filled the night air, enfolding her in a silky veil. His voice was soft at first, but as the song went on, it grew stronger; Luke grew stronger and more confident. The lyrics took on new meaning than from all the times she'd heard them before. His singing voice asked if she wanted him to wait a lonely lifetime for her. But with their history, the question should've been the other way around.

He ended by humming the bridge a second time, his eyes closed.

Front row to a private concert by Luke was teenage Natalie's fantasy come to life. The whole thing made her slip back into that innocent, infatuated mindset, turning her insides warm and spongy.

"Luke," she said softly. "That was beautiful."

"I'm rusty."

"Beautiful."

He glanced at her, strumming the beginning of a new song she didn't recognize. "You're very kind to say that."

She couldn't help biting her lip, but it was okay, Luke couldn't see it clearly in the dark. "I don't remember you playing that in high school."

"I haven't played it for anyone."

"Why did you choose it, and not one of the old standards you've played a million times?"

"I don't know. I was thinking of another song, but with you sitting here and…I don't know, I changed my mind."

His words—that probably meant nothing—made that

spongy, innocent warmth flame in her chest, at the back of her neck. There was nothing innocent about it now. "You said you hadn't played for a while."

"Not for a couple of years."

She pressed her lips together before speaking. "Not since before you and Celeste split up?"

Luke stopped playing and dropped his fingers from the strings. At first, she thought he was angry, but as her eyes focused better, it seemed as though he was blinking out of a fog.

And then something in his expression read gratitude. For her.

The impossible idea caused another wave of heat to wash over her body.

"It's understandable," she said, needing to fill the silence. "It was a terrible time in your life. Playing guitar is a happy thing for you, so maybe subconsciously you didn't want to ruin that positive release while you were going through all the sadness." She wanted to gag herself but couldn't stop speaking. "Do you think maybe that's why you stopped playing? It's good for you, though, mentally. If it makes you happy like it used to, you should play all the time now, and—" She cut herself off. "Oh, jeez. Sorry, it's not like I care—I mean, I do care, I care, but… I'll stop talking now. None of my business. Sorry, mouth zipped."

To stop the madness, she pulled her knees up to her chest, pressed a fist over her mouth and looked away. The shadowy shape of a tree was not too far distant. Maybe she could sneak off when Luke wasn't looking, climb into its branches, and hide. Yes, very good plan.

"Play another song," she said when he didn't say

anything. The silence was too excruciating. "Something loud and frivolous and—"

"Natalie." Luke's voice cut in. The tone was as smooth as when he'd been singing. "I'm done playing."

"Why?" She stared at him with concern. "I'm sorry. It was thoughtless of me to bring any of that up."

"You're not thoughtless. You're insightful, *irritatingly* insightful."

"Then, why won't you play?"

His eyes pinned on hers while he undid the strap and set his guitar to the side. "Because I'll need both hands free."

"Oh." Comprehension was slow coming. "Ohhh."

"It's okay."

Oh crap, oh crap, oh crap. Oxygen hung in her lungs, and her next inhale came in a hot gulp as the gorgeous man of her adolescent dreams crawled over to her.

She opened her mouth; wasn't there something important she should be telling him?

"Shhh." Luke interrupted whatever it was. He knelt before her and ran a finger across her cheek, over her chin until her eyes fluttered closed.

His lips brushed hers once, twice, his breath warm against her chilly skin, making her dizzy. A hand cupped her cheek, rougher and manlier than she remembered. As he kissed her again, his hand slid to the back of her neck. She felt him fist her hair, felt the moment they both stopped breathing.

The calm before the storm…

It was too much to remain still, and she took his face in her hands, needing his mouth to put out the fire. Luke groaned over her lips, and his palms splayed across the front of her thighs, adding fuel to the flames.

Simultaneously, they rose to their knees, and his arms wrapped all the way around her. He was warmer than the blanket that had fallen to the ground. Natalie heard the gasp that escaped her own lips as he pulled her to his chest. Silently, he looked her in the eyes. Some kind of earnest expression sat behind them, but it was too dark and she was too blind. All she could see was that mouth.

So she kissed her teenage fantasy, the popular boy she used to dream would see something special in her and love her forever. The man kissed her back.

Luke's fingers combed through her hair, making her neck arch. She could taste what he'd just eaten, the sweetness of an apple, minty tea, a deeper something she'd tasted before in the tunnel—something that only belonged to Luke.

Gravity changed, and her back was flat on the blankets, with gorgeous Luke Elliott hovering over her. Braced by his elbows, his mouth started on hers, then ran a trail across her cheek, over her jawline. She fisted the back of his shirt in both hands when his lips made contact with the sensitive spot at the base of her ear.

"Hmm, you like that," he whispered, his breath hot and intoxicating.

"I like…everything."

Luke chuckled, then kissed the same spot, slowly, over and over. "Your neck," he said, trailing his mouth down the side of her throat, stopping once or twice for a more thorough inspection. "It's ludicrous, but I swear I taste chocolate coming out of your pores."

"What did you expect?" she said, cradling the back of his head.

He pushed off the ground and gazed down at her, all

his manly hotness right there, hers for the taking. Without a word, he took both her hands, and extended them over her head.

A gush of warmth swirled in her stomach as her core coiled, every other muscle going weak.

"Let me get a better taste." With one strong hand pinning both of hers to the ground, his other swept the hair from her neck, exposing both sides.

She closed her eyes and took it in, took everything in. His spicy smell, his weight, his mouth on her skin, the sounds he made in response to her sounds, the sheer, unspeakable, chemical reaction that happens in the brain when a person is completely blissed out.

A sensation that could never be bottled or even wrapped in Hershey foil.

"Ow," she said. "I think a pear is stabbing my spine." She put her palms on his chest and rolled them so she was on top. "Better," she said, sitting up so she could gaze down at him. "Any fruit digging into you?"

"I have no idea." He reached out both hands and cupped her cheeks.

Another burst of chemistry made her lean down and kiss him, her hands on either side of his head, bracing her weight until they began to shake. With his hands sliding around her back, Luke eased her onto his hard, muscly chest, and she sank into him, their kisses growing deeper, their paces changing back and forth from hot frenzy, to slow and deep.

He rolled them again. Natalie loved his heavy weight pinning her down, their bodies almost as close as they could be. Almost. At the thought, she felt for the bottom of his shirt. She'd forgotten it was a button down, not easily pulled over his head. So she started in on the buttons, their mouths still connected in their latest frenzy.

Wordlessly, Luke rose off of her a few inches, giving her access to that forever long row of buttons. How many were there? Fifty? If she had any strength left, she'd fist the front of his shirt and rip it open like the rock star she used to dream he was.

After she managed to get it halfway open, she slid her hands inside, fingers gliding over his hard, ripped chest. She pushed the shirt back from his shoulders and reached her mouth to his collarbone. At the same time, his hands slid inside her shirt.

It was right then that Natalie caught fire.

L uke smelled the smoke but ignored it. How could he be expected to think of anything besides Natalie's curvy body beneath him? Or her soft skin under his hands as he glided them up and up and up.

Before he'd lost himself completely, the Boy Scout part of his brain kicked awake and glanced to where the kerosene lantern was on its side.

Driven by instinct, he rolled off Natalie, grabbed a corner of the blanket, and gave one hard yank until she and the remains of the picnic flew onto the grass. He heard her yelp, but there hadn't been time to give a warning, he'd only acted, using the wool blanket to smother the fire.

It took a few seconds before the flames were extinguished. Another minute, and it could've been a real problem.

Heart pounding like a marching band, Luke sat back on

his heels and exhaled, wiping his forehead with the back of his wrist. Once he was sure the kerosene had been soaked up, he turned to see Natalie lying on her side, probably in the same position as when she'd landed.

"Are you okay?"

Her tangled, sexy hair was in her face, her eyes peeking through the long, wild strands. "What happened?"

"We kicked over the lantern."

She rose onto her knees. "We started a forest fire?"

"I smothered it before it got out of control." *Before I got out of control.*

His hands, now covered in kerosene, still burned from where he'd been touching her. His mouth needed to be on hers again. Everything felt unfinished, interrupted. Like the rest of his life since seeing her that first night.

Natalie pushed her hair back and crawled to him like a cat. "You're sure it's out?"

"Positive." He moved the blanket to show the area where the spilled oil had spread the flames.

"You didn't get burned, did you? Are you hurt?" She grabbed the soiled blanket from him, pushed it aside, then took his hand and flipped it over, then the other one. He wanted to lace his fingers through hers and squeeze. Then kiss her soft little hand, kiss her mouth, finish this thing like he always had—physically satisfied with emotions untouched.

"I'm fine," he said, knowing he couldn't *finish* anything with Natalie. Luckily, all they'd done was kiss. Yes, again. This time though, he couldn't blame red, wavy lights, or the rocking motion of the boat. He'd known exactly what he was doing when he'd put down his guitar.

What she'd said about Celeste, and how he'd stopped playing music because of her. He'd never thought of it that way, but she was right. For some reason, Natalie helping him see that made her more appealing than ever.

"We need to scrub our hands," he said, moving away from her. "We're covered in kerosene."

"Ew, we stink. And look at the mess."

Luke followed her eye line to the grass where their entire picnic was now scattered. "I'll clean it up. There's a faucet around the corner. No soap, but you can rinse your hands."

She stood but took only a few steps. "I can't see."

"Take the other lantern."

"Then how will *you* see?"

"Okay, we'll stick together." They gathered all their food and wrappers and dumped them in the trashcan. His scorched camping blankets were probably ruined, so he stuffed them in the trash, as well.

Natalie was carrying his guitar and holding the lantern. "I think that's everything," she said, already leading the way toward the faucet. "We're going to need industrial soap to get this off. There's some at the lab."

"Some at the house, too."

They both turned to look up the dark road. Knowing what they'd find up there was a huge house with too many empty bedrooms to count, they said in unison: "The lab."

It made Luke laugh, and then he wanted to beat his skull against a tree for a while. But at least they were on the same page. Both staying here and going to the house was full of unspeakable temptation.

At least at the lab, nothing could happen. It was a sterile, scientific environment. Holy.

Back at the Jeep, Luke extinguished the lamp, and they were on the road to the med center. The safe zone. Seeing Natalie out of the corner of his eyes, thinking about their latest kiss, their *first* kiss, their fire, made him floor it to that safe zone.

Chapter Nine

"I feel like I need a shower, after all."

As Luke said this, Natalie gave him the eye. His shirt was untucked and still halfway open from her greedy fingers. Good golly, his chest, the lines and dents, the speckles of dark hair. She could stare at it all day. They'd both scrubbed their hands clean, which were probably the only parts of their bodies that didn't reek of kerosene.

"They have a few here," she said.

"I'm not about to strip down in the hallway to use one of those Hazmat showers, even if it is the middle of the night."

It took Natalie a few seconds to blink that image out of her mind. Luke stripping in the hall? "Um, there're private showers in some of the restrooms."

"Cool."

"I think I might join you."

"Now *there's* a plan."

She rolled her eyes. "In a different shower than yours."

"Can't say I didn't try." He snapped his fingers. "My clothes deserve their own Hazmat bag."

"Mine too. I always keep another outfit in my car for kerosene lamp oil spill emergencies."

"So do I." Luke slapped a hand on his chest like he was shocked. "Tonight's been full of so many revelations."

"Funny," was all she could say.

Neither of them had mentioned the kiss. Natalie would be content if the subject was never broached. They both knew it was a mistake, so why bother talking about it?

She was a chemist, so she understood the very real chemistry that connects people. She and Luke had been caught in that reaction, and their chemistry was way too explosive when kept unchecked. Since science and plain old human logic were not her strengths when it came to him, they simply couldn't be alone in the dark again. Like ever.

"Your shower is two hallways that way," she said, feeling left over charges from their latest explosion.

"And yours?" He cocked an eyebrow. "In case killer geese attack and you need rescuing."

"Barring any flesh-eating birds, I'll meet you back here after we both—"

"Hose off?"

She snorted a laugh. Classic, reading-her-mind Luke. "Exactly."

She raced out to her car, wanting to get in and out of the shower before Luke even started. The thought of them being naked at the same time only a few walls apart made her feel…uneasy.

No, uneasy is the wrong word. The word you're looking for is sexy.

Please shut up, brain.

Here at the lab, of all places, she could not feel sexy, couldn't think about sexy things or sexy times or how damn sexy she was sure Luke would look with wet hair.

She turned on the cold water full blast and stood under the showerhead for five solid minutes. Hosing off, indeed.

The hotel-type shampoo and conditioner would have to do, but at least she no longer smelled like the inside of a tractor. She pulled on clean jeans and a thin, frilly top she'd never wear to work, but it was the only shirt in her trunk. She usually had gym clothes, including a sports bra, but she didn't even have that. She finished towel drying her hair, tossed her rank clothes in a plastic bag and returned to the lab.

Luke was already there, wearing jeans and a white, semi-frayed Penn Med T-shirt that fit him so perfectly it made her whimper.

"Holy hell."

"What?" Natalie asked, self-consciously twisting her damp hair over one shoulder.

"Your shirt is see-through. You're not wearing a…"

"Oh!" She grabbed a lab coat and quickly pulled it on, buttoning the two middle buttons. "It was the only one in the car…and my…everything else is too smelly to wear."

His wide eyes were unmoving. "Damn, woman, you cannot…" He ran his hands through his damp—and yes, uber sexy—hair. "You can't do that."

"Do what?"

He waved a hand in front of her face and body. "Any of this, all of this. Wet hair, no makeup, transparent shirt, you looking all… And right after we… Just—don't." He spun on his heels and walked away, rubbing a hand along the base of his neck. His T-shirt strained tight over his arms and back. His butt in those jeans looked too good for words.

"Well, then you don't do *that*."

He wheeled around. "I'm not doing anything."

She tipped her chin and *har-harred* at the ceiling.

"Unlike you," he said dryly, "I'm dressed completely appropriate for where we are."

"You might not appreciate a tight-fitting, thin cotton Hanes over a well-defined male chest, but *I* do." *Too much talking, Nat.* "So just put on your own freaking lab coat." She turned away until she heard him pull one off a hanger.

"Okay, look," he said. "Things got out of control earlier— my fault. But it's okay. I don't want to kiss you again."

Natalie spun around, her mouth gaping as she looked for something to throw at him. Ivy's old microscope would do quite nicely.

"No— No," he continued. "I mean I *do* want to kiss you again. But I don't."

"If you think that's a clearer explanation…"

"Sorry, no." He shook his head, looking more perplexed that she felt. "I mean, we both have reasons to not blow off our jobs. Mine happens to be a very important reason. I have a hell of a lot riding on being here."

Natalie crossed her arms. Could Luke's reason be any more important than the mental health of her brother? Or her best friend's job? But she nodded anyway. She didn't care about his reasons; whatever it took to keep his lips out of kissing range.

"Also," Luke said, running another hand through his hair, "I'm not ready to date."

"Date?" she repeated, sidestepping the potential hit to her ego. "Who said anything about dating?

He rubbed his three-am-shadowed jaw, the one that had brushed against her mouth, causing delicious stings. "We could sleep together, though, because that wouldn't mean anything."

Natalie's mouth dropped open again.

"Pause whatever you're about to yell at me," Luke said, preempting the lava of outrage bubbling in her chest. "Dammit, why can't I talk to you like a normal person? I'm usually very well-spoken."

"So speak."

She watched his shoulders lift as he took in a slow breath.

"I haven't really dated since the divorce. There've been women, but nothing even remotely serious. I don't know if it's because I need more time, or if I'm so screwed up that I've got a mental hang-up about relationships now."

Natalie no longer wanted to throw a microscope at his head. She hadn't once considered that Luke's ex had actually damaged him. She worked fast to keep her heart from going all melty and sympathetic.

"Luke, it's fine. We were two consenting adults having a little fun."

"A lot of fun," he said, lifting one of those smoldering grins.

"We broke an amusement park ride."

"Started a forest fire."

She swallowed. "But I can't have fun with you—and it's not only about working together." When Luke's mouth opened, she held up a hand. "Let me finish. You said we could just sleep together because it wouldn't mean anything.

But when I have sex, it means everything, and I don't want an *everything* right now, not with anyone." She paused, wondering if she should tell him why. She thought about Jack the rat—the last guy to break her trust. Then she thought about Luke—the first guy to. "Your head can't do a relationship and my heart can't. See? I might be just as screwed up as you." She laughed, trying to make light of the situation before it got heavy. "And even if somehow your head and my heart were miraculously ready, a relationship would be impossible."

Luke shifted his stance. "Because?"

"Simple." She took a beat. "Hershey."

"What about it?"

"I'm never leaving."

After a moment, Luke nodded, like it finally dawned on him. "And I'll never live here."

Even though she was expecting it, his answer was majorly deflating, the final nail in the coffin. "See?"

He nodded again. "Everything you said makes sense, but you're wrong about one thing."

She made herself laugh again and pulled out a pair of latex gloves. "I seriously doubt that. But I'm curious. Which one thing was I wrong about?"

"What we do together means something to me." The way he looked at her made her heart beat fast. "I like you, Natalie."

She could not let *that* mean anything to her. "That's natural. I'm likable."

He dropped his chin and exhaled. "Fine, never mind. You're right about everything and let's move on."

"Good answer."

It was a relief to be on the same page again, but when she glanced at Luke and caught him giving her body a lightning-fast scan, pausing briefly at where her bra should've been…

Whoa. If his eyes make me feel like this, what will his hands—

"Time to check the molds!" she blurted, turning away. She blew out a breath and ran a hand along the back of her neck. Was it damp from her hair or from Luke?

It hadn't been the full three hours, but most of the molds were set. Maybe this all-nighter was a better idea than she'd hoped. Only a few of the pans were still on the gooey side, probably because they were close to a heater vent. She showed Luke how to carefully pop the squares from the plastic molds, then left him to check her cell.

"I very rarely eat the stuff."

"What?" she asked when she finished reading emails.

"Chocolate."

They started on blending the second batch of samples. He tossed her a box of cold butter.

"With that attitude, I'm surprised they let you cross into Hershey city limits."

He laughed. "You sound like my parents. When they found out why I'm here—to *observe* your project—they had double heart attacks. They even staged an intervention, brought in my brothers and Roxy, and you know Dex is here."

"Take this," Natalie said, passing him a set of clean molds. "Once this is done blending, start filling." She adjusted her safety glasses. "Why an intervention?"

"They think the same way you do, that my sole mission in life is to rid the planet of chocolate."

"Isn't it?" She couldn't help grinning, even as Luke shot her a look through his goggles.

"It's a family thing, too. They worry the Elliott name will be tarnished if one of us goes against Hershey. Roxy was plenty pissed about it. She said I don't come home enough to understand the situation." He moved the mixing bowl onto the counter. "Maybe she's right. I don't come home enough."

"Why is that?" She lifted her glasses so she could really look at him. "Philly's not that far away."

It took a while for him to answer, and it couldn't have been because he was concentrating on filling the molds. This batch was as messy as his first.

"My ex didn't like Hershey," he finally said, keeping his gaze fixed on his job. "She hated it."

Sacrilege! "She what?"

"We had our engagement party here, but after that, she never came back. She didn't like me coming home, either."

Natalie stopped everything she was doing to concentration on Luke, what he'd just said. And what it might say about him. "But your family's here. Sorry, but wasn't that kind of terrible of her?"

He shrugged, spilling more chocolate on the side of the pan. "I'm not making excuses for her, but I saw her point, and I agreed with her—she was my wife, I had to. I love the vibe and energy of big cities. Living in Philly's a perfect fit for me. For now." He rubbed his jaw with the back of his hand, like he had something more to say, but then didn't. "I started seeing Hershey through Celeste's eyes. It happened subtly. First, I didn't come home for my mother's birthday. Then I didn't visit at Christmas. After a few years, I hardly came home at all." He paused and lifted his chin, staring straight ahead. "It hurt my parents. It still does, I can tell. But I don't know how to fix it."

"Just come home more often," Natalie said, even though Luke hadn't asked for her opinion. "All they want is to have their son under their roof, sleeping in his old bed, hanging out in the kitchen."

"You think it's that simple?"

Probably not, but it was a start. Natalie knew firsthand how complicated family dynamics could be. Her own parents were struggling with their marriage, fighting to hold onto what normalcy they had. If she focused on Luke's family issue, she wouldn't have to think about her own.

"Maybe," she said. "I saw your mother tonight. Totally over the moon that you're here."

"She's made me breakfast in bed every morning." He smiled sheepishly. "It's kind of embarrassing."

"Oh, let her spoil you. It won't damage your reputation with the feds."

He laughed. "Thank you, Natalie."

"For what?" She reached for a roll of paper towels to wipe up Luke's misses.

"I don't know. For listening. Not judging me."

Warm spots blossomed in her chest. Not lust this time, but…something like the makings of friendship. Since when did she want to be friends with Luke?

"Who says I'm not judging you? And what's so wrong with settling in Hershey? I grew up in a town even tinier and turned out reasonably normal."

Luke gave her a look. "Uh-huh."

"Shut it."

He snickered under his breath. "This pan's done. Want

me to do another?"

She pulled the mixing bowl away from him. "We can't afford to waste any more product."

"Hey, I'm a rookie."

"You're a suckie."

He unleashed another of those deep, manly laughs. She'd never made a guy laugh so consistently before. It was like he understood her, *got* her unlike anyone else. Thinking that way caused an annoying flutter to erupt in her stomach, so she netted those butterflies.

"See the first squares we pulled?" She pointed to the other side of the counter. "Two of them should fit together like magnets. The little groove on the bottom is where the serum will go."

"Ingenious." He knocked his shoulder against hers. "For a townie."

"You might mean that as an insult, but it's not."

"I wouldn't dare insult you, not while you're wielding a wooden spoon covered in Amazonian cocoa."

Natalie sighed and pushed up her glasses. "Hershey, Pennsylvania is an amazing legacy. I know you studied the town's history; it was a requirement for every student. So you know how the Milton Hershey private school started as an orphanage, and about its current scholarships and free student housing, the factories and jobs, how his legacy is over a hundred years old. And it's not just about selling the best damn chocolate in this country."

"You and Roxy should get together," Luke said. "She's as fired up as you are." He gave her shoulder another nudge. But did this one linger? "And I have no issue that you choose to live here. It's just not my thing."

Thanks for reminding me of that for the hundredth time. "Lucky we're not dating, then."

"Very lucky." He gave her shoulder a third nudge. This time it definitely lingered.

"'Cause if we were," she said, "I'd make you buy me a tricked-out Amish buggy, and we'd cruise Intercourse."

He leaned toward her and lowered his voice. "Can you believe that name?"

"Tourists love it. It's only potty minds like *you*"—she pressed a dot of unset chocolate on the tip of his nose— "that dirty it up."

Luke set down his pan and spoon. "Woman, did you just smear chocolate on my person?" He grabbed a paper towel and wiped it off.

"You won't even taste it?"

"Nope."

With lightning fast speed, she pressed another dollop on his nose, positively not noticing how extra-delicious it made him. Like a sundae with a cherry on top, ready to be devoured.

"You did not just do that."

"Didn't I?" She put her hands on her hips and stuck out her chin.

She was purposefully daring him, and herself. To do what? She didn't know but wouldn't stop until she found out.

Luke took in the sight of her, looking all sassy and provoking. Irresistible in another time and place. But not this one.

Before she could see it coming, Luke flicked his hand, splattering chocolate across the front of her coat.

She sucked in a gasp, looked down at her coat, then up at him. "You…" she said in a low voice. "There will be no food fights in my lab."

"Chocolate's hardly a food."

The spot of it on the end of his nose itched, but he didn't wipe it off. He knew if he ignored it, it would drive Natalie crazy. The way she looked, with her freshly washed hair all curly and wild, and those stupid plastic safely glasses, Luke was suddenly in the mood to make her a little crazy.

He slid the pan of molds he'd just filled off the counter. "What if I sort of lob this at you? Dirty up your lab coat some more."

He was joking, of course, but she narrowed her eyes, those brown eyes that could easily drive *him* crazy.

"I know you won't."

"No?" He cocked his arm, making her suck in another audible gasp. His mind flashed back to how she'd made the same noise when she was pinned beneath him. His vision was about to go blurry, so he set down the pan and backed away, too hot under the collar to make any kind of decision.

Besides, he was starting to respect this woman. He might've wanted to tear her clothes off—he was a man, after all. But he liked hanging with her. And he appreciated her insight when he told her about Celeste and his parents. And even though she'd joked about it, he knew she didn't think any less of him for his mistakes.

She was a good…friend. Huh.

"Hey. You're a betting man," Natalie said, bringing him back to the present. "And we've got time until the rest of the molds set. How about a dare?"

"I eat dares for breakfast."

"Apropos, because I dare you to taste some chocolate." The full lips of his *friend* quirked into a grin. He wouldn't mind tasting chocolate if her mouth was coated with it.

Stop. No mouth, no coated, no tasting.

"Oh, please," Luke said, kicking the image from his brain. "It's not like I've never had it before. I've got a major sweet tooth."

She snorted. "*You* have a sweet tooth?"

"That's why I stay away from it. I know my limits. One taste starts a frenzy."

"No, it doesn't. I've witnessed your extraordinary self-control."

"Unwise to test it," he said, trying to ignore how she was sizing him up with those big eyes. "I'm not as strong as you think so we better change the subject."

"What if I put a tiny dab of it on your mouth?" she asked, still giving him that look, not changing the subject.

"I'd wipe it off."

"What if I put it on *my* mouth?"

His confident smile slipped as he stared at the part of her body in question. Was she toying with him? Daring him? Luke didn't know what the hell was going on. "Tempting," he managed to say, fighting to hold that legendary self-control.

"You wouldn't lick it off me as a favor?"

"Natalie, stop talking like that," he said, hoping to snap her out of this…whatever. "What are you doing?"

She adjusted her plastic safety glasses and gazed off to the side. "I was just thinking."

"About?"

"You removing chocolate from my body."

He still couldn't tell if she was teasing, so he shook his head. "Forget it. I'm not coming near you."

She tilted her head. "You sure?"

Okay, Luke definitely knew that look, and it wasn't a mere tease. Every muscle in his body steeled, trying hard to hold back. "An hour ago, you said you didn't want to do this. Your heart, my head, not ready."

"That's still all true. So answer me this: Are we going to sleep together?"

Luke's heart hammered at the amazing thought. But then he considered her heart when it came to sex. Not ready. "No," he said, then considered his head when it came to a relationship. Not ready. "Are we dating?"

"No."

"Well, then." With that out of the way, he was unsure what to do next. Although he knew what he wanted to do. No interns around, no security camera. His boss would never know; the NIH would never know.

"So," she took a step toward him. "You, me, chocolate. Will you take the dare?"

"Natalie…" He'd meant to continue the sentence with something about working together and ethics and promises and the fact that it was five a.m. and they were both sleep deprived, and a long string of other reasons why she shouldn't tempt him.

But he couldn't remember any of it when she dipped her gloved index finger in the gooey chocolate. Instead of touching it to her lips as the dare, she dabbed it down the side of her neck.

"What about now?"

His goggles knocked into hers as he lunged forward, taking her in his arms, then planting his mouth over the trail of sweetness on her neck.

"This is your fault," he said against her skin.

"I know. Over there," he heard her pant, but didn't know what she meant and could only concentrate on her skin, kissing her clean, taking the dare. Her fingers gripped his shoulders and she pushed their connected bodies away from the counter and to the other side of the lab. "We can't contaminate the good samples," she added, flipping off his goggles then removing her own, along with her gloves.

Luke tore his gloves off with his teeth, then went straight for her lips. "What's in your mouth?"

Natalie smiled up at him, chocolate rimming her lips. She opened her mouth and stuck out her tongue to show a tiny brown square on the tip. "Another trick to get you to try it."

He felt a groan rumble in his chest as he cupped the back of her head and pulled her in. She tasted delicious, every inch of her mouth. When they broke for air, she popped in another piece, richer than the first.

"Your turn."

Ignoring what all the health books say, Luke allowed her to place a square of chocolate on his tongue.

"Let it sit," she said. But it was damn hard for him to stay still, hard for him to not be kissing her, relishing in the sweet frenzy she'd started. Then, the chocolate began to coat his tongue and the roof of his mouth.

She must've noticed something in his expression because she smiled. "Nice, huh?"

"What is it?"

"My own recipe from *deep* in the Amazon. You like?"

He could only laugh, then pulled her to his chest. "Will you and I being here like this mess with your research? Shouldn't this be a sterile environment?"

"All we're doing is sampling products," she said, lifting onto her toes and wrapping her arms around his neck. She held a square of chocolate between her teeth. "That's why I moved us over here. Safe zone."

The chocolate was gone in an instant, but Luke couldn't tell into whose mouth.

He'd also called the lab a "safe zone." He thought they'd have control over themselves here—business only. And he had for a time, until he'd let Natalie tempt him out of his head.

"Not dating, no sex," she said, plucking at a button of his lab coat. "I could never really be with someone who doesn't love Hershey." He was about to reply but was derailed when she pressed her mouth to his neck, her soft lips at first, then her tongue.

Hooooly suuugar.

He clamped his eyes shut and walked them until her back hit the wall, steadying them both. As his fingers dug into her hair, she made that sound again—a gaspy whimper—the same one she'd made in the tunnel, and just hours ago at the park. The sound fed his frenzy, and might echo through his mind forever.

But he didn't have forever. He had less than two weeks. In a matter of days, this harebrained research project would be over, and he'd go back to his life in Philly. Then, if he got what he wanted, Washington DC.

Natalie's teeth nipped his neck, and fire exploded behind

his closed eyes. They could do it right now. He could tear off her lab coat, rip off that flimsy thing that could hardly be considered a shirt, and do what he sure as hell knew they both wanted, right here on the floor.

But he couldn't. Even as she was opening his lab coat one-handed while sliding her fingers around his belt loop with the other, Luke knew he couldn't do that to her. Or to himself.

Her heart, his head, not ready.

Dammit, she was right.

Which probably meant he had to temporarily return his man card, but somewhere down the line, after she'd had time to process, she would resent him. In turn, in his book, Natalie Holden would be nothing to him but sex. His screwed-up head couldn't let her be anything more, and he couldn't stand the thought of reducing her to that.

No matter what she said, being together in this damn lab would compromise everything. Even though he didn't agree with the theory of her research, he didn't want to hurt her.

"Natalie," he said, after taking the time to kiss her once more, tasting heat and sweetness. "Hold on."

"Onto what?"

"Just, hold on a minute." He ran his hands up her arms, resting them on her shoulders. "Let me think."

Those big brown eyes blinked up at him. "You want to *think*?"

"Yeah."

She blinked again, causing a notch of utter bewilderment to form between her eyes. He felt pretty bewildered, too. "Oh, okay." She dropped her gaze from him and bit her bottom lip, but he knew it wasn't to get him going again.

Dammit. Not wanting to hurt her had hurt her anyway.

"Look," he began.

"It's fine. You don't have to say anything. I get it. I honestly don't know what came over me." She laughed but without any trace of happiness. "What's wrong with me anyway? Being around you turns me into this out-of-control maniac who'll do anything to be with you. It's ridiculous— I'm better than that." There was a sharp edge to her voice as she backed away. "Even if we didn't work together, you're covered in caution flags. You're dead set against my research, you're against my work in general, against Hershey—my home—and you told me flat out you don't want to date. I don't want to date, either. All of this is pointless. What the hell is my problem when it comes to you?"

"Natalie," was all he could say when he got the chance to break into her soliloquy. But he didn't have a follow up. Wracked with irrational guilt and confounded by his own incessant attraction, Luke reached out.

"I'm fine." She backed farther away and passed a hand over her forehead. "Damn, I hope I didn't ruin the chocolate. It would suck to have to start over."

"You're worried about *chocolate*?"

"Yes, Luke. It's my job. And is any of what I just said not true?"

He didn't have to think. "No."

"See?" She lifted her eyebrows, but she didn't look right, and he didn't *feel* right.

"What happened in here?"

They both jerked around to see Ivy. Luke quickly re-buttoned his coat.

"Hey," Natalie said. "You're here early."

"It's almost seven. Why are you covered in chocolate? Your clothes and your...your face. Both your faces."

Luke looked at Natalie, really looked at her. Yep, she was smeared with chocolate like it was camo paint, transferred from his mouth to hers and back again too many times to count.

"We were..." Natalie began. "We were just—"

"Sampling," Luke cut in. If Natalie had wanted Ivy to know, she would've come straight out with it.

Ivy crossed her arms. "Sampling?"

"Yeah, I'm interested in her...product. So she let me, uh, try some." Wow, he couldn't have sounded kinkier if he'd tried.

"But it's all over the floor on that side of the lab. Like, *all* over the place. It's even on the wall. How did it get on the ceiling? You must be one sloppy eater."

He forced a laugh. "I am. A real pig." He glanced at Natalie. She'd closed her eyes and was shaking her head. He wasn't sure if he'd made things better or worse.

Probably worse.

"We lost track of time," Natalie said, sounding much more composed. "I'll clean it up."

Ivy frowned. "No, I'm thinking you guys are too punch drunk exhausted to work this morning. You should go home."

"That's not happening, Ivy," Natalie said. "We're already behind, and Mr. NIH over here"—she hooked a thumb at Luke—"insists on observing while any of the trial is happening. And if he's here, I'm here."

Her sternness and blustering made Luke almost want to laugh. Almost.

"We're not behind anymore," Ivy said, sliding her arms into her lab coat. "I did some figuring last night, and I think there's a way to shave off another few days, if we pull one or two more all-nighters."

It was a reflex for Luke to shoot a hopeful glance at Natalie. But she shook her head firmly. Of course. No more all-nighters together.

"I still can't leave," Natalie said.

"Yes, you can." Ivy pulled out her tablet and swiped a finger across the face. "See, we move this here and do this part tomorrow night. Get it?"

Natalie studied the screen for a while. "Ivy, this is brilliant. Nice going."

Ivy grinned while putting her hair in a ponytail. "You can thank me later. First, you need some serious shuteye. I'll clean up and make another few trays of samples to make up for your, um, sloppy little taste test."

Luke didn't like how the redhead was eyeing him so knowingly, but he wasn't about to argue. "I suppose if all you'll be doing is the same thing Natalie and I did all night…" He paused. "I mean, if you're making more molds, I don't have to be here." He looked at Natalie. "You're leaving now?"

"I guess I am." She exhaled. "Go ahead, I'm right behind you—and don't even think about waiting around. No more lurking in parking lots."

This made Luke laugh, but Natalie didn't so much as crack a smile.

Huh. Stopping the kiss really had pissed her off. Or was she upset about something else?

"Lurking in parking lots?" Ivy repeated.

Natalie shook her head while throwing another frosty glance his way. "I'll text the others to reconvene at noon."

"See you then," Luke said. Neither of them said good-bye, so he walked to the door, then down the hall, more than ready to leave. If Natalie didn't want him to even walk her to her car, he wouldn't. *So much for small town charm,* he thought as he tore off his lab coat and tossed it in the back of the Jeep, forgetting it was med center property. *When things don't go her way, she goes as cold as Celeste.*

Before the thought had gotten far, he yanked it back. That was completely unfair. His ex and that feisty blonde were nothing alike—which had confounded him the first time he'd felt real attraction to her. Natalie had a reason to be pissed at him. Even if he didn't know what that reason was yet, he accepted it.

He climbed in the Jeep and drove home, blasting angry rock all the way up the hill.

Chapter Ten

"Spill it," Ivy said.

"Sorry about the mess." Natalie ran a hand through her hair; it was still slightly damp from her shower and had clumps of chocolate in it. She didn't even want to think about how that happened. "I'll help you clean up."

"You're going home to sleep, but not until you spill about Luke."

There was nothing to say except that she was an idiot.

What was going through your mind to do that? You tell the guy ten thousand reasons why you can't be with him for one night—or for the long run. Then your fortitude weakens for half a second and you're smearing chocolate over your body and daring him to lick...

She shut her eyes hard and counted to ten.

And then Luke was the one to put on the brakes because you have no control. She hated what this guy was doing to her.

"It's like I said," Natalie said. "It got late and we…he wanted to try…"

"Mm-hmm," Ivy said, sliding on her gloves. "You can stick to that lame-ass story about sampling chocolate, but judging by the smudges all over both of you, no one with a pair of eyes will believe it."

Natalie puffed out her cheeks, not knowing what to say.

"If you had sex in here, we'll have to throw this batch away."

"We didn't have sex. Jeez, Ivy."

"Oh, please. Look at you."

"I'm fully clothed, we both were," she said as she removed her lab coat and stuffed it in the laundry chute.

"You call that clothing?" Ivy pointed at her. "You're wearing my stripper shirt."

"This is yours? No wonder I didn't recognize it." She fingered the sheer collar. "Back up, why are your clothes in my trunk, and more importantly, why do you have a stripper shirt?"

"Oh, my." Ivy's hands flew to her giggling mouth. "You're not even wearing a bra. Okay, now I understand what went down here—or *almost* went down." She laughed again. "The poor guy. You seduced him."

"No, I…" Natalie crossed her arms over her chest, indignantly. "I mean, okay, maybe it was my fault this time, but he totally started it with all his guitar playing and midnight picnic, and don't get me started about the Kiss Tunnel—that was all him."

"Wait a minute, wait a minute." Ivy held up both hands. "You better back up and tell me what's going on, Nat. I'm your partner and need to know exactly what's up so I can fix it."

Natalie thought for a second, previewing what would

happen if she told Ivy to mind her own business. Yeah, her best friend would grab her in a headlock. Plus, if something really did have to be fixed, Ivy deserved to know. So she took in a deep breath, sank onto a stool, and spilled.

Mostly she stared at the wall, now splattered with smears of chocolate, as she spoke. Guilt and stupidity made it impossible to meet Ivy's eyes. When she finished, she blew out a breath.

"That's all of it. See, I didn't compromise anything."

"The hell you didn't," Ivy argued.

"Luke and I were nowhere near the samples we need for the tests."

Ivy shook her head. "You compromised your *heart*. When it comes to you, that's worse than anything. Forget Jack the rat, you're in no way prepared to handle something like this."

Natalie gazed blankly at her.

"You've had a crush on this guy for what, a million years? Do you call that healthy? Okay, so he's tall and built and he's got that chiseled old-school classically gorgeous thing going on. But the second you learned he was sent by the NIH, Nat, the very second, you should have—"

"I know," she cut in, covering her face with her hands. "I tried. You saw how we were the first day. I wanted nothing to do with him."

"And then you went straight to the Kiss Tunnel and sucked face."

Natalie shut her eyes and groaned. "That was a mistake."

"According to my calculations, you've made three of those mistakes. Are there going to be more?"

"No!" She dropped her hands and looked straight at Ivy.

"Are you sure?"

"No! I mean yes, no more mistakes, I swear. Right before you came in, we had…strong words. He said things and I said things. I was mad and lashed out…though I…I don't know why." She exhaled, feeling disappointed then pissed at herself for it. "Nothing can happen between us now. It's over. My heart is no longer compromised."

They weren't just pacifying words. Natalie knew they were true. She and Luke couldn't continue their kissing fling or whatever it was, because they had to work together. But even if they didn't, even if they decided to somehow go for it after the trial was over, it would never work.

She was a Hershey girl, through and through. She loved chocolate; she bled chocolate. Chocolate was going to help her brother. And Luke wanted none of it. Hell, this was the first time he'd visited his parents for longer than a weekend. He'd tried explaining that away, but how did she know he wouldn't disappear again? He never wanted to live here, and she would never leave. The whole thing was pointless, hopeless, making her stomach sink all over again.

"Get some rest, hun," Ivy said. "And hey, it's gonna be okay. Just stay focused on the prize. Our research is strong, we're going to prove that, and we're going to make a difference with Brandon and other kids like him." She touched her shoulder. "You'll see."

"Thanks." She nodded, feeling choked up, but so grateful Ivy was on her side. "I needed to hear that."

"Please go home. I'll see you in a few hours." She tossed Natalie a sweatshirt. "Might want to put that on before you start roaming the halls in my shirt. It's cute and everything, but even I've seen too much of your ta-tas today."

"If I wasn't so brain dead, I'd make you tell me why you bought this shirt in the first place."

"You don't want to know."

"Probably not, good night." She yawned about twenty times as she walked out to her car. No sign of the Jeep. That should have made her happy, but it didn't.

Thanks to blackout curtains, the bedroom was dark as night. Luke rolled over and grabbed his cell to check the time. It was almost ten. He hadn't slept well. Despite being half a mansion away from Dexter, he could hear his music blaring down the hall. How the guy got work done while being serenaded by 90s grunge rock, he'd never know.

But it wasn't Dex's music that kept him tossing and turning. It was Natalie. How had he let her inside his head? If he hadn't stopped by Hershey Lounge to catch up with Hank, he'd never have run into her, never felt the spark that kept her front and center in his brain. Her silky hair, that stubborn, sassy mouth, how she bit her lip when she thought he wasn't looking, the way she clung onto her cockamamie chocolate theory like grim death.

Getting mixed up with her put everything in jeopardy. If even the tiniest word got out about his behavior here, it could put the kibosh on any chance of being snagged by the NIH.

It was what he'd been working for all these years, and it was more important than a woman who'd straight up told him she didn't want to be with him anyway.

He gathered up his feeling for Natalie and put them in

a box. Sealed tight.

With tired strength that only came from frustration, he punched his pillow and rolled over. But it was no use. Five minutes later, he blindly grabbed one of the robes from the back of the bathroom door and wandered into the kitchen. His mother had left a note for him on the table—not a text or voicemail, but a handwritten note, like he was fifteen again.

Everything about being in Hershey brought back memories, probably because he hadn't stayed under this room for longer than a week since high school graduation.

Hersheypark, working at the med center, even Bullfrog Park caused memories to resurface. Though new memories included one other person.

Dear Luke, We didn't want to wake you, so your father and I booked 18 holes at the club first thing this morning. Please play nice at work today, don't forget to eat, and I won't ask where all my fried chicken went. Love you, Mom

Luke pressed a hand against his chest. His mom was pretty damn great. Unconditional love at its purest. He'd felt that kind of love for Celeste at the beginning, before it all fell apart.

He reread the note and smiled, recalling what Natalie had said. How just being here, sleeping here, eating here made his mother happy. Would he ever feel that kind of love? Could he love someone with everything in him, forgive no matter what, forever?

He wanted to. He wanted intimacy and friendship,

someone he could laugh with, someone who turned him on and challenged him into wanting more out of life. A woman who kicked his ass and made him a better man. A woman to grow old with, their family surrounding them.

Exactly what his parents had.

When he imagined a future like that, he didn't picture Philly. The jarring fact was, he pictured Hershey.

"'Sup, bro?"

Luke glanced up when Dexter came in, saving him from his whacked-out thoughts.

Dex laughed. "Nice threads."

Luke hadn't bothered checking what robe he'd put on, but it was obviously one of Roxy's. Short and pink and way too many ruffles.

"Would you rather I take it off?" Luke said, searching the cabinets for a mug.

"I'd rather you put on clothes like a human," Dexter said, pointing at the cabinet next to the fridge. "Why aren't you at work?"

Before replying, Luke poured a tall cup of coffee. He had no idea how long ago it had been brewed, but it was hot and highly caffeinated. Though ethically against relying on chemical stimulants, he needed it today. He'd been breaking all kinds of rules lately.

"I worked late," he said, "I told you that when we stopped by last night." He sipped at the steaming liquid then winced. "What is this?"

"Coffee," Dexter said, pouring is own cup.

"No, it's not. It tastes like…"

"A Hershey bar?" His brother grinned. "Mom infuses everything with it."

Luke took another investigatory sip. It was chocolate, all right. As the drink ran down his throat, a memory from last night—or this morning—shot to the front of his mind. Natalie with smears of chocolate on her mouth, her face, neck. He couldn't swallow another drop.

"You get used to it." Dexter chuckled and took a long gulp. "So, were you with *her* all night?"

Stalling for time, Luke took a drink. The taste triggered another memory—one he blocked out, boxed up with the rest of them. "Yes, it was just us."

"You were holding out on me, brother. She's smokin' hot."

"Don't say that."

Dex lifted his eyebrows. "What's with you?"

"Nothing." He sank onto a stool and cradled the mug between his hands, wishing the caffeine would hurry the hell up. "It was a long night, that's all."

"You two seemed cozy. Did something happen?" It was a mistake for Luke to not answer right away, because Dex set down his cup and leaned forward. "Oh, man. Something happened, right? Tell me I'm wrong. Tell me."

Luke ran a hand over his face. "I need to shave."

"I'm right, aren't I? Dude, you're totally sleeping with the enemy."

Luke glared at him. "She's not the enemy, and we're not sleeping together. It was only a kiss." He shuddered, remembering how he'd thrown that line at Natalie about their time in the tunnel. Only a kiss. He was such an ass.

"You kissed her?" Dex said. "Once?"

"No." He shut his eyes, trying to keep a tight lid on that box. "More."

Dexter sat on the stool beside him. "How much more?"

"We're not thirteen and this isn't a locker room."

"Fine, fine. Just remember, I had to watch Dr. Phil with Mom for two months after I had knee surgery. I'm practically a psychiatrist."

You're practically about to get your ass kicked, Luke thought. But then he exhaled in defeat. Maybe talking would help. But what the hell did he know? And what the hell would Dex know? Despite his better judgment, however, and with limited detail, he told Dex about last night.

"You were together in the lab, just the two of you, and you're telling me you didn't get a little…" He closed a fist. "Bird-in-Hand?"

"You're an idiot. We weren't kissing the whole time."

"You were literally waiting for chocolate to solidify in a pan. What the hell else did you do?"

"I don't know. We hung out. She's cool."

"Cool? What does that… Ahh." He pointed at Luke. "You're into her. You're into the Intercourse dairy farmer's daughter."

"Apple farmer," Luke corrected.

"She's hot, man," Dex added. "I don't blame you."

Luke jerked around to face him. "I mean it, stop talking about her like that."

"Sorry. Touchy subject." Dex sat back. "I take it that particular part of your relationship is over? I know the signs; you're defensive and you sound wrecked."

"I'm not wrecked, I'm just…" He scratched his morning beard. "Conflicted. I shouldn't…want what she wants—it's doesn't fall in line with the future *I* want. My life is totally my own again, no way I'll let that go. I won't make the mistake of letting anyone control me."

"Who's trying to control you?"

Luke shook his head. "I don't know." He already regretted bringing up the subject. He should've taken his coffee-chocolate concoction back to his room. Or given Dexter that ass kicking. Maybe that would've cheered him up.

Dexter leaned his elbow on the counter. "We knew this was coming."

"Knew what was coming? And who's we?"

"Me and Rox. Mom, too."

Luke put down his mug and sat ramrod straight—fully awake now. "I swear, if I have to sit through another intervention…"

"This is about Celeste. It's all on her."

When Luke furrowed his brow and blinked, it made his head ache. "What is?"

"The way you are with women, or were. You're different about this one. You like her."

"Her name is Natalie."

"You like hanging out with her, you think she's cool, and you've macked like champs."

Luke didn't need the reminder. "Do you have a point?"

"When you had to think about it going past what's easy—a relationship and not just sex, you bailed. And that's Celeste. She messed you up."

Dex was an insensitive hound when it came to the unfortunate women in his life, but he might've been onto something here. Luke wasn't about to admit it, though. "This has nothing to do with her."

"She cheated on you, publically. That sucks big time, but it wasn't your fault. You gotta get out there, man. Not every relationship will work out, but on the flip side, not every woman is out to control your life. You have to get over it."

"I am over Celeste."

"You're over *her*, but what she did still affects you. You're sitting here in Roxanne's bathrobe because you and Natalie got into a tiff. Dude, that's lame."

"There's a lot at stake for me," Luke said. "My job, my reputation. Did you know I'm being headhunted by the National Institutes of Health? I have my future to think about, and that future has nothing to do with Natalie. It's more complicated than you think."

This reminded him that he was due to check in at work. His boss had emailed twice asking for a new update. He couldn't be expected to do that while being *conflicted* over a woman.

"Man, every chick is complicated," Dexter said. "But that's no reason to give up."

Luke didn't want to talk about it anymore. He'd already figured out what to do with his feelings. He'd boxed them up. And he didn't need his brother throwing armchair relationship psychology at him. As if wham-bam-thank-you-ma'am Dexter knew a damn thing about relationships.

"I gotta get going," Luke said, walking to the sink and pouring out the rest of his coffee.

"I'm here if you need to talk."

"I won't," he threw over his shoulder. Then he felt like a dick. "But thanks, man."

He let the shower beat over his head, as he tried to get back to the place where things made sense. His job, his future, progressing in his career, not letting a woman screw with his priorities. Not until he'd put another mental layer of duct tape around that box did he get in the Jeep and drive to the med center.

Chapter Eleven

Natalie sensed the moment Luke entered the room, because her heart did that annoying skip thing, and her lips felt hot. Since she couldn't be expected to control physical reactions, she didn't bother looking at him.

"You're late."

"It's three minutes to noon," he said.

She lifted her chin to eye him.

"Sorry. I'll make it up to you."

She narrowed her eyes.

"Or not." He dropped his keys on the table.

At least he wasn't wearing another skin-tight T-shirt, but one of those boring, tailored, million-dollar button downs. Thank goodness. There was no time for distractions today. If he'd only put his lab coat on faster, she wouldn't have to notice how that very boring shirt was tucked into his black pants, showing off his trim waist and lovely flat abs.

"Nat? You ready?" Ivy stood before her with the clicker

for her laptop.

"Yeah." She cleared her throat. "Now that we're all here"—she couldn't help shooting a glance at Luke—"we'll get started."

She probably shouldn't kick off the day by giving him grief. After all, she'd only arrived at the lab twenty minutes ago. But Luke didn't need to know that, or that she hadn't gotten a wink of sleep. Stupid gorgeous man in a lab coat.

"Gather around, you guys. As you know, we're starting the preliminary injections today. The real serum won't be ready for another seventy-two hours, but we need to make sure once the two halves of each mold are sealed properly they'll hold the full injection. Got it?" She clicked through a few slides, but it was purely a refresher; her team knew what to do.

"The makeshift serum we're using today is the same consistency but with chemical substitutes." She demonstrated by toggling to an overhead projector hooked to her microscope. "See?" She displayed two slides, one of the final serum, and one of the prototype. "The chemical compounds are the only difference."

"Since time's an issue, instead of using a prototype, why not use the real thing now?"

Natalie switched off the projector and looked at Luke. The sound of his voice did something to the rhythm of her heart she didn't like. Or *did* like. Or whatever. Grrr

"You heard me say two seconds ago that the serum isn't ready," she said. "And it's called *practice*."

"Doesn't that mean wasting the molds we made last night?"

She put a hand on her hip. "We have plenty of molds."

"We actually don't," Ivy said. "We should have a lot more, but some of them got, shall we say, redistributed."

One of the interns raised his hand, but Natalie ignored him. "I counted this morning, and we have just enough. We're good to go. And I'll be extra vigilant about no more *redistributing* incidents." She heard Luke attempt to cover a chuckle with a throat clear. Was he being deliberately annoying? Or unintentionally charming? "Anyway, let's get started. Who's first?"

"Outta my way." Ivy pushed up her sleeves, slid on her goggles and approached the counter. She filled the syringe, sealed the two chocolate bars, then inserted the serum like a pro. "And that's how it's done," she said, snapping the cuff of her glove.

The interns went next. Each with steady hands and dead on precision. Afterward, they went to their own station and got to work.

"Don't I get a try?" Luke asked, approaching her workstation just as Natalie was about to clean up.

"No."

"Why not?"

"Because you're here to observe—no touching. Just because last night I let you—"

"Touch?"

She closed her eyes impatiently. "*Help*...doesn't mean you're allowed to touch anything today. Or ever again."

"Fine." He pulled out his tablet and started tapping.

"What are you writing?" she asked, trying to get a look.

"Observations." He angled to the side so she couldn't see.

Grrr, this guy! Deliberately annoying, for sure, even

though his cocky grin did add a tiny touch of charm. For a second, she thought about apologizing for being prickly this morning. But why bother bringing it up? She should stay prickly toward him for the rest of the two weeks. That would keep them apart, at least.

"You said the chemical compounds of the prototype differ from your serum," Luke said. "How so?"

She was about to refer him to her proposal when he said, "I read it, but I'm not a chemist. I need you to explain it to me." He slid his hands in his pockets and leaned back, stirring the air between them just enough that she breathed in his aftershave.

No—too distracting. Stay away, sexy smelling man.

She tried to breathe through her mouth, but that only meant she could taste the aftershave, activating another sense. If only he smelled like kerosene.

"We swapped out two main ingredients," she said.

"Which ones?"

"Since their chemical names won't mean anything to you, suffice it to say, they're herbs and root oils from the Amazon."

"Oils?"

"They're precious and extremely rare, which is street talk for majorly expensive—hence, our grant and our need for additional grants to move forward. That's why we're not using the real stuff during the pre-test phase."

"I see." He glanced down at the serum and the pile of chocolate squares. "You insert that between the two bars, and it seals them together. In effect, the end result is similar to chocolate covered cherries?"

"Sort of, but the serum solidifies instantly, so it won't be liquid at the time of consumption."

"I assume you include additives to make it taste good, since it's taken orally."

Natalie tried very hard to not lose her patience. "They're not additives. They're organic. But honestly, the serum has very little taste. There's a light fruity tang, like mango water."

"Mango?" She noticed Luke's eyes brighten, though he examined the serum skeptically. "I like mango."

"Want to try? Just a little drop." No, this was not another dare. "It won't hurt you. It's a hundred percent pure."

Luke looked at her then down at the serum, his eyes still narrow. "Sure, I'm curious." He held out his hand and Natalie picked up the syringe, squirting a dollop of the clear liquid on the tip of his index finger. He eyed it for a moment, then touched it to his tongue, blinking as his taste buds reacted. "Not bad."

She capped the syringe and carefully placed it back in its holding stand. "Told ya. You'll feel no reaction since it's aimed at stimulating the adolescent brain, only." She fought back a smile as she added, "Though there're minor side effects in male adults."

"What side effects?"

She cocked an eyebrow and lowered her voice. "Spontaneous prolonged erection, big guy." Luke's face went bedsheet white, and it took everything in Natalie not to burst out laughing. "In some test subjects," she added clinically. "A lot of those early tests were done on gorillas, and everyone knows they have less testosterone than human males. Even so, those were some impressive results. Boy, oh, boy."

"Water," Luke said, grabbing his throat like he was choking. "I need some water."

"You okay, fella?"

"Uh." He dropped his gaze to the front of his lab coat, about two thirds of the way down. "I'm not going to, I mean, will I…"

"Not that I can see—yet," Natalie said, then she couldn't take it anymore and broke into a laugh so hard she could barely breathe. "Relax," she said, patting his shoulder. "This is the prototype, remember. I'm sure you'll be fine."

He stared at her for a few moments, maybe gauging if his ears and brain and other parts of his body had heard right. Then a deep notch cut between his eyebrows. "Not cool."

"But funny," she said in a sticky-sweet voice. "Didn't mean to scare you."

"You didn't. I'd be fine with… I could handle… Never mind." He grabbed his tablet. "I *won't* be reporting on this." He shot Natalie a menacing look, but she caught more teasing in it than anger.

The guy could take a joke. She only hoped he wasn't into equally measured paybacks.

Even hours later, just thinking about Natalie's little *trick* made Luke's palms break out in a sweat. No matter what the sitcoms said, no guy wanted to be inflicted with that particular side effect. At least not in public.

He glanced at Natalie, who sat behind a desk making notes, pulling at the end of her ponytail, chewing the cap of her pen. *Definitely not in public.*

"Okay, guys," she said, pushing back from the desk to stand. "Thanks to more of Ivy's brilliant scheduling, we're able to move some things around. If all goes well, the day after tomorrow should be the last of the big push, which makes the following day more waiting—molds to set, serum to process. So if you need to take care of anything personal, pencil it in for then. Though things always change. Remember that."

"A day off in the middle of a major time crunch," Luke said, coming up behind her. "Why do I find that suspicious?"

"Because you're a gorilla who can't trust anyone?" She gave him a saccharine smile. If it were twelve hours ago, he'd kiss that sass right out of her.

But the fact that she'd called him untrusting gave him pause. Was she right? Was Dexter right? Hell, Natalie didn't know him well enough to pick that up, even if it was true.

"I'm not a gorilla."

She glanced down the front of his lab coat. "Not yet."

He was not going to get sucked into another inappropriate flirt-off with this woman. No matter how much he enjoyed their banter. Especially since he knew it couldn't end with a quicky drift through Kiss Tunnel.

While Natalie and Ivy went over some procedures with the interns, Luke read three emails from his boss. He shot back a reply, running down what they'd gone over that day. No more than five minutes later, his cell rang.

He stepped into the hall before answering. "Elliott."

"I read your update," Melvin said as a greeting.

He didn't like his boss all that much, but Luke had been with Penn Med for five years, was damn great at his job, and had a solid reputation. Solid enough that the feds had come knocking.

"DC is breathing down my neck," Melvin said.

Luke glanced around and lowered his voice. "I can't talk now. I'm at the lab. But I'll send you another message when I can."

"Do that." The line went dead.

Luke scoffed. "Dickweed." More than ever, a job with the NIH was appealing as hell. Climbing the ladder in a government position meant he could make real changes… once he cut through all the bureaucratic red tape. That was one part he wasn't looking forward to, but it would be worth it.

He shut off his phone and returned to the lab. Natalie had her laptop and projector out, running through slides with graphs and charts. This PowerPoint was in the proposal packet he'd received from the NIH.

"Go back to the last slide," he said, stepping closer to the screen. "This data's a hypothesis at best."

Natalie lowered the clicker. "Are you saying that as an observer?"

"No, as a microbiologist, concerned citizen, and future father."

Natalie tilted her head. "Father?"

"Someday. But that's not the point. You're talking in gross generalities here. There's no way to know if it works or not."

"That's why we're running *tests*. This is a research lab. A clinical pre-trial."

Even though he heard irritation in her voice, he had to take a stand one last time. "And you intend to feed an already sick kid a bar of chocolate and think that will make it all better? Doesn't that sound even the least bit counterintuitive?"

"That's a lot of talk for an *observer*."

Luke gazed around the room, waiting for one of the other faces to show an inkling that they agreed with him. But they were as stone-faced as Natalie. Unbending. Controlling.

Okay, maybe it wasn't fair to think that. He knew she wasn't out to intentionally hurt anyone. But her aims were misguided. Shouldn't someone set her straight so she could get on with her life?

"I don't get it," he said, sliding his hands in his pockets. "You're so damn smart about everything else in your life, why are you doing this to yourself, wasting time when you know it won't get anywhere, and for no reason?"

Natalie stared at him. At first she looked merely insulted, then plain old pissed off. "Who says there isn't a reason?"

He crossed his arms, ready to hear it, and then fight it, no matter what it was. "Tell me."

"Luke," Ivy cut in, "just drop it."

"No." He kept his eyes on Natalie. "If she's got a personal agenda, shouldn't we know about it?"

"My *agenda* is none of your business," Natalie snapped. "Just because you don't think this study is important doesn't mean it isn't. This might end up being *very* important to someone out there, some kid, someone's son or brother who needs help because nothing else works."

Luke clearly noted a hitch in her voice. For a moment, he thought he'd pushed her too far. But no, she'd never make it in the real world—the world outside sugar city—if she couldn't defend herself.

"Your argument is weak, too personal."

Natalie didn't reply. Stone-faced, she marched over to him, close enough that he could catch the golden flecks in her brown eyes. "You're being an ass," she hissed.

He moved his focus from her eyes to take in her whole face, the stress lines that looked way too out of place. He'd managed to truly tick her off this time. "Hey, don't take it personally," he said. "We're debating. It's what we do."

"Not about this," she said before turning on her heels and storming out the door.

Luke balked in confusion. What just happened? "Natalie," he called, and was about to follow her into the hallway when Ivy grabbed his elbow.

"Let her go," she said, her voice held a hint of sadness. "I told you you should drop it. Why do men never listen?"

Luke stared at the open doorway, waiting for Natalie to come back. Five minutes later, she did. But it made his insides feel twisted and tight when she wouldn't look at him. He hadn't meant to upset her, not really. They couldn't one-up each other anymore in the way that had become familiar and fun—because that always led to more.

Did that mean they couldn't even be work friends?

The next two days at the lab, Natalie barely said a word to him and refused to speak to him alone. He wanted to explain, to apologize and make things right between them. He'd grown used to the awesome feeling he got when they'd catch each other's glances, share a quick look when someone mentioned the *redistributed* chocolate molds, or how she'd roll her eyes when she acted like she was annoyed with him for asking a question.

She was all business now, and he didn't like that one bit.

Chapter Twelve

"Ivy has kindly volunteered to oversee production of the molds tonight and tomorrow," Natalie said. "So we won't meet back here until Tuesday morning. Everyone cool with that?"

She didn't bother looking at Luke, but she heard him clicking his pen. She hadn't seen him outside his lab coat in two days, which helped keep her lustful thoughts at a distance. He'd also stopped contributing to the discussions. Sometimes she wouldn't hear him speak for hours. When he would chime in, the sound of his voice made her heart do that skip thing she liked. And then she'd yell inside her head that her heart had no business skipping over any part of Luke.

He'd obviously never understand her or her position or how important this trial was. So why bother with the façade of friendship?

She was the last to hang up her lab coat and was halfway across the parking lot when Luke stepped into her path.

"Do you have a second?"

Her heart went all skippy-skip. "No. I promised Ivy I'd bring her TexMex." She gripped her purse strap. "I have to go."

He stepped in front of her again. "What about later?"

"I'll be asleep."

"No, you won't. You'll be going over the project in your head. You won't be able to sleep."

He was right, but she wouldn't let him charm her by pretending he knew her so well. "Nevertheless, I don't have time. I'm very busy." When she tried to walk around him, he blocked her path. She exhaled. "Fine, you wanna talk, I'll meet you later."

"Where?"

"I don't care." So long as it was somewhere public—lots of people, please. No dark tunnels.

"Phillip Arthur? I'll buy you a sundae."

No, you won't.

"Fine."

"In two hours?"

"Two hours." When she confirmed, he finally stepped out of her way. As she started her car, she felt a little guilty. Luke would be waiting a lot longer than two hours for her to show up.

Her parents' outdoor back porch was her favorite place on the property. While she sipped her café mocha, she fixated on the *Holden Apple Farm* sign swaying lazily in the morning breeze. Dad really needed to repaint it or make a larger one, even though he spent less and less time actually running the farm, and more time in Hershey or making deliveries.

Consequently, Natalie was out at the farm a lot more. There was always something her parents needed or had forgotten. Who knew what would happen if she wasn't around to help all the time. Not that she minded, though, not really. Taking care of others was good for her. Right?

"Morning, honey."

Natalie's mom joined her on the porch. If anyone belonged in Lancaster County among the green farmlands and winding country roads, it was her mother.

"Morning." She took another sip of coffee, heavy on the mocha.

"We were surprised you showed up last night."

"I needed to decompress."

"You only decompress here when you want to hide."

She was kind of hiding, but Mom didn't need to know why. The farm could be a sanctuary sometimes. True, she resented it when she was a teenager and lived so far away from any kind of regular teenager life, but now, she understood its peaceful beauty.

If only Luke could say the same thing about Hershey. But he couldn't wait to finish the job and go straight back to Philly where he belonged.

He'd never belong in Hershey, let alone in a place like Intercourse. In her wildest fantasies, Natalie could never picture him chilling out on the porch or strolling through their three acres gathering apples to sell at the farmer's market. No way.

"Is Muff awake?"

Mom looked over her shoulder into the house. "I heard his TV. I think he's been up for a while." She sighed and sat beside her at the table. "He had a few good days this week, but yesterday…"

Natalie didn't need Mom to finish the sentence. For the millionth time in a week, her heart ached triple time for Brandon. This trial had to work. If it didn't—

She wouldn't allow her brain to finish the sentence. There was way too much at stake.

Though she'd never admit this to another human being, she wasn't in complete denial about what Luke had said about her product. Legitimizing the theory of dark chocolate infused with organic anti-depressants was probably a long shot. Maybe it wouldn't make it onto this year's clinical trial list, but maybe it could find a home in specialty stores, organic markets, new-age shops…

She flinched at the last thought. *New-age.* Hadn't that been what she'd mockingly called Luke that first night at the Lounge? Why couldn't he have been just plain Luke Elliott? Local dude back in town for a few weeks, the boy who'd kissed her in a boarded-up boathouse once, the guy who'd tiptoed in and out of her fantasies since she was thirteen. The grown-up man who made her feel things with a single look through his fogged-up safety glasses.

"What's the matter, hun?" Mom asked.

"Nothing. Everything." She exhaled. "I've got a lot on my mind. Meanwhile, I think I'm *losing* my mind."

Her mother put a hand on her shoulder. "I'm sorry if this is too much for you. We've all been relying on you, waiting for your grant to get approved. You're under too much pressure from us. It's not fair."

Natalie blinked back the tears that had been hovering since she'd left the parking lot of the lab last night. "You haven't been pressuring me. I do that on my own. But every time I think about Muff, I… I have to try, Mom. I have to do everything I can."

"I know, Nat." Her mother patted her hand. "Is that everything that's bothering you?"

"No." Natalie tugged her bottom lip. "But it's everything I want to talk about now."

"Okay." Never one to pry, Mom smiled and gave her hand a squeeze. "It's still a little early to eat, but how about I make us an omelet to share. I picked up some bologna from the Bird-in-Hand butcher shop on the way in."

Natalie's stomach clenched. Not at the thought of bologna, but from the thought of the last time someone made an omelet for her—or tried. "Sure." She smiled up at her mother, gratefully. "Thanks."

As Mom headed to the kitchen, Natalie heard tires crunching over gravel at the front of the house. "Is Dad already out?"

"Don't think so. He was still sawing logs when I left the bedroom."

"That's funny. I hear a car."

"You sure it's a car?" Mom said from the kitchen. "Might be that nice Amish boy who your father hired to fix the irrigation pump. Grab the door, will you, hun? Don't make him come up and knock. He's so shy."

Natalie didn't think it was a buggy. No sound of horse hooves. But she zipped up her hoodie, slid into her flip-flops and opened the door. The front porch faced east, so the bright, early morning sunlight shone right in her eyes. When she heard a car door close, she used her hands as a visor.

Then her heart jumped up her throat. "What are you doing here?"

Luke was marching across the gravel to the porch. "You didn't show last night."

Natalie bit the inside of her cheek and crossed her arms. "Sorry."

"No, you're not. You stood me up on purpose."

The nerve of this guy. "You left at seven in the morning and drove forty miles to lecture me some more?"

His forehead crinkled. "I'm not lecturing you. And I left at five. Took me a while to find this place. The sign out front needs to be bigger."

"I tell my dad that all the time."

Luke pulled at the top button of his shirt, then rubbed his palms together. He wore faded jeans with a hole ripped in one knee. The way the sunlight made his hair look almost auburn made her want to run her fingers though it to catch the light.

"You still haven't answered my question," she said, forcing an edge to her voice. "Why are you here?"

"Can I come in?"

"No."

"Nat?" Mom was on the porch now. Crap. She should've made Luke leave the second he'd arrived.

"Mrs. Holden," Luke said, trotting up the steps right past Natalie to shake her mother's hand. "It's nice to meet you. Sorry for dropping in so early. I'm Luke. We met the other night in the Hershey Lounge parking lot. Well, we didn't actually meet, but we were both there—"

"Why are you talking?" Natalie said from the corner of

her mouth.

Luke turned to smile dotingly at her. "I'm saying hello."

"Didn't you see the other sign out front?" She pointed up the gravel driveway. "Trespassers will be shot on sight."

"Natalie." Mom cut in. "He's not a trespasser. Look at his shoes."

The three of them stared down at Luke's black sneakers. They might've resembled Chuck Taylors, but they were probably a designer label.

"He was just leaving," Natalie said.

"Oh?" Mom frowned. "You wouldn't like to come in for a cup of hot cocoa first? I'm heating the milk and about to add the Hershey's syrup."

Yeah, right. An offer like that will send Luke running and screaming for the nearest paleo market.

"Sounds delicious," he said. "I'd love some, thanks." As he followed Mom into the house, he sent Natalie a smug smile over his shoulder.

She narrowed her eyes at him but didn't speak, didn't give him the satisfaction that he'd used his Elliott dreamy good looks and manners to charm Mom into letting him in the house. Maybe if she didn't speak at all, he'd get the hint and leave. The sooner the better.

Luke hadn't been out to Lancaster County in years. But after waiting on Natalie at Phillip Arthur for three hours last night, he'd been so furious that he'd actually cruised the streets of Hershey looking for her. After a fruitless hour of that, and after looking in to see if she was with Ivy at the lab, he'd gone home.

At four in the morning, he'd thrown back the covers and Googled *Holden Apple Farm*. There was no physical address, just one for the Intercourse Farmer's Market. If a girl like Natalie was royally pissed, she'd want to be surrounded by something calming and familiar. Thanks to the never-ending winding stretches of Intercourse's back roads, it had taken him a few hours to find it.

"Would you like whipped cream on top?" Mrs. Holden asked, holding out his steaming cup of cocoa. "It's chocolate flavored. You can never have enough!"

The description made Luke feel like his teeth were about to start rotting. But he smiled and said, "Yes, please."

Natalie sat in the kitchen chair across from him. After his answer, she released a snarky chuckle under her breath. It was the first almost-word she'd uttered since he stepped foot in the house.

"Cocoa for you, Nat?" her mother asked.

"I'll just take a big ol' bowl of the whipped cream," she replied. "All the vitamins and minerals I need for the day."

She hadn't looked his way, but Luke knew the comment was aimed at him. He wouldn't let her goad him, not today, maybe not ever. Yes, he'd been livid that she hadn't shown up when he'd clearly only wanted to apologize. When she wouldn't allow him to do that, he had to track her down.

But he didn't feel like apologizing now. He felt like giving her another lecture. He wanted to get it into that thick skull of hers that she was speeding toward a dead end. Why wouldn't she listen or let him help? She was so frustrating, this head of a research team.

Not that she ever really looked like a chemist gunning

for a clinical trial, this morning, especially. Her unruly blonde hair was tamed within two loose braids, and she wore a pink zip-up sweatshirt, yoga pants, and flip-flops.

She looked… Well, she looked freaking adorable. Except for the scowls she shot him whenever her mother's back was turned, she also looked relaxed, comfortable, at home.

Luke hadn't felt that way for a long time, anywhere.

"Well, your father loaded the truck last night," Mrs. Holden said, wiping her hands on a dishtowel. "I hear him in the shower now, so I think I'll drive the apples to the market myself."

Natalie sprang from her chair. "I'll do that."

"No, no, it'll be faster if I go. I want to pick up some shoo-fly pie on the way back. They make it fresh on Saturdays." She grabbed a set of keys on a hook by the sliding glass door. "Nat, why don't you show Luke around? The orchards are finally dry after the rain."

"He can't stay," she said before Luke could open his mouth. "He has to get back to the lab."

"Oh. Well, it was nice to meet you."

Luke pushed back his chair and stood. "Very nice to meet you, too, and thanks again for the…the…"

"The hot chocolate with chocolate whipped cream, Luke," Natalie finished for him. "You can say it aloud. The NIH won't hear you."

"Yes, thanks for that." He smiled at Mrs. Holden, and felt like spanking Natalie. "It was delicious."

The second the door closed, Natalie rounded on him. "Satisfied?"

"By what?" he asked, walking his mug to the sink.

"By…whatever you came here to see."

"I didn't come here to—" Luke broke off when he spotted a tall, thin blond kid hovering by the doorway. "Hi," he said.

The kid didn't reply, but Natalie immediately approached him. "Muff," she said in a quiet voice, like she was trying not to startle him. "Mom just left. Everything okay?"

He didn't speak but only shrugged his slumped shoulders. He lifted his eyes briefly. They were the same shade of brown as Natalie's, but they had purple shadows beneath them. He stayed huddled by the door and put up the hood of his sweatshirt, shielding his face.

"Who's he?" The kid pointed his chin toward Luke.

"He's a…friend from high school," Natalie replied, in that same slow and soothing voice. "Luke, this is my little brother, Brandon."

"Hey," Luke said, not moving to shake his hand or give a fist bump. Something told him the kid wasn't cool with strangers.

"Hey," he mumbled in reply. "That your Jeep out front?"

"Yeah. Are you into cars?"

Brandon shrugged.

Luke sensed something was up, something unspoken and private, almost like he'd shown up on a day meant only for their family. If that was the case, Natalie would've said so right away and kicked him to the curb. So what was this vibe?

"Bran, you do like cars," Natalie said. "Those classic muscle ones, right? Luke's Jeep is ancient. Still has a tape player, no iPhone jack."

Brandon's gaze flicked to the front window, then away.

"I'm sure he'll let you check it out if you want."

"Stop mothering me," Brandon muttered in a low voice

while staring at the hardwood floor.

Natalie lifted both hands and backed up. "Okay," she said. She was looking at the floor now, too. That relaxed, comfortable stance from earlier was gone. As she lifted her gaze to her brother's lowered eyes, Luke caught the expression on her face. She looked completely broken.

It was right then that he figured it out. He looked at Brandon, his slumped posture and shielded body language, then he looked at Natalie looking at Brandon, the helplessness in her eyes.

No wonder she was obsessed with finding a new angle to ease teenage depression. Her own brother was suffering from it. Cement poured into Luke's chest—he was the hugest asshead in Pennsylvania.

It was wrong and intrusive for him to have just shown up, determined to make Natalie hear him out just to reiterate his own opinions. Maybe Brandon was having a really bad day, so the family had retreated to the farm. Crap, he was such an asshead. Now was not the time to make some grand apology.

"Thank your mother again for the hot chocolate," Luke said, totally in the way, and completely unwelcome. "See you at the lab."

Natalie gave him a stiff nod, barely meeting his eyes. She looked embarrassed, which made him feel like an even bigger jerk. Depression wasn't something you *caught*. It's a disease, and nothing for any family to be embarrassed by. Knowing Natalie's schooling and background, he was sure she knew that.

What she was embarrassed by was Luke knowing about it.

Asshead.

"Nice to meet you, Brandon," he said, not expecting the kid to reply. He was probably dying for Luke to get the hell out of there, too. Luke hesitated at the open door to give Natalie another look.

"Just go," she mouthed. The combination of sadness and pleading in her eyes made Luke's chest feel like a ten-ton semi was parked on it.

He sat behind the wheel of his Jeep for a few moments, gathering his thoughts before he hit the road. While reaching for his seatbelt, he glanced in the rearview mirror. Brandon was on the bottom step of the porch, looking his way.

I should just go, he thought. *This is none of my business and Natalie doesn't want me here.*

"Hey," Luke said, flat-out ignoring his own advice. "I think the engine needs water. Got a hose?"

"By the shed." Brandon said.

The Jeep didn't need water, but Brandon was showing an interest. From his own studies, Luke knew it was sometimes good to cater to that, if the interest wasn't unsafe. He put the gear in reverse and circled back to the shed. Brandon didn't say anything and kind of hung back while Luke lifted the hood and topped off the washer fluid.

As he was coiling up the hose to return it to the shed, he noticed Brandon gazing into the back of the Jeep.

"That your guitar?" the kid asked. "Do you play?"

Luke didn't reply at first but noticed Natalie standing on the front porch, watching them. For some reason, Luke's gut knew a lot was riding on what he would do next.

Chapter Thirteen

Natalie felt a little paralyzed, unsure if she should call Muff inside or see what happened next. She hated that Luke was here, bearing witness to her personal life. His family was so perfect while hers belonged on an After School Special.

She couldn't hear what he was saying to Muff, but hopefully he wasn't machine-gunning him with questions, causing her brother to shut down even more than he already was.

For a second, it looked like Muff was gesturing at Luke's guitar case in the backseat, but she was too far away to be sure. Her brother used to love music. Their parents had even bought him private guitar lessons for Christmas three years ago. He'd begged for them four months earlier, but by the time Christmas rolled around, he'd lost interest in everything he used to love. The big change had happened that fast.

Luke was pointing at something in his Jeep, then kicked a tire. Seriously, how dare he just show up at the farm like this? From the pitiable look he'd shot her right before he'd left the house, she knew that he knew the situation with Muff.

But she didn't want his pity.

Maybe it should've been a relief that her secret was out, that Luke now knew she had a "personal agenda." But… what if he included it in his report to the NIH? Would that help her cause, or somehow put her already-slim chances at risk?

She didn't know enough about the political end of trials and patents to be sure.

"Morning, sweetie." Her dad joined her on the front porch. He held a mug, his thinning hair was combed back, and he smelled like the same aftershave she'd given him every Father's Day.

"Hey, Dad."

"Did I hear Abram Yoder a while ago?" He took a sip of coffee. "He hardly ever comes inside the house."

Natalie squinted into the sun. "That was Luke, a member of the research team."

"Huh." Dad noticed the Jeep by the shed and took a few steps that way. Then he stopped. "That's your friend talking to Brandon?"

"Work colleague," Natalie corrected, "but, yeah. He's here to…uh…" She didn't know how to finish because she still didn't know why Luke was there. "We had a problem at the lab," she continued, scrambling for a simple explanation. "But it's all good now."

"Well then." Dad set his mug on the top porch railing. "I best introduce myself."

"You don't need to." She reached for his arm to stop

him, but he was already going down the steps. She didn't follow him across the wide gravely driveway but stood in horror as her father approached Luke Elliott.

She still couldn't hear what they were saying, but all at once, the three guys turned to look at her. She froze halfway down the second step, then treaded back up, losing both flip-flops. Luke lifted his hand and waved, looking completely at home. Her fingers gripped the railing but she let go and waved back politely. Luke kept his eyes her way for another moment, then leaned forward like he was trying to hear what Dad was saying. The two men laughed, and had Brandon *smiled*?

Needing to know what was going on, and exactly what Luke might be telling them, she launched down the rest of the stairs and onto the driveway in her bare feet, but Dad and Luke were already walking her way.

"I was just telling your father that I came here for some cider," Luke said.

Nice save.

"You know where it's stored in the utility barn," Dad said to her. "But I'm making a fresh batch today."

"I'd love a fresh batch," Luke said.

He might've been able to charm her mom with all his dashing hotness and smiles, but that wouldn't work on her. "I'll bring it to you at work on Monday," she said, shooting him a subtle glance that she hoped he'd interpret correctly.

"I guess I can wait," he replied, giving her an even sub-tler nod. At least the man wasn't dense. "See you then."

Natalie exhaled as Luke jingled his car keys in his hand and turned toward the Jeep. "Yeah, see ya." She looked at her dad and brother. "You coming in? I'm about to hop in the shower but I'll make us a huge breakfast after." She nodded toward the house, then slid her gaze to watch Luke open his car door.

Her feet stung from standing barefoot on the sharp gravel, so she didn't bother waiting for him to drive off but headed straight for the bathroom. The scalding hot water and steam felt good as it poured over her. She always used her mom's minty-smelling shampoo when she visited the farm. It made her scalp tingle, energizing the rest of her body and mind.

With a towel wrapped around her, she padded across the hall to her bedroom. It hadn't changed since she'd gone away to college. The same framed photos hung on the walls, same complete set of Nancy Drews on the shelves, same CD player on the dresser covered with stickers.

After sliding a no-muss-no-fuss sundress over her head, she combed out her hair, scrunching the ends so they'd dry wavy. She frowned at the CD player. Had it just switched on by itself?

No, but she definitely heard music.

Following the sound, she walked down the hall, then stopped before entering the living room. The scene she found around the corner was so out of context she had to do a double take.

The music was an acoustic guitar; the player was Luke.

Brandon sat on the opposite end of the couch, flipping through a three-ring binder. "This one?" he said, holding up the page for Luke to see.

"You know your classics," Luke said.

Muff shrugged and looked down. "I used to be into music."

Luke glanced at him, then returned his gaze to the guitar strings, his fingers strumming. "No one who's been into music ever really stops being into it. It's in your soul forever. Maybe it gets buried deep under piles of shit for a while, but it's always there, waiting to make you happy again. A good friend told me that recently. At least that's how it is with me. Know what I mean?"

Brandon brushed the hair away from his eyes and nodded. "I guess."

Luke made a few more strums then stopped. "Your turn." He unfastened the strap and passed his guitar to Brandon. But her brother didn't take it. "It's cool," Luke said. "No one's watching. It's just you and me, man."

But someone was watching, and Natalie felt a sob in her throat when her little brother slowly lifted a hand and took the guitar.

"Know how to fasten it?" Luke asked. Muff secured the strap across his back, settling the guitar on his lap, his hands moving into the positions like he was about to play. "You said you know a few chords?"

"*G* and *C*…*E*-minor."

"Let's hear 'em."

Brandon clenched his left hand into a fist, then stretched his fingers over the strings. He strummed a couple of times with his right hand.

"Now the *E*," Luke said.

He readjusted his fingers and strummed another chord. Before Luke could request the next one, Brandon switched again, then back to the first. The sound was like an angel to Natalie's ears.

"To go from *E* to *G*," Luke said, "put your third finger

on the *D*. That's it." He sat the open binder on the couch between them. "You'll need A-minor for this song, but it's way easy." Without touching him, he explained where Brandon's fingers should go. "You got that, too. Throw in a *D* and you're set."

"Isn't the *D*...?" He adjusted his fingers and strummed, but he got the positioning wrong. Natalie held her breath, hoping this minor setback wouldn't derail her brother.

"Close," Luke said. "I make the same mistake all the time. Press your pinky on the—" The strum cut him off. "That's right." Natalie released her held breath. "Okay, can you see the page from here?" Brandon nodded. "It starts on *G*, goes to *E*-minor, then back to *G*."

"Got it," he said. Then with no sign of fear, her brother was playing.

Natalie didn't recognize the song, but watching her brother play, showing an intent interest was amazing. Luke leaned back on the couch, a hand at his chin, staring into the middle distance while his head bobbed to a beat Natalie couldn't follow.

"You know the coolest thing about this song is the lyrics, right?" Luke said. "Gotta hear you sing it."

"I...don't sing," Brandon said, shifting his position on the couch.

Please don't give up, Natalie pleaded, not sure which guy she was talking to.

"Neither do I," Luke said with a chuckle. "But I do it anyway, and I don't give a rat's ass what anyone thinks. Come on, I'll kick it off. Hit the *G* to *E*-minor intro."

Natalie could see her brother's shoulders tense up, and she wrung her hands together, fearing the inevitable: for

Muff to shut down.

But a second later, he strummed the first chord.

"'I'm drivin' in the caaaar,'" Luke sang. "'Turn up the radiooo…'" His head was bobbing again, his foot tapping, keeping time to Brandon's accompaniment. He sang the next line of the verse, then Brandon—shaky and timid at first—joined in, and the two guys sang together.

Natalie clenched her fists so tightly that her nails were leaving imprints in her palms.

"'Now Romeo and Julieeeet'—you take the next line, man," Luke said.

"'Sampson and Deliiiilah,'" Brandon sang on his own.

They continued switching back and forth until the end of the song, both of them crooning the last note like wannabe rockers.

"Woo-hoo, yeah," Luke exclaimed. "Springsteen's got *nothin'* on us."

"Nothin'," Brandon said, his hair falling over his eyes. But the smile on his face stole Natalie's breath. "What about this one?" he said, flipping to another page of Luke's binder.

"You man enough to play John Denver?"

"Hell, yes."

Natalie stepped into the kitchen, pressed her back to the wall, and quietly slid to the floor, spending the next hour listening to Luke and Brandon riff. They covered the classics from Dylan to Morrison to the Stones. She couldn't think of the last time there'd been live music at the farm, or the sound of her brother's laugh.

"Oh," she heard Muff say. "That's my alarm. It reminds me to take my…pills. And I gotta do some other stuff, too."

"That's cool," Luke said. "I have to head out, anyway."

She heard them both stand up from the couch, the wooden floorboards creaking. "Hey, why don't you keep the guitar for a while? Your sister will get it back to me when you're done."

"It's okay."

"No, man. I won't be needing it anytime soon. They won't let me audition for American Idol anymore."

Brandon exhaled a quiet chuckle. "Okay, um, thanks. I swear I'll take care of it."

No more talking came from the living room, but Natalie heard the floorboards creak as the two guys went their separate ways.

"Hey."

Startled, she sucked in a breath and looked up.

Luke stood over her. He tilted his head and his eyebrows pulled together, examining her more closely. "Hey," he repeated, but the tone had changed from casual greeting to something soft like compassion.

Only then did she realize she was crying—silently sobbing in the kitchen for who knows how long. Her eyes to the base of her throat were wet from a steady stream of tears.

"Natalie," he said, crouching down so he was at her eye level. "Nat." Before she could form any kind of reply, let alone get her mouth to open, Luke took both her hands and gently pulled her to her feet. "I passed by the back corner of the apple orchard when I drove in. Will you show me the rest?"

Luke hadn't known Natalie had overheard him with Brandon. In fact, he had no clue she was anywhere near them. He figured after all the glares she'd thrown his way when he'd been talking to her father, that she'd taken off, too annoyed to be on the same plot of land.

He deserved her wrath. After meeting her father, he'd been about to drive away when something had stopped him.

Brandon had been checking out his guitar again, and Luke got the overwhelming feeling he should ask the kid if *he* played. Next thing he knew, he was in their living room giving an impromptu lesson.

Luke had no idea what kind of depression Brandon had, but in their short time together, he'd seen the kid open up, just a bit. He hadn't realized what a big deal that was until he'd found Natalie slumped in a corner of the kitchen, hugging her knees to her chest, crying.

It was a knife to his gut.

He didn't need another overwhelming feeling to know he wasn't going anywhere.

"Let me put on some shoes and get a sweater before we go to the orchard," Natalie said, touching the back of her hand to her wet cheek, not meeting his gaze. She didn't need to be embarrassed about crying. She didn't need to be anything but herself. Her kind-hearted self.

She met him on the porch wearing a pair of knee-high black rubber boots—a charming contrast paired with her little white and blue-striped, spaghetti strapped dress.

"Ready?" she asked, sliding her arms inside a white cardigan, glancing at him quickly then away. Wordlessly, she led him to the other side of the house, past a big red barn, and through a gate. Luke knew where the orchard was and could have explored it by himself if he'd wanted. But he needed to be with Natalie, though he didn't know why.

Beyond the gate were dozens of trees, maybe a hundred, standing in precise rows, each bearing more red apples than its neighbor.

"Whoa," Luke said. "That's a hell of a lot of cider."

"It takes four pounds to make one liter," she said, walking to stand between two trees. "That's nearly sixteen pounds to make a gallon. The taste used to make me gag." She shook her head and dropped her chin. "I was so ungrateful. I had no idea what I had. Life can change so fast." She was blinking rapidly.

"Natalie."

"I don't want to talk about it."

"Let me just say—"

"Luke, don't." Tiny tears clung to her lashes, gutting him again. "I don't want your pity—I couldn't stand it. Not after…" She stopped like she couldn't say the next word. "Not after everything."

"Pity?" he repeated, wanting desperately to understand, but falling short like he always did with her.

She turned to him, looking pale and so unhappy. "I know that's how you feel, and I know what you're thinking."

She knew what he was thinking? *He* didn't know what he was thinking, or what he was feeling. When he looked at this woman in the short dress and rubber boots, her hair blowing in the breeze around her tear-streaked face, he tried to pinpoint his feelings, name them. But there were so many he couldn't grab hold of a single one.

All he knew for sure was he admired the hell out of her.

No, it wasn't admiration he felt. It was something else,

something that made his heart pound when he looked at her, when he thought about her kindness, her stubborn determination, the way everything she did made him want a bigger life than even *he'd* planned, while driving him absolutely out of his head...his screwed-up head that wasn't ready for a relationship.

Or was it?

"You have no idea what I'm thinking," he said. "No idea what I'm feeling—about you." He walked to her, reached out and touched her cheek. "But we both need to find out."

Chapter Fourteen

She couldn't let it happen again. She'd compromised everything, made the worst possible decisions since the second she'd seen Luke at Hershey Lounge. But the way he touched her cheek, the way he was looking at her...

"Luke, please don't," she whispered, almost completely out of energy. "I can't think straight about anything. I'm so exhausted."

"I know you are," he said. "Give me five minutes."

She bit the insides of her cheeks and shook her head. "I don't have five minutes. You saw for yourself what's going on. But what you don't see is my family is falling apart. I have to take care of them, my parents, my brother. And Ivy's dating this new guy who's awful, and because of me and this impossible deadline, her job's on the line—"

"Okay, I hear you," he said. "You do a lot for other people."

Natalie was about to say she had no choice, but didn't

bother.

"Will you just… Let me do one thing for you, Natalie. Please." Slowly, he closed the distance between them, opened his arms and wrapped them around her. "Five minutes of this," he whispered, cupping the back of her head, easing it to his chest.

How did he know this was exactly what she needed right this second? To be held by him and no one else in the world. When she inhaled a snivel, Luke tightened his grip and his hand ran a circle across her back.

She closed her eyes and pressed her cheek to his chest, feeling his heart beat against her. It was strong and steady, and just hearing it calmed her. Everything about being inside Luke's embrace calmed her, made her warm in spite of the autumn air. She fisted the back of his shirt and he dipped his chin, nuzzling his face to the side of her head. Her own heart was pounding now, because, despite all the laundry lists and caution flags, this was where she wanted to be.

And that scared the hell out of her.

She thought her heart was safe from him. Their physical chemistry was like fire, but she also wasn't safe from the goodness he'd shown her today. She'd never seen it on display like that. He'd had no personal motivation to hang with Muff, to treat him like a friend and not like a patient. He'd done it because that was who Luke was.

"My five minutes are up," he said, his soft words drifting to her ear. She felt him loosen his hold.

"*No*." She hugged him greedily.

"Okay." He laughed into her hair. "You'll hear zero complaints out of me." He tunneled his fingers through her hair, resting his hand at the back of her neck, skimming across her skin. She repositioned her cheek against his chest, feeling his muscles contract, his heart pick up speed. His other hand ran up and down her spine, awakening the tender corners of her insides.

Since when was she content to just hug Luke? They'd always been in a hurry, caught in a frenzy, as Luke might say. It was like they both knew it was okay to slow down now. She loved the security of his arms around her, not just his lips.

"I love hugging you," Luke said. "I love how our bodies fit when we're still. But I..." His fingers pressed into her back. "I feel like a broken record when I say I *know* there are a hundred reasons why we shouldn't, but Nat, I really want to kiss you."

So do I! Her already erratic heart slammed against her ribs. She pulled her head from his chest and met his gaze, those piercing blue eyes seeing all of her for the first time.

"Think we can put a pin in our problems for a second?" he asked. "Research project will keep, our jobs will keep, but I can't keep." Before giving her a chance to answer verbally—the answer was clear on her face—he leaned down and kissed her.

Heat shot straight to her lips. Instead of kick-starting another frenzy, Luke held the sides of her face, kissing her slowly, deeply. His sweet, steady thoroughness made her muscles go weak and new tears spring to her eyes.

They pulled back at the same time when they'd depleted their oxygen. "We're in the middle of the orchard," Natalie said.

Luke touched his forehead to hers. "I like kissing you in the daylight. It's a new concept for us." He ran his index finger from her temple, over her lips, down her neck. "And I'm not through."

"Neither am I." She stood on her toes, ready to get back to it, but Luke pulled away.

"When I am through with you, we need to talk." He cocked his head. "Okay?"

She knew they had to talk, too. There was still so much she needed to get straight. When her mind started flooding with all the glaring conflicts, she put a pin in that too, took Luke's hand and gave it a tug.

"Follow me." She led him to the far inside corner of the orchard where the fences intersected. "This is the most privacy we'll get," she said, stepping backward up onto the middle railing.

Luke's mouth curved into a sexy, heart-stopping grin as he moved in front of her, a head shorter than her now. He held her hips to make sure she was steady. She was, and to prove it, she took his face, tipped his head, and kissed him.

Like before, their connection began slowly, but then his body bolted forward, pinning hers to the fence. She wrapped her legs around him, her dress riding up her thighs as he balanced her in his arms. The sun was on her face, his breath on her neck; she smelled ripe apples mixed with a heavenly, intoxicating scent that seeped from the top of Luke's head.

"I think it's time to talk," he said in a husky voice, even as he hoisted her body higher.

"Shut up," she whispered.

Luke's shoulders shook from a silent laugh. "I'd set you down, but you seem to have lost your boots."

While attached to his body like a lumberjack to a redwood, Natalie peered over his shoulder at her feet. Sure enough, she'd somehow kicked free of her rubber boots and was barefoot. "Huh."

"That's the second time you lost your shoes today."

"You saw that with my flip-flops?"

"Baby." He smiled. "I see everything you do."

The rest of her stubborn, work-obsessed core melted like a Hershey bar in the sun. "You can put me down. My feet are tough."

But Luke didn't let go, not at first. "If I put you down, that means we'll have to talk."

"And you're worried about that?"

He walked them until they hit the fence, but she was high enough now that he slid her onto the top railing to sit. "No," he said, running his knuckles under her chin. "But you are."

L uke hadn't been even close to wanting to let go of her soft body that had been clinging to him. And though holding her had given him the strength of twenty men, in about a minute, that strength would've been channeled into an act that would traumatize the Amish population of Intercourse.

Natalie had told him her heart wasn't ready for that. And maybe…his wasn't either. Because now, it really would mean something.

Also, their talk was overdue.

"I am worried," she admitted.

He ran his hands down her long legs, all the way to her cute bare feet. "Tell me why."

"We're taking the pins out? All of them?" she asked, sliding off the fence and onto the ground.

He put his hands on the tops of her shoulders and eased her forward, kissing both of her lowered eyelids. "Yes," he said, stepping back to give them plenty of space. "Start wherever you want."

Her eyes remained closed for a moment, as if still feeling his kiss, then she looked up. "Brandon's been suffering from depression for three years."

"Okay."

She took a deep breath and blew it out. "When I was writing my senior thesis, I read about a study in the French medical journal, *La Revue de Médecine Interne*—two studies, actually. They weren't connected at all, one was about this root in the Amazon, and the other was about a cocoa plant that grows only a few feet away from the root." She paused and smiled. "Chocolate, of all things."

He laughed. "Go on."

"It wasn't what I wrote my thesis on. It wasn't even my field of study as a food chemist. By then, I knew my career path was Hershey, but both studies stuck with me." She dropped her chin. "This kind of depression can run in families, but Brandon didn't show signs until he was thirteen."

"Nat." He knew their touching time was over, but he couldn't help cupping her chin, making her meet his eyes. "It's nothing to be ashamed of. You know that."

"I do," she said. "Intellectually. And it's not that I'm ashamed—that'd be like being embarrassed you have cancer; it's no one's fault. Once my career got going in the R and D labs, I saw firsthand how ideas went from someone's daydream to being patented and on the shelf." She turned toward the sun and squinted. "When Muff got sick, I remembered those studies about the root and cocoa plant, and I wondered what would happen if they interacted. I researched some more, talked to a lot of experts, and before I knew it, I had an actual recipe. I had results and statistics and a plan that didn't get me laughed out of the room when I presented it to the submission board. I know you don't agree, but I truly believe in my soul that what we have will work." She paused and twisted her fingers. "We just need this chance."

Her explanation moved him and made him want to take her in his arms and tell her what a brave, caring, inspiring woman she was. It did not change what he'd studied his whole professional career, however. How *he* felt in his soul about it.

But Natalie's research project, the whole reason they'd been thrown together, was not her side against his side. Chocolate versus broccoli. "You're getting your chance right now," he said. "And you're doing great. I've had a front row view of it."

"Good thing, too. Last night, I read the clause in the contract about you."

He lifted his eyebrows. "Missed me that much, huh?"

"Um, no." She tugged a strand of hair. "I was actually seeing if I could fire you."

He threw his head back to laugh. "And?"

"Seems once a proctor is contractually required, the trial can't continue unless *he's* there." She poked his shoulder, but then she touched his cheek, slid her fingers along the side of his hair, making him able to only halfway concentrate on what she was saying. "So it looks like I'm stuck with you."

Luke closed his eyes and breathed. *Yes, you are.*

"I've been thinking about something else, too."

"Mmm-hmm?"

She didn't answer, so Luke opened his eyes.

"You know that…that part of my body that wasn't ready to move forward with you?" She placed a hand over her heart.

Luke tried to swallow. "Uh-huh."

"I think it is now."

Of course, he knew what she meant. *My head, her heart, not ready.* Something had changed for her. Something had definitely changed for him, though it had happened so subtly, he couldn't remember when.

Every single muscle in his body tightened, ready to enfold her right that second, Amish onlookers be damned. But they were at her family's farm. Her brother was inside the house. He'd sipped hot chocolate in her mother's kitchen. Natalie was at the farm that day for a reason.

He'd have to wait. And he would. For her.

"Um, I don't think we should be in this orchard anymore," he said. "I'm having visions of you wearing nothing but strategically placed apple blossoms." Natalie was blushing and smiling and biting her damn lip. "Weren't you talking about making a big breakfast for everyone, even though it's almost lunchtime now?"

Food. That would take his mind off…her.

"I could eat," Natalie said, while staring toward the house. "But you already said good-bye to Brandon, and my parents think I'm working and won't expect me to be here…" She tilted her head. "How about lunch at my apartment?"

Luke's mind jumped two steps ahead. "Can Brandon

bring your car to you later?"

Natalie was right with him. "Let's go." She left her rubber boots by the fence and took off in a feminine run, her bare feet kicking up dust. Luke stood and watched for a few seconds, captivated by the sight. "You coming?"

He followed after those long legs in the little striped dress. When they reached the back porch, Natalie whirled around, holding her index finger over her mouth. "Meet me at the Jeep." He nodded as she tiptoed up the stairs and disappeared behind the screen door.

Luke wanted to laugh. All this sneaking around. They were twenty-eight years old, for hell's sake. But it brought out the kid in Natalie. And he wanted to give her that, let her escape for a while.

A few minutes later, she bolted across the driveway wearing sandals and carrying a grocery bag. "I swiped food," she said in a breathless giggle, sliding into the passenger seat.

"Got any bologna in there?" He craned his neck to look in the bag.

"And the rest of the chocolate whipped cream, just for you." She winked.

Luke winked back, slammed the Jeep into first, and—despite their earlier stealth—peeled out, the tires spraying gravel in their wake. Natalie squealed a girlish laugh and grabbed the dashboard.

While they cruised west down Old Philadelphia Pike, Natalie gave Luke a driving tour of Lancaster County, stories about things she'd done in tiny villages with names like Dutch Wonderland, Lealock-Leola-Bareville, and Fertility. Her hair blew in the breeze as they slowed to a crawl behind two Amish buggies on the outskirts of Zooks Corner.

Luke tipped his chin and inhaled, feeling warmth on his face, enjoying the smell of farmland and the feel of sunlight, easing him into a slower way of life without a second thought. He'd never considered settling down here—never. It was unheard of. Even though Natalie had freely admitted she hadn't loved growing up in the nothing town of Intercourse, he could see she loved it now. It fit her, too…just like Hershey. Like Philly or DC never would.

But he put a pin in that thought.

"Take a right on Cocoa Avenue," she said. "Then a left on Maple."

Pedestrians and bikers spilled onto the sidewalks, enjoying the sunny weather. Luke had never noticed how people-friendly Hershey was, though it shouldn't have surprised him. He'd just never taken the time to appreciate it.

"In there." Natalie pointed to a cluster of red brick buildings. "My unit's on the end."

"You actually live in Sugar Central Apartments?"

"You expected less?"

He laughed, and without thinking, put his hand on her knee. After realizing what he'd done, he didn't draw it away, but ran his thumb along her skin, testing the water.

The water didn't need a test. They weren't here to eat lunch, and they both knew it. From out of nowhere, Luke felt a rush of nerves. He was that kid in the boathouse, psyching himself up for his first real rite of passage with a girl. The one he'd shared with the woman in the seat next to him.

Thinking that should've chilled him out. This was Natalie.

But it didn't. Because, hell…*this was Natalie*.

"I'll get the food," he said after finding an open parking space.

"Thanks. Top floor."

If he was reading her right, Natalie was nervous, too. Instead of joking and laughing like they'd been during the drive, they climbed the stairs in silence. Luke couldn't help drinking in the way her dress rode up in back with each step. An even bigger jolt of nervousness shot through him when they got to her door.

Chapter Fifteen

A blast of cool air from turning the heater off when she'd left the night before greeted Natalie as she stepped inside her apartment. It made goose bumps pop up all over her skin. Or maybe the goose bumps came because she felt Luke behind her.

Why was she so freaked out over this?

"The, uh, kitchen's through there," she said, hearing the silly, nervous tremor in her voice. She followed Luke in where he set down the bag of food on the counter. He slid his hands in his pockets and looked around.

"Nice place."

"Thanks." The sun shone through the open blinds, and except for the empty Hershey wrappers on every flat surface, her apartment was clean and smelled homey. Completely acceptable for a…visitor.

When the thought made her stomach flutter, she pressed both hands over it.

"Hey," he said, fingering a handle of the grocery bag. "I owe you an omelet. You brought cheese from the farm, but do you have eggs?"

Oddly enough, relief flooded her, easing the nerves. Not because she didn't want to tear Luke's clothes off, but because this was a huge deal, and she was thinking *way* too much about it.

Luke Elliott was in her home. The boy who'd light her up then break her teenaged heart on a daily bases. The boy she used to think she didn't deserve because there was no way she'd be enough for him. The man who shattered all those doubts by just being here now.

"You want to eat?" she asked.

"Might take the pressure off."

She was taken aback. "You feel pressure, too?"

"Are you kidding?" He laughed and pushed a hand through his hair. "Do you have eggs?"

She couldn't help smiling, amazed by how in sync they could be. "I should."

"I'll check." He pulled open the fridge then made a disapproving *hmph*. "No Holden Farms cider. But eggs and milk, a couple of sad-looking vegetables."

"Might want to check the expiration date on that milk," she said, grabbing a skillet from the cabinet. "I can't remember how long ago I bought it."

"I'll need a blender, too," he said, transferring the food from the bag to the fridge, then inventorying all of it.

"What are you planning to make? I don't have anything to blend."

"It's a surprise." He unbuttoned his cuffs and rolled up his sleeves, showing toned forearms. His expensive black shoes had a layer of Intercourse dust over them from when they'd been in the orchard. She couldn't help biting her lip.

"I love surprises," she said, leaning a hip on the counter while peeling off her cardigan.

"Too late for your flirting, Ms. Holden." He butted his forehead to hers. "I'm melting butter in a pan."

She tried to control herself by watching him crack eggs one handed, then add salt and pepper, just like he had in his mother's kitchen less than a week ago. Maybe they'd actually eat this time.

"So, I kind of feel like a jerk," she said, after Luke had moved the mixing bowl to the fridge and thrown in more mystery ingredients.

"Why?"

"Besides being a sugar Nazi, I don't know much about what you do. You work at Penn Med, but how does that involve the NIH? Sorry, I never let you talk about your job when we're alone."

"Our time was better spent." They smiled at each other as he added the egg mixture to the pan and whipped it with a fork. "The National Institutes of Health hires contract proctors to sit in on all pre-clinical trials that've applied for federal grants—like yours. I've done a few for other foundations, but this is the first for the NIH. It's how they test out potential employees, so I was more than willing to step in short notice." He shook the pan and flipped the eggs.

"You want to work for them," Natalie said. "You want to move to DC."

Luke looked at her. "Yeah."

This wasn't exactly news, but Natalie's spirits got a tiny reality check by hearing it out loud.

"They're a huge government agency," Luke continued, "which I don't love, but it's the most efficient way to make progress. I like to stay busy, work fast on multiple projects. Where's a plate?"

Natalie already knew all this about him, too. If her logical brain was running this scene, she might've asked him to drop the spatula and leave right now, save herself potential heartache.

But her brain had left the room at the same time as her nervousness.

She pointed to the cabinet behind him and Luke pulled out a plate, dishing all the eggs onto it.

"Eat," he said, pushing it over to her.

"What about you?"

He shook his head. "You first. I'm guessing you have nothing in your system besides your mom's death by hot chocolate."

She laughed but didn't argue, and took the fork he was holding out. She'd never tasted eggs like this. They were tangy. Were eggs supposed to be tangy? They were eggs made by Luke, which made them the most delicious dish she'd ever eaten.

"Back to the NIH," she said, after another bite, eager to hear the rest of his story.

"If they're seriously considering me, being here is a big break." He rinsed the pan in the sink. "I feel really lucky that they specifically asked for me. It could be huge for my career."

Natalie lowered her fork. "And I've been trying to undress you the whole time."

"That's one way of putting it." He stood across from

her, leaned against the fridge, and shot a smoldering, spine-tingling smile her way. "Though I haven't been fighting you off very vigorously."

She shoveled in another mouthful of eggs, thinking she'd need a whole lot of vigor if he kept looking at her that way.

"So, the NIH is your dream job."

"I have a lot of dreams." Another smolder.

Good gracious.

"It's what I've been working for all this time; it's the goal."

Natalie knew he was talking about the NIH, but that smolder in his eyes made her feel like *she* was the goal.

A second later, the smolder was gone. Luke took in a breath and looked up at the ceiling. "If I'm being really honest with myself, though, I'd like to head my own team, take on projects *I'm* passionate about, the ones that drive me, personally." He leveled his gaze to her. "Like what you're doing now. I'm pretty jealous, you know."

She couldn't help being flattered, especially since they'd never seen eye-to-eye about short-term or long-term nutrition goals. "Why don't you start your own business?"

"Startups take a lot of capital."

"Aren't you kind of swimming in capital?"

He sighed and scraped a knuckle along his square jaw. "That's my family's money. A big chunk of it is legally mine, but I didn't earn it. It'd take something pretty damn important for me to tap into that particular well."

Natalie thought for a moment while chewing her fork. All these layers of Luke were unfolding right before her eyes, each one making him a better man than she'd thought before.

"So the whole time you've been observing me," she said, "you knew you were being observed by the feds."

"Well, I don't think they're spying on me."

Spying? The thought caused ice to run across the back of her neck. "Luke, if that video of us at Hersheypark gets out…"

"I know. Not that DC isn't brimming with scandals, but if that surfaces, I can kiss the NIH good-bye. Definitely my job at Penn, too. They're really cracking down on personal reputations."

"It's been a week. I'm sure they've recorded over it by now." *They damn well better have*, she thought. Then she made a mental note to drop by the admin office the first chance she got. She'd trade anything to get the master of the tape and destroy it.

"I wouldn't mind watching it," he said, pushing off the fridge and taking a step toward her. "Have you ever made a sex tape?"

Natalie almost choked on her last bite of egg. "No!"

Luke laughed, but the look he gave her, like he was remembering what they'd done in that tunnel, made her stomach do a backflip, her whole body flush and prickle like she was burning up from lust fever. Why wasn't she pulling the buttons of his shirt off with her teeth?

"Me neither," he said, keeping his eyes on her. "That video of us is the closest thing."

"The feds will never find it on my watch."

"Speaking of DC." He reached out and fingered a lock of her hair. As his hand brushed her cheek, her stomach backflipped again, and an almost painful heat bloomed from her abdomen to her chest. "What'll happen if I get the job?"

"You'll spend your days filling out lengthy bureaucratic forms and going to Red Skins games."

He cupped her cheek, intentionally this time. "I mean, what'll happen with us?"

Natalie's wide eyes resembled two Reese's Peanut Butter Cups. He'd caught her off guard.

Good. Now they might actually talk about it.

"Us?" she repeated softly, almost under her breath. "I… don't know."

"Moving to Washington isn't a done deal," he said, tucking a strand of her hair behind an ear, "but I live in Philly. That's where my job is, my work."

Natalie nodded. "I know."

"And yours is here."

She rolled her eyes and sighed dramatically, as if she hadn't needed him to point out the obvious. It made him want to hug her and then do other things. He removed his hand from her silky soft cheek and stepped away…but only until they'd finished this last conversation.

"Not to mention the minor detail of the trial," she said, then her expression changed. "Luke, listen." She stood up straight and poked a finger at his chest. "From now on, everything at the lab has to be completely professional and above board. Do you understand? Everything you do." Her voice was demanding, but not in a controlling way. Not like Celeste's. "*Everything*." She poked him again, harder.

He grinned, loving when she got all feisty. "Okay, Nat, okay."

She used her fist against his chest this time. "I'm serious."

"I can tell."

"Listen to me. I won't let you jeopardize your job or your chance with the NIH because of me."

Luke's smile dropped, but his stomach lit with a new fire. He was sure Natalie was just as concerned about her trial as he was about his job. But it was concern for *him* she voiced. For *him* that she pounded her fist on his chest.

This was a game changer. Enough with indecisiveness.

He placed a hand over hers that was now fisting the front of his shirt. "It's your turn to listen to me." He squeezed her hand. "This phase of your trial ends on the twenty-eighth, meaning I will no longer be your proctor." Another squeeze. "On the twenty-ninth, all bets are off."

A stunning flash of hopefulness shone in her eyes. But a second later, it was gone. "On the thirtieth, *you'll* go back to Philly. Seems pointless."

Luke kissed her before she could say another word. "We're trying anyway," he whispered, clasping both of her hands inside his.

"Trying what?"

"Us," he said, not even stumbling over the word. "On the twenty-ninth, we're an us. We'll make it work."

"How?"

He kissed her again. He kissed her hard until she stopped trying to speak, stopped trying to ask questions. Finally, she let herself go, and Luke was there for her to hold onto. Their play was different now between the kisses. She slowed down and just hugged him, held him, allowing their panting, shaking bodies to reset.

But with each reset, they both grew more determined.

He hoisted her onto the table. She was better focused than he was, because he hadn't noticed his shirt was unbuttoned. He moved his hands up her arms and slid the thin strap of her dress off one shoulder, his mouth there to take its place. Natalie tilted her neck and exhaled a sweet moan that made his insides coil like a damn jack-in-the-box.

"We're still not dating," she whispered, easing herself back on the table, guiding him with her.

"Yes, we are, gorgeous," he said, balancing on one knee beside her thigh, knocking a stack of mail to the floor. "But it's our little secret for now."

She beamed at him then drove her fingers into the back of his hair and clenched her fists, pulling him on top of her. "I can't even think about dating until the trial's over."

Luke's head swam as she wrapped her legs around him, her sugar-sweet tongue sliding across his lips. "Then don't think."

She broke their kiss to flash a smile. "Done."

Damn, she was the most stunning thing he'd ever seen. Right now, with her hair spilling around her face like a sunflower, and her bright, beaming soul that was as addictive as the creamiest chocolate.

He kissed the sensitive spot below her ear that he knew she loved. He knew she'd love even more what he'd do next...

"Uhh." She wiggled under his body.

Luke grinned and kissed her there again, slowly, taking his sweet time.

"Ow." She wiggled again, and rotated to scrape the top of her shoulder against his chest.

"Are you lying on something?" he asked, pulling back to

suspend his weight off her. He hadn't bothered checking the table for any knives or...or who knew what Natalie might have around. "If you're not comfortable, I say we take this party to the—"

"*Ow! What the—*" Natalie bolted into a sitting position, knocking her head against his. She slapped her palms flat over her collarbones, pressing in the heels of her hands. "Stings," she whispered in a confused voice, staring down at herself.

When she lifted her chin, her eyes were dewy, there was a layer of perspiration above her upper lip, and right where the adorable dimple on her cheek should've been, was a cluster of tiny pink welts.

"Are you okay?"

All she did was stare wide-eyed at him for a moment, then she slapped a hand over her mouth, pushed him aside and ran down the hall. Luke was hot on her trail and found her crouched on the bathroom floor.

Right as she made a sound like a dying animal, he dove behind her and held her hair back just in time. For a solid minute, she hacked and coughed, her whole body jolting. He kept a hold of her hair with one hand and rubbed her back with the other. When the worst was over, Natalie flushed then rested her cheek against the bowl.

"What did you feed me?" she asked in a weak voice.

"Eggs," he replied, grabbing a towel off the sink. He wet one end and held it out to her. When she didn't move, he pressed it to the corners of her mouth.

"But what was in them?"

"Nothing." He ran the other side of the towel over her forehead. "Butter and water, cheese, a few mushrooms."

Natalie's eyes flew open. "You used those yellow-striped mushrooms from my fridge?" She swiped the back of her hand across her mouth. "Luke, those were sent to me as a gift with the roots for my study. They're edible, but I'd never eat strange fungus from the Amazon without testing them first."

"What?" His words were cut off by another dying animal groan, as Natalie's face plunged toward the bowl. Luke dropped the towel and held her hair back with both hands. "Shit, Natalie, I'm sorry."

"Ughhh," she groaned. "Shut up."

He rubbed her back. "Is your throat swollen? Are you going into anaphylactic shock?"

"Stop talking, shut up," she panted, resting her forehead on the open lid of the seat.

Well, her airway definitely didn't seem to be affected—that was a good sign. He didn't speak, just kept rubbing a slow circle across her back. After she hadn't moved much for about half an hour, he figured this first phase was over. "I'll get you some water," he said, shifting his weight.

"No," Natalie whispered in a pitiful voice, lifting a shaky hand to shove him away. "Just go. Don't want you to see me…like this."

"Too late," he said. "And I'm not going anywhere."

The hand she'd used to try and push him away was now clutching his arm. Heat seared from her skin. She already had a fever, and that tiny cluster of pink welts on her cheek had spread down her neck and shoulders, across her arms. Maybe everywhere.

Hives, he thought. *Not dangerous, but if they didn't itch like hell now, they were about to.* She was also nauseous with a fever of at least 102, judging by his quick assessment. Of course no one could be sure what Amazonian mushrooms might cause next, but if these were her only symptoms, she'd be fine. In about twenty-four hours.

"I'm going to leave you for a minute," he said. Natalie's shaky grip tightened. "Just to go to the kitchen."

She exhaled what might've been "okay," but the sound barely came out.

In the kitchen, he did a quick rummage through drawers until he found some peppermint tea, filled a mug with hot tap water and tossed in the bag. He also found some half-crushed, saltines that might've been ten years old. He carried the crackers, tea, and glass of ice water to the bathroom, grabbed a washcloth from the shower rack, soaked it in cold water, then knelt beside her.

"You're hot," he said, pressing it to her forehead.

"Your timing stinks."

He laughed under his breath. "You have a fever caused by a histamine release from the mushrooms, plus a minor food intolerance."

"Minor?" She opened one dewy eye.

"Drink this," he said, holding out the mug. She took a few sips, rested, then a few more until the minty drink was gone. "Eat." He unwrapped the cracker and tried to move her into a better sitting position, but the second she brushed against him, her hands flew to her arms, nails raking across her skin.

"Don't scratch," he said, grabbing her hands as she struggled.

"It feels like fire ants are crawling on me."

"I know." He squeezed her hands tighter inside his,

keeping her still. "But you can't scratch. It'll make it worse."

She slammed her eyes shut and bucked against him. "Let go. It's driving me crazy."

"Shh-shh." But she wouldn't stop squirming to get free, so Luke flattened her to the floor and pinned her hands to the tile. "You can't scratch—hey!" She tried to knee his junk to get away, which left Luke no choice but to lower himself on top of her. "You *can't*, baby. It's like chicken pox, you'll scar."

"Luke, I'm so not in the mood for love."

"You think *I* am? I want your body, but not when it's covered in hives." Well actually he wanted her body so badly he wouldn't give a damn if it was crawling with real fire ants. But Natalie was suffering and her fever was climbing, he could tell by the heat of her forehead as he pressed his lip to it, gauging the temperature.

After a good ten minutes of holding her down, she finally stopped thrashing. It was bound to happen, once the fever hit a certain pitch, it would wear her out. The itching wouldn't stop, though, but she'd be too weak to fight him.

"If I get off you, I need you to not move," he said in a calm but stern voice. "Do you have Benadryl?"

"No," she said in a sobby whimper.

"Dammit. Any hydrocortisone cream?"

"Um…" She tilted her chin toward the linen closet.

"In there? Okay." One-handed, he soaked a towel in cold water and the ice. "Sit up, put your hands on your lap." But as he unpinned her and sat back on his heels, she didn't move. "Sweetheart, you need to sit up."

Finally she did, slowly, miserably. Her chin bobbed like she had trouble holding up her head; it might've been from how he'd been restraining her, or it might've been fatigue from the fever. He'd find Tylenol next time he was in the kitchen.

"Put your hands on your lap and I'll lay this here." He draped the wet, icy-cold towel over her arms. She didn't fight him or try to scratch, which he knew was only temporary. In the linen closet, he found a bottle of Calamine lotion and cotton balls.

"Let me see," he said, gently taking her chin in his hand to examine her face. When her eyes lifted to his, he could see the fever burning away. He soaked a cotton ball with Calamine and dabbed it across her cheeks. "It's okay, it'll help," he said when she winced. She nodded but began to fidget under the towel. He wasn't as slow and careful as he applied lotion to the infected areas down her neck and arms, needing to get the medicine on quickly.

When he was done, he eased her back to prop against the wall. "Does it itch anywhere else?" Her eyes fluttered closed and she rubbed her wrist across her chest. Luke stared at the location and swallowed. *All righty, then.* He soaked another cotton ball, then slid a finger inside the top of her sundress, pulling it away from her body. He swallowed again when he saw the trail of welts that disappeared into the cup of her strapless bra.

"Nat," he whispered. "I'm sorry but I have to…um…" But she barely stirred. Of course he'd do anything to ease her discomfort, so after a steadying inhale, he gently yet clinically applied lotion everywhere it needed to go. He was just relieved she hadn't scratched any other place he shouldn't be without her permission.

"Want to…lay down," She sounded completely wiped

out from trying to shove him away while her body worked overtime to fight the funky rainforest bacteria swimming in her blood.

Luke had had his fair share of hangovers and knew the most desirable spot was flat on the cool bathroom tiles. So he took her shoulders and was about to ease her to the floor, when she changed direction and her head landed on his lap.

He gazed down at her, at this miserable, beautiful girl covered in dots of pink lotion, whose dress was twisted around her body, hair tangled on one side, and who was clutching the bottom of his shirt with both of her hands.

Clutching his heart.

He stayed with her, allowing her to rest, while allowing himself to unwrap that sealed box in his mind, the one that was supposed to contain and restrain all his feelings for Natalie.

But they were too strong. He hadn't even realized how much being with her had changed him…made him happier, more complete. And finally, finally ready.

When she stirred, he had her sit up and drink some water. Tears clung to the corners of her closed eyes and her bottom lip quivered. She was barely awake, in that feverish stupor between consciousness and sleep. Doing his best not to rub off the Calamine, he scooped her up and carried her to the bedroom.

It was dark now, but a street lamp outside her window showed the way. He pulled back the covers and laid her on the bed. Her sandals were still on, so he unfastened them and slid them off her feet, the same feet he'd tickled when she'd sat on the fence. He thought about taking off her dress so she'd be more comfortable, but decided against it. One, she'd be mortified in the morning if he did. And two, the first time he saw this woman fully naked was going to be the best night of his life.

So he did his best to make sure her dress wasn't constricting her anywhere, then he draped the top sheet over her body. Until her fever broke, and unless she was naked, she wouldn't need any blankets.

Enough with the naked talk, Luke inwardly yelled. *Nat would punch you in the stomach if she knew what you were thinking.*

He put a full glass of water on the nightstand and was about to leave the room when Natalie stirred, not all the way awake, but in that limbo zone.

"You're okay, baby," he whispered. "Go to sleep."

Her body moved under the sheet. Luke hoped she wasn't about to have a scratching attack. "Stay," she exhaled in a breathy whisper, one eye opened a crack as she stretched her arm out to him.

Luke's chest and heart and head constricted at the same time, squeezed with a desire to take care of this woman who took care of everyone else. "I'll be on the couch if you need me."

"Luke," she said, her hand reaching for him. He took it and felt the fever invading her body, but the angry welts were already fading. "Stay," she repeated. She weakly tugged his hand toward her, then with probably all the strength she had, shifted her weight like she was offering to give him room on the other side of the bed.

He didn't know what to do. He obviously wasn't about to take advantage of the situation by hopping into bed with her.

She tugged his hand again. "Come…here…"

It was no longer a decision. Keeping every stitch of clothing on including his shoes, Luke sat on the bed, then re-clined, resting his head on the pillow. She squeezed his hand and tried to slide over to him, but didn't have the strength to get far.

So Luke did it for her.

Natalie smelled like minty tea, medicated lotion and clean girl sweat. And he loved it all. He rolled to his side and held her to his chest, feeling the moment her body fully relaxed. He listened to her breathe, waking up each time she stirred, as she slept semi-restfully through the night.

It wasn't until late-morning the next day that her fever broke.

Chapter Sixteen

The inside of her mouth tasted like something had died in there, her skin felt drier than the Sahara, and her abs were so sore it felt like she'd done sit ups in her sleep. And why was her bedroom so bright? Had she fallen asleep with the light on?

The second she opened her eyes, her head pounded, and when she tried to sit up, the whole room tipped on its axis.

"Morning."

Her focus steadied, and she saw Luke leaning on the doorframe of her bedroom. His hair was more tousled than usual and…wasn't that the same shirt he'd been wearing at the farm?

The farm? Luke? In her apartment?

She closed her eyes and held her head in her hands. "What happened?"

"Shrooms."

"That's right." She lifted her chin; her head weighed fifty

pounds. "You tried to poison me."

"Pretty sure I succeeded in that." He took a step into the room. "How do you feel? I mean, besides like crap."

"Nope, crap sums it up." He was holding a glass out to her. She took it without question and sipped. Ginger ale. "Thanks," she said, taking a moment to gauge what effect the first thing hitting her stomach in hours would do. When it felt good, she took another sip.

By the time she'd finished half the glass, Luke was leaning against the doorframe again. He looked tired and really rumpled, but still oh-so sexy—though her brain had a hard time processing sexy this morning. "You took care of me."

"You were raging like the exorcist."

"Was not," she said, hoping like hell that wasn't the case. Talk about *un*sexy. She braced her weight on her hands and pushed into a sitting position. Luke's lips peeled apart. He cleared his throat and looked away, like she'd just caught him in an ogle.

Still bleary-eyed, she looked down at herself, vaguely remembering she'd broken out in a rash. But except for some dried Calamine lotion, her arms looked clear, so did her chest, and stomach and—

"Um, why am I wearing nothing but a hot pink bra and matching thong?"

"Do they match? Hmm, hadn't noticed." He smiled, his eyes lazily scanning over her without hesitation.

Her cheeks burned and flushed. The memory… It was like waking up to the worst alcohol-induced blackout. "What the hell happened last night?"

"Bad reaction from the mushrooms. And it wasn't pretty. Well, some of it was more than pretty."

She pulled the sheet up to her chin.

"Relax." He chuckled. "I didn't undress you. Ivy did."

"Ivy?"

"I asked her to put you in your pajamas." His smile twisted. "I guess that's what she thinks you sleep in. I approve."

Ivy. She'd kill her. Well, at least she hadn't dressed Natalie in the Naughty French Maid costume at the back of her closet, complete with feather duster/whip combo.

"When was Ivy here?"

"Few hours ago."

"*Hours*?" Forgetting her state of undress, Natalie flung off the sheet and slid off the bed. "What time is it?"

"Almost two."

"In the afternoon?"

"I'll bring you food so you can eat something. Don't worry, I didn't make it."

"I don't have time to eat." She pushed past him. "I should be at the lab. We only have three days left. How could you let me sleep half a day away?" When she entered the bathroom, she stopped in her tracks. The place was spotless and smelled like her lavender all-purpose spray.

"Did you clean?"

Luke shrugged. "Not a lot to do at five in the morning."

She ran a finger over the top of the commode. "You held my hair back while I barfed, applied Calamine lotion to…I don't even wanna know where, stayed with me all night, and then cleaned my bathroom?" She laughed quietly and shook her head. "Even though the only reason you came over was to…"

"That's not the *only* reason I came over." He took a step toward her, and the cool, steady look in his eyes made her feel pin pricks all over her body. "But we won't get into those other reasons now. First, you need to take a shower. Second, you need to get to the lab right after you shower. And third, I can't just stand here while you're only in that." His glance left her eyes for a split-second. "My head's about to explode."

She squeaked and grabbed for a towel. But the only one on the rack wasn't large enough to cover even one demi-cupped boob, not to mention 90 percent of her butt was on display.

Luke's lazy smile returned. "There's food in the kitchen—rice, saltines, bananas, toast. Eat something before you get in the shower, and drink as much water as you can. Take something with you to work. Rash is pretty much gone. You should feel even better in a few hours."

"Um, okay."

He hovered by the door. "Also, Brandon still has your car, so Dexter's on the way here. He's driving me home to shower and change. Keys to the Jeep are on your table. First gear can stick."

She didn't know what to say. He'd really taken care of her, thought of everything she'd need. She wasn't used to that, but she liked it. Oh, how she liked it.

"Luke, thank you," she said, her throat feeling tight. The only thing stopping her from jumping his bones was she probably smelled like the bottom of the sewer.

"You're welcome." He turned to leave, but then turned back. "Since we won't be talking about it until then, don't forget, we have a date on the twenty-ninth." His gaze traveled to her skimpy lingerie. "Bring that." He winked. "See you at work."

Natalie was finishing a second piece of dry toast when she got to the lab.

"Looks like you feel better," Ivy said, popping squares of chocolate out of their molds.

Natalie felt a lot better, actually. She'd managed to keep down all the food and water, and only a few little pink bumps dotted her stomach. "You gonna tell me why you dressed my unconscious body in my sexiest sexy-time outfit for Lu—"

"Nat!" Ivy's ear-splitting call cut her off, and she shot a look to the back corner. Mark the intern was holding a large beaker while Ken was adding the contents of a syringe. Both were staring at her. Luke was at his desk, also staring.

"Uhhh," Natalie said. "M-morning, everyone."

"Afternoon," Luke said, shutting his laptop. Though he didn't come over, he sent her a look, which she returned, and then an almost telepathic conversation happened between them.

You're okay?

Yes. Thanks to you.

That's good. I wish I could kiss you right here, right now.

Me too.

But we can't.

I know.

We'll talk about it in four days. In the meantime, I'm picturing you in that sexy-time outfit...imagining how I'm going to slowly peel it off your body with my—

"So." Ivy clapped her hands, shaking Natalie away from Luke's penetrating gaze. "We've been rerunning the sixth test. The compounds are a perfect match. Check it out." She pointed to the microscope at her workstation.

Natalie fanned the front of her shirt then grabbed a lab coat, buttoning it as she crossed the room, feeling Luke's smoldering eyes on her the whole time. She flashed Ivy only the tiniest glance before peering into the lens. "Looks good. Wait, this is the slide from two days ago, why are you—"

"I'm trying to help." Ivy's muffled yet sharp voice cut in.

"Um, help what?"

Ivy subtly tipped her chin to the back corner. "You guys were having eye sex in front of the interns," she whispered. "They'll be scarred for life."

"Oh," Natalie whispered back, pretending to adjust the slide. "It won't happen again."

"The hell it won't. I was there this morning. I saw you *with him* this morning. He called at five a.m. and told me what happened, asked me to stop at the grocery store and bring you sick food. When I got there…well…"

"What?" Natalie tried to keep her voice low, then "*hmm'd*," scratched her head, and took another look at the bogus slide.

"You kept mumbling his name in your sleep, or your half sleep. I couldn't tell if you were awake, though you pitched a pretty decent fit when he left the room so I could put you in your PJs—you're welcome, by the way." Now it was Ivy's turned to fake-examine the slide. "The second he came back in, he knelt by your bed, and you grabbed his shirt and yanked him to you like he was a security blanket. He said you were like that all night."

"I…" She touched her forehead. "I had a fever."

"I'll say. He sat there with you and stroked your hair

while you practically strangled him with your crazy-powerful fever strength. Remind me to never bring chicken soup if you have pneumonia."

"I was strangling him?"

Ivy smiled. "Didn't seem like he minded. The man was in heaven. I didn't know you were a couple."

"We're not." Natalie couldn't help sneaking a glance at Luke in the far corner. *Not yet, anyway.* Warmth and gratitude and other tingly sensations filled her body. "Thanks for your help," she said to Ivy, pushing the microscope aside.

"You're welcome. So," she said in a louder voice, "what's next, boss?"

For the next few hours, they worked fast and efficiently. Luke stayed at his desk, typing like a madman on his laptop. *Those fingers...* Natalie caught herself thinking, only once or twice, or twenty times.

It was impressive, even to her, how much they were able to accomplish in just a short amount of time, especially with the schedule cut and other setbacks. At the end of the day, she felt more revitalized than ever, mentally and physically. She'd even eaten half a hamburger.

Luke was at his laptop as she hung up her lab coat. They were the last ones there. "Feel like an omelet?" she asked.

He laughed but stayed seated. "I might never eat one again."

"I've also got rice and mashed bananas. And Calamine lotion."

Luke closed his eyes for a moment. "We should probably sleep in our own beds tonight. Sleep," he repeated. "I know you're not one hundred percent."

"I'm close enough."

He laughed again, but it was wrapped around a groan from his chest. "We've come this far. You need to stay focused, which means I need to stay out of your way. You're almost at the finish line, babe"—he cleared his throat—"Natalie, I mean."

She loved the familiarity of a pet name coming from him. Luke was no longer the fantasy boy she had a crush on. They had real feelings for each other now. Though she might've been in denial about facing a long-distance relationship, she knew she had to try…because she had a sneaking suspicion she was happier with Luke than without him.

"Go home," he said, gazing at her with those swoony blue eyes. "Brandon dropped off your car a while ago. I'll lock up when I'm done. I won't be long."

"Okay." She exhaled contently, and couldn't wait for the day when she could crawl onto his lap. "Thanks again, for everything."

"Any time."

She did sleep that night, and before that, ate applesauce and half a PB&J. She also found a disgusting-looking green smoothie in the fridge with a note attached: *Drink one cup mid-day and before bed until it's gone. Electrolytes and vitamin A.*

She couldn't help rolling her eyes, but then hugged herself. Luke.

The next day was even more productive, and Natalie was bouncing off the walls with energy— No, it had *nothing* to do with that green smoothie that tasted like lawn clippings. Time had flown so fast that it was a shock when she realized it was after seven.

"Sorry I kept everyone late," she said. "But we're set for

the final two days. We nailed this trial, I can feel it."

Ivy came to her side and put an arm around her. "Me too. And just in time." They shared a relieved smile.

After Ivy and the interns left, Luke's cell bleeped from across the room. "That must be Dexter," he said, pushing back from the desk. "He's early—we're hanging out at home tonight, just the family."

"Good," Natalie said. Luke's warm smile in return was filled with such meaning she wanted to give him the biggest hug ever. Then jump him.

"Oh, huh, it's not a text from Dex," he said, "It's an email from…the NIH."

When his expression went blank and he didn't go on, Natalie went to him. "Is anything wrong?"

"Not a thing." He blinked down at his phone. "They're giving me the job."

Being human, Natalie couldn't help it that her initial reaction was disappointment. Philadelphia was a little over an hour away, while Washington DC was a three-hour train ride. But that was a selfish thought. Could she help it if she wanted him as close to her as humanly possible? Luke wanted this job, though, and she'd be nothing but supportive.

"That's great! Congratulations. I mean it. We should celebrate tonight, or maybe you should keep the plans with your family and we'll celebrate later. But wow, Luke, you really deserve this."

Had he even heard? He was still staring at his phone, running a finger over the screen.

"No, wait, it's…" He trailed off.

And then Luke Elliott's jaw actually dropped.

"Oh, man. *Sweet*! Signing bonus, executive package,

travel, and… No way. I'll be heading my own team." When he finally looked at her, his expression had transformed. She'd never seen him so excited. He was practically glowing. "Do you know what this means?"

"Oh…um…" She displayed an open mouth grin, widened her eyes and nodded up and down to demonstrate excitement and support, even though she didn't know what he was referring to.

Luke was reading his phone again. "Okay, okay, here's the… *Excellent.* They want me to start right away. I'll leave tomorrow morning—no, tonight."

"Tonight?" Now *her* mouth fell open. "But you can't."

"Nat, don't worry. We can handle the long-distance thing, right? Oh, baby!" He swooped her up in his arms and swung her around. "It's happening. Just like I planned."

"I'm happy for you—so happy," she said sincerely. "But you can't go tonight."

His animated smiled morphed into the sexy one that had the power to make her melt. "Missing me already, are ya? Come here." He pulled her close but Natalie put the heels of her hands on the front of his shoulders.

"If you leave, you won't be our proctor."

He grinned. "Even better. No more ethical conflict. Now come here." When he tried to kiss her, she extended her arms to hold him back. "Are you feeling queasy again?"

"Um, sort of." She blinked. "Luke, think about it. If we have no proctor, we can't continue the trial."

He looked concerned for a second then shook his head. "There are other proctors besides me. No big deal."

"It is a big deal."

"Nat, it's fine. Just ask for another one."

Was he really trying to blow this off? She couldn't help exhaling a bleak chuckle. "You think I can just snap my fingers and the federal government will do what I say?" She wiggled out of his arms and stepped back. "I don't get everything I want at the drop of a hat. I'm not an Elliott."

Luke's sharp jaw clenched. "Wait a minute—"

"The NIH will understand about the timing," she said, the heat of panic building in her chest. "Just tell them you absolutely cannot leave yet. Tell them, Luke."

"Think about my side." He folded his arms. "I'm not about to tell the people who just handed me my wildest dreams on a silver platter that I won't drop everything to be where they want me to be."

She swallowed then took a deep breath. "What about me?"

"We knew there was a chance I'd be moving. It's just happening sooner, because I have to go now."

"No. I meant, what about my *trial*? We only have the lab for two more days. That's it. If the NIH can't magically overnight me a proctor, there's no way we'll finish in time." She thought about Muff, her project failing, and her stomach rolled. Then she thought about Ivy's job. "You might think you know how imperative finishing this trial is, but there's more to it. This is really important."

"And this job offer is really important. I'll see to it you get another proctor as soon as possible."

"Can you promise one tomorrow?"

He didn't reply, but the sudden trace of apathy made Natalie jump to the worst-case scenario. "So you're picking your job over me. That's basically what you're saying."

"That's not at all what I'm saying, but if that's the way

you choose to see it, I can't stop you." He walked to his desk.

Natalie stared at his back, baffled, blindsided. Until she stopped and thought about it for a second. *Oh, girl. You are such an idiot*, she inwardly lectured, fighting back the rage. *A blind fool. You should've seen this coming.*

It was happening again. Everything she feared, everything she'd sworn to protect her heart from... What she needed didn't matter to Luke—that was clear. Which also meant, deep down, *she* didn't matter to him, either. At least not enough to sacrifice two tiny days to keep her trial from going under.

A wave of the old, painful teenage insecurities crashed over her head.

I'll never be enough for him. He didn't see me then. Why would he really see me now? And up until five minutes ago, I was willing to give him everything, my trust, my heart.

The sound of him zipping his laptop case shook her awake. "Luke, please don't go yet," she said. Desperation to save her research project made her prepared to say anything, beg him if she had to. "Tell them you broke your leg or your great-grandpa's sick or something—anything." When he didn't stop packing his things, she switched gears. "Do you really want to leave Hershey this soon? Remember what happened before. Think of what you put your family through, your mother."

She hoped the new angle would soften his heart, but when Luke wheeled around, his expression was frighteningly cold, distrusting, matching his tone. "What did you say?"

"I—"

"This is my life, my decision," he said, hardness coloring his voice now. "I'm not about to change it because you told me to. I won't let anyone control me again. Ever."

"Luke." Her own heart immediately softened, knowing how her words must've sounded to him. "I'm not trying to… I'd never do that."

She could tell he wasn't listening as he hooked the strap of his laptop case over one shoulder.

"Luke, hold on." She followed after him as he walked toward the door. "Don't leave like this. Let's talk about it."

"There's nothing to talk about. I see how it is with you."

She was close to grabbing his arm, but right as he got to the exit, he stopped. For a moment, some of the tension in his shoulders seemed to leave, and she held her breath.

"I can't believe you brought that up, what I did to my family before," he said, his back to her, chin lowered as if he was looking at the floor. "I can't believe you tried to manipulate me with it."

Slowly, he lifted his head. Natalie still couldn't breathe, waiting for him to turn around and face her, to work it out.

But he didn't. And the next thing she knew, she was staring, unblinking, at the empty doorway.

Chapter Seventeen

Luke had yet to calm down when Dexter pounded on his car window two hours after he'd left the lab. No, he'd *stormed out* of there — like an obstinate teenager.

He rolled down the window and growled out what had happened.

"You're a fat, stupid idiot," Dexter said when he'd finished.

Luke glared at him, ready to kick his brother's ass to the dark side of the moon just for the hell of it. "Shut up."

"And now you're stewing in the driveway all pissed at yourself because you know she's right."

"Not even." Luke exhaled a sarcastic laugh and stared through his windshield at the house. "I told her about the job offer and she completely freaked out on me."

"Because you also told her you were leaving her project high and dry."

Luke shook his head. "No. I told her I'd line up another

proctor."

"Any reason why she should trust you to do that when you were about to walk out the door?"

Luke opened his mouth, ready for a rebuttal, but then closed it. "Still doesn't give her the right to try and manipulate me like that."

"How did she do that, again?" Dexter asked, an annoying lightness to his voice that made Luke want to kidney punch him.

"She…" He rubbed his chin. "She asked me to stay. Practically begged me."

"Oh, poor you."

Luke huffed and rolled his eyes. "When I told her I couldn't, she laid out all that crap about what happened with Celeste and…and how I should think about what I put Mom through, what I put all of you through."

Dexter shook his head. "Fat, stupid idiot."

"I'm done talking. It's over." Saying it aloud made his gut clench, so he swung the Jeep door open, nearly bashing it into his brother. "I have to pack."

"You're really leaving for DC tonight?"

"I have to," Luke said, walking toward the house. *And the sooner the better. Get me out of here,* he thought, though his gut clenched again at the falseness of the statement.

Just as he got to the front steps, Dexter called from behind, "You don't think the NIH can survive without you for two days?"

"Of course they can," Luke snapped. Then he stopped walking, remembering that Natalie had said the same thing, and he'd blown her off. He stared at the ground as a flicker of realization flashed through his brain.

No, I did worse than just blow her off, he thought, replaying the scene. *I chose my job over her…just like she said.*

"Fat, stupid idiot," Dex repeated.

Luke didn't bother denying it, but sat on the bottom step, the rest of that heated conversation—especially what he'd said at the end—coming back with a fury. "I told her she"—he paused to swallow—"and then I accused her…" He trailed off, unable to finish the phrase.

"See? She was right," Dexter said, sitting beside him.

"I didn't know what… I mean, I didn't see it that way. I got the email, and it all happened so fast." He held his face in his hands, his skin hot with regret, his gut knotting at what he'd done.

"As your younger brother, it pains me to say how completely terrible you are with women."

"You're one to talk," Luke said through his hands. "You haven't had a steady anything in years…if ever."

"Bro, we're not discussing me. You were happy with her. I haven't seen that in a very long time."

A fist squeezed Luke's heart. He had been happy with her. *She* made him happy. More than that, she made him hopeful and excited about the future. He wanted different things out of life, bigger things, by just being around her.

"You're the relationship guy," Dex cut into his thoughts. "The example to us all."

Luke scrubbed his face and finally looked up. "Some example. I'm a two-time failure," he said, picturing Natalie's face, how hurt she'd looked when he'd accused her of manipulating him. "Totally screwed up."

"I wouldn't be so fast to write it off. Natalie's obviously more level-headed than you. It was one argument. Do you think that's enough to ruin your whole…whatever you two had going?"

Luke thought for a moment, his churning stomach settling a bit. "Maybe not," he said, staring straight ahead into the darkness. "Hopefully not." His head ached when he recalled the harsh, untrusting things he'd said, for no damn reason except *he'd* been untrusting. Dexter was dead on when he'd called him a fat, stupid idiot…with a dollop of chocolate whipped cream on top.

No doubt about it, Natalie had been right, including about how Luke didn't have to leave for DC so soon. He arrived at the lab early the next morning, ready to apologize like hell and tell her just how right she was about everything.

Ivy was the only one there. She stood before a stack of flat cardboard boxes, trying to assemble one.

"Morning," he said.

"Hey," Ivy replied, dully.

He set his laptop case on a desk and watched her for a second. "Want some help with that?"

"Sure." She passed over one of the un-built boxes without looking at him.

Natalie must've told her about our fight, he thought, accounting for her coolness. *I guess I deserve it.*

"I didn't see Natalie's car in the parking lot. Did she drive in with you?"

Ivy tore off a long piece of packing tape to secure the bottom flaps of the box. "She's not here. And she won't be."

Luke stopped what he was doing. "Why?"

The redhead didn't answer at first, but then she sighed and muttered, "Clueless."

The ocean of regret he'd been swimming in the previous

night was trying to pull him under again. "Ivy." He moved to stand in front of her. "What do you mean, she *won't* be here?"

She blew out a loud, exaggerated breath and looked at him. "Because it's over. And I can't believe you had the gall to show up after what you did."

Luke nodded and rubbed the back of his neck. He deserved the stab. "We had a fight and I want to apologize."

"How *big* of you. Nat sent a dozen emails last night, and spent hours on the phone trying to secure another proctor, but no one's available until next week."

Another stab, right in the gut. He should've called her last night and told her he would stay until someone could take his place. But he'd been fuming and stubborn and not thinking straight.

By then of course he knew Natalie hadn't been trying to manipulate him. Her heart didn't work that way. She might've been desperate—hurt and disappointed in him—but never controlling.

"It's fine now, back to normal," he said firmly, to himself more than to Ivy. "I'm here, we can keep going."

"We…" Ivy muttered under her breath.

"Call her," Luke said, trying to breathe through the newest stab. But this one stayed in place, making his stomach whir like a blender from hell. "Call her now, tell her I'm staying. Never mind, I will." He went straight for his cell. He'd get her to this lab if he had to drive to her apartment and drag her out.

"You don't get it," Ivy said. "She let the interns go last night. One already flew to Johns Hopkins to work on another project. It's over—scrapped." She put down the tape dispenser with a loud bang. "And now she thinks she's let everyone down. Her family, her brother, the team, *me*. I told her a million times it isn't her fault—I'll figure out how to keep my job."

He looked up from his phone. "Why does this trial affect your job?"

Ivy blinked. "She didn't tell you about the lab hour requirements?"

Luke thought for a moment. "She mentioned something about it once, but…" He read Ivy's expression and connected the dots. "Oh. Your contract is up soon. You needed this."

She nodded. "And Nat blames herself, which is nonsense. She thinks she has to take care of everyone, and if she can't, she feels like a failure. You know her."

He did. He knew how Natalie's huge, caring, giving heart worked, and that she'd take full responsibility, even though none of this was her fault.

"It's mine," he muttered, jaw clenched, while the weight of a pile of boulders dumped onto his shoulders. "My fault— all of it." But just standing there, taking the blame wouldn't do shit. "We have to get her to this lab. Wait. Why, exactly, isn't she here now? She'd never abandon this project because of me. I know *that* about her, too."

"It's not because of you," Ivy said in a small voice, pressing her lips together. "It's something else."

The dreadful look in Ivy's eyes and her hesitant manner turned his stomach into a cold void. "Did something happen to her?" When she didn't reply, he wanted to shake her by the shoulders. "Ivy, tell me what's going on. Where is Natalie?"

"I don't know."

The non-answer was like an invisible hand wrapping

around his throat while he waited to hear more.

"Late last night she got a call," Ivy finally continued. "Her brother's in the hospital. They think he tried to…" She stopped and looked away.

Luke pictured Brandon jamming on the guitar, singing Springsteen, and then he felt the floor drop out from under him. "Is Brandon hurt?"

"He's okay, I think. Nat texted this morning saying she wouldn't be in. She's staying with him because her parents have to appear before some legal panel about rezoning their county. They have to be in Harrisburg for the next two days. See, she's trying to take care of everyone again, and she doesn't know we're down one intern. Not that it matters. We're screwed."

"No, we're not," Luke fired back, fists and jaw clenched. He gathered all the energy in his body that made him a fat, stupid idiot and channeled it into sharp focus. He seized Ivy's open laptop on the counter and spun it around to face her. "Find the schedule. We're fixing this now."

She just stood there. "You can't touch anything. You're the proctor."

"I'll have a replacement here in ninety minutes. It'll cost me, but I have connections." He grabbed his phone and typed a short yet firm email to his buddy at Penn Med, promising him anything if he'd get here.

"But how can *you* help?"

"I have a degree in science just like she does. Where's the schedule?" When Ivy still hadn't moved, Luke stepped around her and clicked through to find today's agenda. "I'll do it all myself, if I have to," he added, as he speed-read the spreadsheet. "But I sure as hell won't let Natalie's dream, what she's worked so hard for, disappear. No way."

"Huh. I can see why she was strangling you that night."

Luke looked at her impatiently. "What?"

"Nothing." She shook her head. "We're really behind now, and two men down."

"Where's the final serum?" Luke said, ignoring her as he charged across the room for a lab coat.

"Over there." Ivy pointed to a fridge in the corner. "Bottom shelf."

"Is this the version susceptible to temperature?"

"Yes."

"I won't take it out until we're ready." He rubbed his chin and tried to think like Natalie. "Okay, I need three beakers, three syringes, and clean gloves. *You*"—he snapped his fingers at some random intern who happened to walk in—"get me gloves and two trays of chocolate, no three. Come on, let's move."

"Did you call her yesterday?" Luke asked as Ivy loaded the first of the final set of slides.

"Yes."

"Did you tell her?"

"She knows we got a replacement for you." Ivy paused and looked at Steve sitting at the desk Luke had used as proctor. "But when I mentioned your name, she threatened to light my hair on fire if I said another word."

"Dammit." Luke muttered as he removed the slide from its latches. "I need another one. Haven't had to use a microscope like this since grad school."

"You've been behind a desk too long," Ivy said, pulling out a whole box of blank slides, even though they only needed five. "You need to get your hands dirty more often."

Luke chuckled under his breath, but it felt like his chest was caving in. He'd felt like that for two days. "You sound like Nat." He tried not to let his hand shake when he spoke her name.

While he, Ivy, John the pinch-hitting intern, and Steve had worked, he'd tried not to think about her. Too much was at stake to be distracted. But now that the rush was winding down, Luke thought about her a lot. Worried like hell that he'd blown the greatest thing in his life.

"She knows the project is still moving forward?"

Ivy nodded. "But she has no idea you've basically taken over her lab."

"Good." He loaded the next slide and refocused the viewer. "No reason she ever has to."

They worked quietly for a few minutes, then Ivy said, "Does she know about the other thing?"

"No." Luke looked at her, annoyed. "And *you* don't know about the other thing, either. Remember your promise?"

"But it's a huge deal. You should tell her."

At the moment, he wasn't in a position to tell Natalie anything. She wouldn't take his calls or allow Ivy to speak his name. Besides, Luke had already thought through the "other thing." It was a done deal.

"What if I tell her about it and she resents me—resents *it*? What if she resents me enough to not accept it?" That "if" was probably moot; it was clear Natalie already did resent him. The thought brought on another wave of the agony and helplessness he'd been living with. "No." He shook his head firmly, channeling those heavy feelings into motivation. "This is the one thing I can control, and there's no way she can find out."

Ivy sighed. "Then I won't tell her."

"Thank you."

Another stretch of silence rolled by until Ivy broke it again. "Her parents are driving back from Harrisburg this afternoon, but not in time for her to make it to the lab before the data's due."

"We'll make it," Luke said. *Or this will all be for nothing*, he privately added.

"Are you going to try to make contact with her when we're done?"

"She doesn't want to see me." He exhaled and tried to work out the kink in his neck, but the aching had taken over his entire body, though the worst of the pain centralized around his heart. "I've left messages. She'd call back if she wanted to talk. She must be so pissed at me." He heard misery in his voice and didn't care.

"She doesn't know what she is," Ivy said. "*I* know what she is, even if she doesn't. Even if *you* don't."

Luke didn't have the extra energy to follow what she was saying. He could barely concentrate on anything but the task at hand. He clamped in the next slide and made a checkmark in his notebook. "I'm leaving for DC tomorrow. I planned on staying for a while, but it seems futile."

His heart beat like a fifty pound slug whenever he thought about leaving. Because he wasn't just leaving Natalie, but his parents, his family. He'd be leaving Hershey—his home, and the damn enchanting way all its street lights were shaped like chocolate Kisses.

"Hey. Check it out." He slid the microscope toward Ivy. "That's it."

Luke held out a pen. "You do the honors."

Ivy grinned, and Luke tried to find some kind of satisfaction in the moment, but it was hollow. He was hollow. So hollow and so out of time.

It was the second day in a week Luke found himself driving toward Amish country before breakfast. Not until he spotted the "Welcome to Intercourse" sign did he finally take his lead foot off the accelerator.

He'd banged on her apartment door and even begged Ivy for her parent's address in Hershey. She was nowhere. Which meant, she was at the farm.

He waiting impatiently behind a buggy at a four-way stop but was flying again by the time he turned onto the gravel driveway. Her car wasn't there. Neither was her father's truck.

Luke marched up the stairs and knocked. Once. Twice. Three times. He was about to make himself at home on the porch swing and wait all damn day when the door opened.

"Hey," Brandon said.

Luke was surprised. He knew from Ivy that he'd been released from the hospital the day before, but he didn't expect to see him here. "Hey. Is your sister here?"

He shook his head.

"Was she?"

The kid hesitated, then nodded.

"Is she coming back?" When Brandon didn't reply, Luke

backed off. "It's cool. I'll wait in my car if you want, but I'm not leaving 'till I see her."

"She went with my parents on a delivery." He gripped the door jam. "It was a big one, and she knew it'd take them all day if she didn't help."

"So they left you *alone*?" He regretted it the second it escaped his mouth. "Sorry, man."

"It's okay." Brandon shifted his weight. "I guess you heard what happened."

"Only that you were in the hospital." He did a quick visual sweep of the kid's wrists. No bandages or scars from a razor. Then he hated himself for even thinking that.

"It was an accident." Brandon took a beat, then held the door wide open. "Wanna come in?"

He sat in the armchair across from where Luke sat on the couch. "I was building a model," Brandon began. "This three-D puzzle of the Charger from *Fast and Furious*. I kept getting the tiny pieces mixed up, so I emptied a few of my med bottles so I could use them. I tried to keep all the pills separated, but a bunch fell down the sink. Then I couldn't remember which pills went in which bottle, I don't pay attention. There's one I'm supposed to take only right before bed." He shrugged and tugged at his cuffs. "I guess I took the wrong one with dinner 'cause I woke up in the ER after they pumped my stomach."

Luke felt pain behind his eyes. He swallowed and asked, "Are you okay?"

Brandon nodded. "It was a stupid mistake, and even after I explained what happened and why some of the pills were gone, they made me spend the night there. I wasn't trying to OD, but Mom…" He stopped and ran a hand across his mouth. "They finally believed me when only a tiny bit of meds showed in the blood test. They look at me different now. Well, Nat doesn't, but she never has." He picked at the frayed cuff of his sweatshirt. "I think she made them all go on the delivery today. She knows I can't stand when they look at me like that."

Brandon sat back, shook his head and looked down. "Sorry, didn't mean to unload all that on you."

"It's cool," Luke said like he was shrugging it off, even though he'd listen to whatever this kid wanted to say. "I'm glad everything worked out."

"Yeah." His eyebrows suddenly squished together. "Hey. Nat thinks you're already gone."

"I'm supposed to be, but I need to talk to her. She hasn't been at the lab." Luke was tugging at his shirt cuffs the same way Brandon had. "We finished without her."

"Nat didn't finish because of me?"

"Um. No." Luke backtracked, cursing himself for the insensitive slip-up.

"*Shit*." He made white-knuckled double fists on his lap. "It's my fault."

"It's not, I swear. I turned in the trial results right on schedule. Nothing happened because of you."

"Wasn't it Natalie's project, though?"

"It still is."

Brandon opened his mouth but didn't speak for a minute. "You helped her finish it? But I've heard her call you the candy cop."

"Sugar Nazi." The term made him want to laugh now. *If Natalie only knew the truth…*

"But you helped her anyway." The kid eyed him for a

moment, his gaze as perceptive as Natalie's. "You're the guy who was following her in the parking lot that day."

"Uh." Luke started bouncing his knee. "Sort of. But it's not what you think."

"Wait." His eyebrows lifted. "You're the guy she got caught on tape making out with at Hersheypark."

"She told you about that?"

"She tells me things all the time. I don't think she knows I'm listening, but I am."

He sat back. "When you were here the other day, it wasn't for work. You like her."

Luke was bouncing both knees now. "I like everybody."

"No, you *like* her."

"Yeah." He stopped twitching, and stared at the floor between his feet. "Yeah. I like her."

Like. What a stupid, useless word. Like wasn't at all how he felt about Natalie. It was too hollow and small. She made him feel full and electric, like he could fly her to the moon and back, and then hold her in his arms. He wanted to be a better man when she was with him, even when she wasn't with him.

Two days ago, when he'd decided to finish the trial, he feared he might've been throwing away the future he'd worked so hard for, the future he thought he wanted. And then, only a few hours ago, he'd *willingly* thrown that future away.

At least, that was what the NIH had told him.

Because of Natalie, Luke wanted even more out of life, more from his job and the future. But none of it meant anything if that future didn't include her by his side, inside his arms.

"I love her."

"Awesome."

Startled, Luke flinched and looked up. He hadn't realized he'd said the words aloud. He'd hardly had time to think them or to feel their strength and realness in his soul and in his head…his head that had been too broken to trust her.

"Don't say anything to her," he asked. "I mean, I never told her." But suddenly, it was the only thing he wanted to say. The phrase was burning a hole in his brain. "She won't"—he paused and raked both hands through his hair—"she won't talk to me."

"'Cause she's all pissed off," Brandon said. "She's so stubborn."

"Tell me about it. The only time she ever listens to me about a subject she wants to avoid is when I catch her off guard."

"So do that."

"Yeah." He laughed drearily under his breath. "Should I jump out of a cake holding a sign?"

"Dude, no. But you gotta do something. Right?"

Of course he did. And it shouldn't have taken a sixteen-year-old to make him see that. Luke was in love with a crazy, sexy, chocoholic, kindhearted, brilliant woman, and he'd do anything to make her listen. Absolutely anything to win her back.

Suddenly, he was so restless, he jumped up and began pacing the room, while his heart pounded in his chest so hard he had to clench his teeth.

Catch Natalie Holden off guard when he couldn't even get in the same room with her. How the hell would he do that?

Wait a minute. He froze in place. The idea smacked him in the face like a line drive, and before long, the plan was brewing.

"I know what to do," he told Brandon. "But I'm gonna need your help, man, *and* your mad guitar skills. You up for it?"

Chapter Eighteen

Natalie pouted in the backseat of her father's car. It had been years since she'd had a serious moping fest, and today seemed like as good a day as any, even though they were on their way to get ice cream.

Ivy had called so many times that Natalie had finally turned off her phone, but at least the trial hadn't been a total loss. When she'd seen the text from Ivy that it had been finished on time, she'd been surprised. But very, very grateful.

So why didn't it feel right?

The landscape of Lancaster County rushed by as she glumly stared out the window.

Yes, she'd gotten what she'd wanted and proved her theory was legit in the lab, but...the cost felt too high, like she'd lost more than she'd gained. The only solace was maybe she'd get to try again. But she wasn't a fool. It was highly unlikely she'd get another miracle grant for phase two. This research project so dear to her heart was over.

She slouched down in her seat and crossed her arms. She wasn't in the mood for ice cream, anyway.

Luke had called her, too. And she hadn't picked up. She'd been playing make believe in her heart for too long. She should have known that the boy she'd dreamed of didn't truly care about her, make *her* the priority. Neither of them were ready to trust again, maybe even love each other. It had all been wishful thinking, which brings nothing but heartache.

And she'd been right all along.

She was better off with just work. Just a quiet apartment and a refrigerator full of deadly mushrooms and eight bags of Hershey's Kisses to keep her company at night.

Luke's eyes were on a government position in DC, while all Natalie wanted was to help make the world a sweeter place. Sure, she did that by inventing delicious ways to sell chocolate, but what was wrong with that? Worst of all, Luke considered living in Hershey beneath him.

Had he ever said that, though? Or had Natalie made that jump? And just because she was a food chemist and he was a nutritionist didn't mean they couldn't get along. They got along great, actually. She felt closer to Luke than anyone.

Her breath suddenly caught and she sat up straight. Why, exactly, was she a self-inflicted prisoner in this car in the middle of Amish country and not on a train bound for DC?

Because she'd refused to talk to him, and now he was gone.

She held her breath then pushed it out, concentrating on not crying. Which, of course, made her want to break down in hysterical sobs.

She glanced at Muff in the other backseat. He had his ear buds in and was tapping his foot to whatever song he was listening to. He was also moving the fingers of his left hand like he was playing guitar.

This made Natalie's already broken heart shatter. Did Luke have any idea what he'd done for her brother? She'd tried to thank him, but she couldn't remember if she'd even gotten the words out. She'd probably just grabbed him and kissed him instead, letting her actions speak.

Gah!—the uncontrollable passion she felt for that ridiculous, gorgeous sugar Nazi was almost embarrassing. *Will I ever feel that strongly about anyone ever again?* she wondered, as she swiped a tear rolling down her cheek.

Muff snapped his fingers in front of her face to get her attention.

"What?" she growled, miserably.

With his headphones still on, he pointed at her cheek, made the pantomime of ugly crying, then wagged his index finger.

"I'm not crying," she said, crossing her arms. "It's allergies."

Muff rolled his eyes, wagged his finger again, then looked out his window.

"Who has allergies?" Mom asked from the front seat.

"No one," Natalie replied, scrunching further down in her seat, getting back to her pouting party.

"Your great-aunt Toby was allergic to the color turquoise," Dad said, looking at her from the rearview mirror. "A *color.*" He chuckled. "Can you imagine?"

"She wasn't allergic," Mom said. "She just hated it."

"Same thing."

"No, it's not."

Natalie wished she was wearing ear buds, too. Her parents… They were trying so hard, so lovingly absurd. Like right now. Brandon said he was craving a Phillip Arthur special, so the next thing she knew, they were packed in the car, driving eighty miles round trip so their son could have ice cream. Natalie just wished Muff hadn't insisted she come along. She'd rather have sat on the back porch and thrown apple cores at crows until she stopped feeling like crap.

"You sure you won't come in?" Mom said, as the other three got out of the car at the ice cream parlor.

"I'm sure," Natalie replied, she had some pouting to do, after all. No more than two minutes later came a tap on her halfway-lowered window.

"Thought it was you," Dexter Elliott said.

"Hey." Natalie sat up and glanced past his shoulder, making sure his brother wasn't with him. "What are you doing here?"

"It's root beer float night. Never miss it when I'm in town." He gestured at the parking lot. "That's why the place is packed."

"Oh." Dexter looked too much like his brother, so she turned to examine her nails.

"Why aren't you inside pigging out? I know you're not against sugar."

She exhaled a halfhearted laugh. "Not in the mood."

"Come on." Dexter opened her door. "We'll split one. That way I won't look as pathetic when I devour three on my own."

She could've begged off and stayed right where she was, but she didn't have the energy to be contrary. "I don't want to talk about your brother," she warned, walking with Dexter to the entrance.

"Which brother?"

She shot him a look.

"Oh, that brother." He opened the glass door for her. "I won't bring him up if you don't."

"I won't."

Dexter nodded somberly, then pointed his chin to the back. "Looks like the party room's the only place with open tables."

Natalie glanced around at all the full seats and booths. "That must be where my family is, too." She followed Dexter as he weaved through the main dining room. As soon as he entered the party room, all the lights in there went out, making her run into his back.

Three flat screens mounted on the walls flickered on. "There's a private event in here," she whispered. "We should leave."

An image was slowly fading in on all the TVs, and music was playing, not from the TV's speakers, but someone was strumming a guitar at the front of the room on the little stage. The same stage she'd seen Luke grace back in high school.

Her heart suddenly lurched and panged. Maybe it was being with his brother, or maybe it was stupid Phillip Arthur, but she missed him so badly it hurt. Hell, she'd missed him even when she wouldn't speak to him.

Why hadn't she answered all those times he'd called? She'd wanted to hear his voice, his laugh. But she'd been stubborn because he'd said something hurtful, and then she'd said something hurtful back, and then… Well, she couldn't remember what happened after that, only that he was gone. He'd left for DC that night, angry, and she hadn't even tried to apologize. Instinctively, she reached for her phone, but she hadn't brought her purse along.

"Can't I get one tiny break?" she muttered under her breath.

She closed her eyes and saw him that first night at Hershey Lounge. She saw him stammering while introducing her to his parents. She saw him covered in chocolate, felt his arms around her, his sweet, passionate kisses. She saw him the morning after she'd been sick, and he'd taken care of her, selflessly. She thought about that green smoothie and realized that was the moment she'd fallen in love with him.

Her heart pounded up her throat. She loved Luke, and their insignificant differences didn't matter enough to stop that. She should've tried harder to be with him, and not given up when she didn't get her way. If his life was in DC's fast lane, hers could be, too!

She opened her eyes, realizing she was still in the dark and crowded events room at Phillip Arthur, wasting precious time at someone else's party.

"Dexter," she whispered in a rush. "Do you know what hotel Luke is staying at in DC?"

He flashed a quick glance at her then away. "What do you think? He's my brother."

"I need the address or just give me the name and I'll find it." Her heart pounded in an ecstatic, nervous rhythm the second she had a plan. "*Dexter*." She poked him when he didn't reply. "I need to find him. Never mind, I'll call him from the road, and if he doesn't answer—"

"Shh." Dexter linked an arm through hers and pointed

at the TVs on the walls. "Check it out."

Words suddenly flashed across the screen: *Warning. Do not try this at home. Boathouses only. Arms and legs inside the ride at all times. Killer Canadian geese.*

Huh?

An image took its place. It was a photo of…her. She was seven years old, braids in her hair and holding a red balloon from the county fair.

Puzzling.

The background music wasn't a solo guitar anymore. Someone was singing a power ballad version of that Maroon 5 song about…sugar. Natalie blinked as another image appeared on the screen. It was her again. She was fourteen, displaying the trophy she'd won at her first science fair and grinning like it was an Oscar. Another caption: *Only you can prevent forest fires. And Hazmat showers.*

What the hell?

The next photo was of Natalie at her college graduation, wearing her black robe and yellow *cum laude* honor cord. She was also holding a Hershey bar.

Caption: *This woman has secrets: She loves apple cider, green smoothies, and me… The last one shouldn't be a secret anymore.*

The crowd in the room started to murmur and whisper. Natalie squinted into the darkness. Was that the back of her mother's head? Dad's bald spot? That was definitely Ivy's red ponytail. She even recognized Eileen Elliott's immaculately-styled dark hair.

Holy shiz. What was going on?

Just as she was about to break away from Dexter and demand an explanation from whoever was in charge of this

little stroll down memory lane, her eyes landed on the singing guitarist on the unlit stage. There were two of them now,
both playing, but only one still crooning about sugar, about
how he's hurting for her, hurting and broken and needing
just one little taste.

"Luke?" she couldn't stop from calling out.

"Hey, Nat," he squeezed in between verses. "How do we
look?"

"We?"

He flashed that grin that made her knees weak, while
pointing the neck of his guitar at a screen.

Caption: *Natalie, I'll never go to your house hungry,
unless I want mushrooms. Or your chocolate. Lots of your
chocolate.*

As her photo disappeared, one of a preteen Luke took
its place. She knew it was him, because, no matter the age,
she'd recognize that face.

*The bottoms of your feet are ticklish. So are some other
parts.*

Natalie couldn't help smiling, and her cheeks felt flushed
with happy embarrassment.

Next, Luke was fifteen with floppy hair, holding a guitar.
Then he was in his own graduation robe, one arm around his
mother.

*You sing Madonna when you have a fever. And do other
Madonna things I won't mention in public.*

"Nice." This came from Dexter as he grinned and
nodded his approval.

Natalie laughed as the last photo of Luke shattered
apart on the screen, then pieced back together. But it wasn't
of just him now. Each of their photos was edited so they

were together in the picture, as if they really had known each other forever.

Ask her about Amazonian cocoa. But not about the Calamine. That's my secret.

Luke's song picked up tempo, more urgent and pleading, matching the feelings in her heart she had to get out before she burst.

"Luke!" she called between her cupped hands. "I need to talk to you!"

But he just grinned and strummed the musical bridge of the song.

"Luke!" she said, weaving her way toward the stage, bumping into chairs. "This can't wait."

"It's almost the end, baby. Watch!"

She turned to the screen where a new image was slowly coming into focus. It was gray-green and grainy like a cop car's dash cam. It took Natalie exactly two seconds to figure out what it was. A tiny, two-seater boat bobbing on the water, an out-of-focus couple kissing in the darkness. His fingers running though her hair.

"Ermrgrrrrrrd," she whispered, cover her smile with her hands.

Before all the blood in her body could rush to her cheeks, the image was gone, leaving the screens glowing white. A second later, the room erupted with whoops and applause.

"You know what you did to me that first day," Luke said. "You made me see stars. I've been seeing stars ever since."

The whole room was bright enough now that Natalie saw Brandon was the other guitarist on stage. He stood farther back than Luke, but he was up there, strumming along just as confidently.

How had this happened? And was her pounding heart about to beat right out of her chest?

Just as Luke hit the last note of his song, and he and Brandon strummed their final chords, one final caption flashed across the screen: *See you soon, Intercourse!*

The room erupted in cheers, applause, and ear splitting catcalls.

"Subtle," Natalie said, unsure if she wanted to kiss him or strangle him. Then their eyes locked across the room, and she had no intention of strangling him.

"Well, that was memorable," she heard Ivy say.

"Get some good tips, Red?" Dexter replied.

But she saw only Luke.

He held the mike close to his mouth. "Natalie," he said, drawing out the name. "I have to tell you something. Alone."

She had to tell him something, too—now. She wanted to call it out right then. But she kept her eyes on him as he wove through the crowd toward her in a hurried, determined clip, ignoring everyone he passed.

When he got to her, he didn't break stride, just took her hand and pulled her out the emergency exit at the back of the room. She barely had time to catch her breath or notice they were in an empty alley before he was in her face.

"I'll get to the apologies and explanations and groveling in a minute—and there will be plenty of that," he said, his words just as fast and determined as his pace had been. "But this first." Like he was psyching himself up, he rounded his lips, pushed out a breath, then focused those blue eyes right on her. "I'm in love with you. And if you're pissed at me and want to throw Hershey bars at my head, I'll still love you. And if you tell me my singing sucks and you hate my car, I won't care, because I love you. I love all of you. So much."

It wasn't possible for Natalie's heart to beat any faster, soar any higher into the heavens. She should speak—it was her turn. But hearing that flood of words from Luke turned her into a tongue-tied pile of happy goo, too dizzy and dazzled to form any cohesive reply.

"Looks like you need convincing," he said. "I hoped you might." His lips curved into that cocky smile she loved, and then those lips crashed into hers, making her stumble back and lose her footing, until his strong arms went around her.

He wouldn't let her breathe, and she didn't care. He kissed her until she felt more flushed and dewy than while in a mushroom-induced fever. All the while, her heart was turning cartwheels. His hand moved to cup her head, the other slid down her spine, and then he bent her into a dip, her arms flying around his neck to hold on.

"I love you," she panted the first chance her lips were free.

Luke opened his eyes. "What was that?"

She grinned. "And I don't care if you throw Brussels sprouts at my head"—she squeezed him—"I'll still love you."

Luke smiled back with a glow in his eyes that she knew shone in her eyes, too. Gently, he pulled her to stand upright, but before she could regain balance, he kissed her again. It was slow, penetrating, filling her with beautiful words still unspoken. She felt his love though every inch of her body.

"I'm so sorry about what happened that night," Luke said, his voice husky, breath uneven.

"So am I."

"No, I mean really sorry. I can't believe I said those

things to you."

"It's okay." She ran a hand through the back of his hair. "I said some things, too…because I was hurt, and so mad you were leaving that I really was about to pummel you with Hershey bars."

Luke laughed and pulled her into his strong, solid chest. "You should have."

"But listen." She took in a deep breath and lifted her chin so they were eye to eye. "I know you didn't make that decision lightly, and I know it'll be hard for you to be away from your family again. But Luke, it was stupid for us to pretend the long-distance thing would work."

He looked at her, his mouth set in a confused frown. "What do you mean?"

Finally, she could tell him the rest. "Your life's in DC now. I'm a Hershey girl, and I never thought anything would make me want to leave. Until you." She grinned when Luke blinked in surprise. She'd caught *him* off guard for once. "I can't bear the thought of living even a train ride away from you. One of us has to compromise, and I've decided it's—"

As a thought dawned on her, her own gasp cut her off.

"Luke, the video of us in the tunnel!" She clutched his arm. "Why didn't you destroy it? You know if it gets out, the NIH will never touch you."

"Exactly."

"And you'll get fired from Penn Med."

"Can't fire me. I quit."

Her mouth fell open like a fish, utterly confused now. "Why?"

He paced a finger under her chin to close her gaping mouth, kissed her forehead and tucked some hair behind her ear, each touch making Natalie melt a little bit more. "My turn to talk again?"

She nodded.

"The *why* is simple. I'd be an idiot to not do everything in my power to be where you are. Since you're here, I'm here— end of discussion, Hershey girl." Reading the bewilderment on her face, Luke took both cheeks between his hands. His rough touch setting her whole body alight. "You're a nutty, beautiful chemist, and you opened my mind, *re*opened a lot of things in me."

He hesitated before going on.

"But I screwed up big time, Nat. I reverted to that closed-up guy who couldn't trust anyone. When I realized how utterly wrong I was, I wanted to tell you I'm sorry, but you were gone, and I couldn't find you. Everything went wrong so fast, your trial was about to go to pot, and I couldn't let that happen." He shook his head and stared into the middle distance. "I had to do something. I had to help the only way I knew how. I did what I had to, and I don't regret anything I did to complete the—"

He paused again and looked away. It took Natalie a few seconds to understand. When she did, she wondered how it was possible that she loved him even more?

"*You* finished the trial."

His eyebrows furrowed like he was ready to deny it. But then he nodded. "How angry are you about it?"

"Angry?" she echoed, her throat growing tight with gratitude. "But why, Luke? It cost you your career."

"I couldn't let all you worked for just evaporate—it's too important. Along with all the other things you changed in me, I know what direction to take my career now." He took her hand and placed it over his heart—its strong, thrumming beat beneath her fingers. "If you'll let me, I want to partner with you during all the future phases of your project. I want to see it through the developmental stages, the clinical trials, as far as we can take it." He squeezed her hand between both of his. "Because I believe in you."

All she could do was gaze at him, dizzily speechless. *Luke, the holistic microbiologist, wants to defend a theory based on chocolate?* If she hadn't already been crazy-ass in love with this man...

She swallowed around the love lump in her throat. "That's sweet, really so sweet, but I'll never get any more funding. It sucks, but I'm dealing with it. Someday another researcher will pick up where we left off. I know it."

He opened his mouth, shut it, opened it again and then looked at the ground. "Um. There's one other thing I need to tell you." He rubbed his jaw. "It's a little embarrassing. I didn't want you to know."

"Luke." She swatted his arm. "What is it?"

"You're kind of fully funded, like forever." Before she could wonder what he meant, he added, "I always said I'd only touch my inheritance if something really important came up." He brushed a warm hand across her cheek. "It finally did."

She knew her eyes were wide and unblinking with amazement, but she was too overwhelmed, too full of love and wonder to speak. She tried to say thank you, and the words hopefully made it out of her mouth before she kissed him.

Tears stung her eyes when he enfolded her in his arms, filling her with hope and warmth and better daydreams than she'd ever had. And then his mouth was on her neck, and a raging heat replaced the warmth as he whispered her name over and over, repeating those three little words she'd never tire of hearing.

"Ya know," Natalie said, "right before your little slide-show in there, I was ten seconds away from leaving to track you down in DC."

"Oh yeah?" He touched his nose to hers. "Couldn't live without me?"

Heat spiraled around her core as she breathed him in. Why deny the truth? "Not for another second."

"Since it's finally clear that neither of us is leaving Hershey, how about we try for that omelet again."

"Mmm. Excellent idea." She slid both hands inside the back of his shirt, feeling hard, warm muscles and skin. *Just a preview*, she thought, so ready for the full unveiling.

Luke pulled her against him and exhaled a sexy groan from deep in his chest. Natalie wanted to groan right back. He kissed her mouth, her forehead, that spot under her ear. And then he drew back and just stared at her neck until her panting, expectant breaths were as loud as his.

"Time to get you off the streets, woman," he said, then took her hand and led her shaky-legged through the parking lot.

That was when Natalie noticed the T-shirt he was wearing had *Kiss me, I heart Hershey* printed on the front. She grinned and squeezed her delicious sugar Nazi's hand even tighter, knowing she'd never, ever love any chocolate bar as much as him.

"So," he said, stopping in front of the Jeep, "will I get to see your special PJs again?" He dragged his gaze up her body, making her tingle with sweet thoughts, as well as a few savory ones.

"I was mad at you, so I threw them on the compost pile with the rotten apples."

His expression crumbled. "Babe, no."

She ran her thumb over his bottom lip. "But I have something else in the back of my closet you'll like."

"Sounds nice, for tomorrow." He grinned a smoldering, knowing grin. "Tonight, though, we don't need anything…except maybe a little chocolate whipped cream." She shrieked as he swept her off her feet and into his arms. "But that's all for me."

Acknowledgments

Thank you to Scott and Mark from The Hershey Company for the fabulous behind-the-scenes peek at chocolate heaven and for answering all the questions a romance author could have. Thanks to the usual suspects at Entangled Publishing — Alycia, Stacy, Debbie, Crystal and Jessica — for once more allowing me to live my dream. And to the phenomenal writerly/readerly women — Nancy, Sue, Lisa, Ginger — who helped me through every step in creating this book. Special thanx to Lindsay Emory and Alexandra Haughton for their bril and smexy plotty ideas. (tee-hee) Lastly, huge chocolaty kisses to my Hershey, PA family for, well, for just living in the "sweetest place on earth." I'll be visiting again soon! xoxo

About the Author

USA Today bestselling author Ophelia London was born and raised among the redwood trees in beautiful northern California. Once she was fully educated, she decided to settle in Florida, but her car broke down in Texas and she's lived in Dallas ever since. A cupcake and treadmill aficionado (obviously those things are connected), she spends her time watching arthouse movies and impossibly trashy TV, while living vicariously through the characters she writes. Ophelia is the author of KISSING HER CRUSH in the new Sugar City series; AIMEE & THE HEARTTHROB; CHALK LINES & LIPSTICK; DEFINITELY, MAYBE IN LOVE; the Abby Road series; and the Perfect Kisses series. Visit her at ophelialondon.com. But don't call when *The Vampire Diaries* (or *Dawson's Creek*) is on.

www.ingramcontent.com/pod-product-compliance
Lightning Source LLC
Chambersburg PA
CBHW020818260626
47169CB00003B/715